She heard a shor then a dull thud. He the bed.

"Open the cuffs. No sudden moves. I've got a gun"

She turned the round-barreled key once, twice - and her feet were free. "I've done it," she said, rubbing her ankles to get the blood flowing.

"Now get up, quick."

She put her feet, still numb from constriction, on the floor and pushed, but her head was reeling. Straining her eyes and ears, she took a hesitant step into the darkness that seemed filled with invisible tripwires.

"I can hear where you are. Don't try any tricks. I want you in front of the window." On tottery legs, Jessica walked over.

"And now dance." he ordered. "Dance your last dance."

*To Richard
Enjoy the
rhythm of life*

THE
RHYTHM
OF
REVENGE

The First Inspector Terry Mystery

Christine Spindler

Christine Spindler

avid
press LLC

Brighton, Michigan USA

AVID PRESS, LLC
5470 Red Fox Drive
Brighton, MI 48114-9079
http://www.avidpress.com

Copyright 1999 by Christine Spindler

Published by arrangement with the author
ISBN: 1-929613-18-0

For information contact Avid Press, LLC.

First Avid Press printing October 1999

To the memory of my mother,
who taught me the magic of words

I want to thank

Natalie and Joachim, for their love and support,

Olwen, Neasa, Jane, Gabi, and Chris for their valued critique and enthusiasm,

and the officers at Albany Street Police Station in London for their friendly help, with special thanks to Michael Bernard.

Chapter One

After a rainy winter day, a sudden drop in temperature had covered the pavement with crystals of ice. The reflections of headlights shimmered like stage spots. Carefully steering through the London evening traffic, Jessica pictured how dazzling it would be to dance all on her own. She turned into Duke's Road and let the car skid to a halt in front of The Caesar. She was glad that she had brought a pair of overshoes, which she put on meticulously before she stepped out. She closed the door firmly, as if to convince herself that she was doing the right thing. With no rehearsal scheduled today, she had had no excuse to drive to the theatre; not on Roger's fiftieth birthday, when he expected her to act out the role of loving wife for his guests.

In the yellow light of a street lamp, she glanced at her watch. Ten past five already. She should have come earlier instead of helping Roger decorate the living room with garlands, where she had created a mess when a packet of drawing pins slipped from her hands and spilled its contents over the Chinese silk carpet.

Alan's call had been the last straw. He couldn't come to the party because he was developing a cold and didn't want to pass on his virus to his principal dancers so shortly before the première. Tonight, Roger's cronies would pollute the air with cigarette smoke, they would blather away about sinking interest rates and speculations on the stock market, and without a chance to escape for a chat with Alan, Jessica would feel left out of things. Roger had also invited David and Susan, but you can't discuss choreography for hours. Dancing is for practice not for prattle. Irritably, Jessica had grabbed her coat and shouted in the direction of the living room that she would drive to the theatre whether Roger liked it or not, and that she would be back before the guests arrived. He would be peeved with her, but he often was so it made little difference.

What did it matter now? She was where she belonged, and instantly her concerns faded. Cautiously placing her feet on the slippery ground, she walked to the entrance. The building lay dark except for the illuminated signboard over the door with "The Caesar" written in huge gaudy lettering on a black ground. Because of the exhaust fumes from nearby Euston Road, Alan had to repaint the sign every three or four years. Last autumn he had chosen fluorescent orange and green. Fourteen years ago, the same letters, painted pink and turquoise, had encouraged her to walk in and ask if they had tap dance classes for children.

A chilly wind began to blow. Jessica turned the key with stiff fingers. Inside, safe from the world that bothered her with its manifold demands, she switched on the light and raised her feet in turn to remove the overshoes. On the wall opposite the box office hung the poster of their new production, *Taming of the Shoe*. With a few brushstrokes, Alan had portrayed her in mid-dance—her swirling bob of black hair, her dark eyes and ivory complexion, her slender body in a red mini dress. Magically, he had also captured the thrill that suffused her when she danced. The poster was fantastic, perfect but for the names printed diagonally across the lower right edge, *Jessica Warner & David Powell*. The P under the W looked ugly and misplaced. *Jessica Warner & Alan C.*

Widmark would read much better. Her name on top of his, the Ws in a perfect parallel. Jessica let out a long-practiced sigh and went downstairs. Why did it have to be David? At first, she had been impressed by David's inventiveness on the dance floor and his keenness to make the most of her talent. When he had wanted more, she had still been so naive as to think that he was just another penis-piloted adorer who was potty about her but would lose interest after a few passionate encounters. His persistence had surprised and scared her, and only a nasty shock had given her the determination to ditch him once and for all.

She opened the red door of her dressing room, placed her ruck-sack on the table and began to undress. The heating was turned low and she hurried to put on her tracksuit, then bent down and picked up the heavy-plated practice shoes Alan had given her for her eighteenth birthday. She went through the routine of check-ing if the screws that fixed the metal plates were tight. Pressing first the right then the left foot against the make-up table, she laced each shoe with a double bow. The thick black leather enclosed her feet like a second skin.

Jessica climbed the spiral staircase that led to the stage, pushed open the electrician's room door and switched on the foot-lights, leaving the auditorium in velvet blackness. In four days, at the première, spotlights would clip her out of the darkness, music would roar wildly and she would be intoxicated by a blend of con-centration and consummation. She longed to share this experi-ence with Alan.

She warmed up until the clacking of her shoe-plates sounded like drum-rolls, then began her dance session with fragments of David's choreography. Soon she was taken over by her passion for jazz elements. Her ankles moved like friction-free gearwheels, her jumps became higher, her turns wilder. The styles began to mix as if of their own will. She shifted into flamenco peppered with Irish jigs, swirled her feet like an overwound clockwork toy, gal-loped across the stage and leaped into a split. It felt better than having an orgasm; it was like being an orgasm.

Two exploding sneezes brought her to a sudden halt that almost tripped her. For a shameful second, she felt as if she had been caught in an auto-erotic act. The auditorium lights went on and she saw Alan shuffle down the aisle toward the stage, bleary-eyed, unkempt and dressed in blue flannel pajamas.

"Sorry," he said. "I didn't want to make you jump. Or rather, I didn't want to stop your jumps so abruptly." He sneezed once more and pressed a crumpled handkerchief against his face.

"I'm the one who should be sorry, Alan. I woke you up, didn't I?"

He gave her a lopsided grin. "Your footwork may be nifty but it's not loud enough to penetrate two storeys of bricks and concrete. It was Roger who woke me. He called and wanted to know if you're still here."

Jessica made a cool-down stretch. "Just because he's old enough to be my father doesn't mean he can treat me like a child."

"He said he was worried because it was already twenty to seven and—"

"Twenty to seven! Are you sure? Shit. He'll be furious."

"I'll call him back and say that you're on your way."

"You're a darling. You know, instead of driving home to that silly party, I'd rather stay with you, make you some tea with lemon and cool your forehead. You look very unwell."

Alan inspected his handkerchief for a place to blow his nose. "Why are you here anyway? Just to spite Roger?"

She shrugged. "One of my whims, I suppose. I had better leave now."

"Take care. The streets are icy," Alan's voice croaked after her.

Five minutes later she was out again in the frosty, hostile winter.

David was so nervous he couldn't knot his tie properly.

Working with Jessica was one thing; meeting her in her private surroundings quite another. There had been a time when every moment in her presence had been filled with hopeful yearning and feverish longing, to be replaced a few months later by the exuberance of fulfillment, which lasted only a year. Then, out of the blue, she had ended their affair. David felt amputated and was wracked with all the symptoms of emotional phantom pain. The part of him that had been Jessica's lover was aching like a severed leg; it was throbbing with sadness, burning with desire and itching with rage.

David tugged at the ends of his tie until the knot came loose again.

"I'll do it for you," Susan said. She completed the knot and then embraced him from behind. He felt a stab of annoyance as Susan's fingers moved up and down his chest.

"You smell good." She rubbed her cheek against his shoulder blade.

He disentangled himself. "It's half past six and you haven't even started your make-up."

Susan sighed, reached for the hairbrush, and combed her blond curls with long, sweeping strokes. "I don't feel all that well, you know. Maybe we should stay at home. There's black ice on the roads."

"It's only a short drive and I've never had any problems with icy roads," he said testily. The evening was problematic enough without Susan's endless carping.

Susan tapped the back of the brush against her palm. "I don't think Roger really expects us to come. It was purely out of politeness that he invited us. Or maybe he didn't want Jessica to feel so terribly outnumbered by his clan and colleagues."

David unnecessarily straightened the knot of his tie and said with studied composure, "You're not getting one of your headaches or your monthly?"

"No, it's just that Roger makes me nervous. He has a short

fuse." Susan put down the brush, poured a measure of liquid foundation on a small sponge and dabbed her skin with it. "I know better ways to spend a Saturday night. And Nurit's cooking is always so spicy. The smell alone makes my stomach revolt." She looked at David across the mirror. "Do we really have to go?"

"What's the matter with you?" David turned around. Leaning against the washbasin, he observed indifferently how beautiful she was, her slim body outlined in a white silk dress. He associated women with flowers. Years ago, he had called Susan his water-lily, had seen in her a creature of calm, remote beauty, afloat and vulnerable, shaped to painful perfection. Jessica represented an exciting contrast. She was his red rose, strong-stemmed, thorny, rich in scent and promises. When she took off her clothes, her beauty unfolded as if she were a rose opening its calyx.

"You should stop making up excuses," David offered. "Just tell me if you have a good reason for staying at home."

He saw Susan's jaw line stiffen. Suddenly apprehensive, he realized that even though his affair with Jessica was long over, he was still dreading that Sue could have learnt about it. Instead of answering, she picked up her lipstick and ran it along the contours of her mouth. God, what if she knew? She had disliked Jessica from the start, so it had been impossible for him to tell if jealousy was an ingredient of her hostility.

"You're right. I've got a problem with that party—and it's not Roger." Her green eyes turned dark like an overshadowed pond and David's heart sank. He was not so much afraid that Susan knew he had wanted to leave her for Jessica, but that she had found out the embarrassing truth that Jessica hadn't wanted to leave Roger for him.

Susan screwed in the lipstick with elaborate slowness. "It's because of Clara," she finally said.

David relaxed. "Who's Clara?" he asked.

"Roger's daughter by his first marriage. We met her at the garden party last summer. She must be eight months pregnant by now."

So that was it. Goodness. He smoothed back his hair with cold fingers. "Oh, come on now, Sue. You can't go on avoiding pregnant women for the rest of your life."

"She'll carry her womb like a trophy. She's the kind. It's too much of a facer for me." Susan was close to crying now and David felt helpless.

"Maybe she won't be there at all. Clara and what's-his-name?"

"Kenneth."

"Kenneth, yes. They live in Greenwich, don't they? Kenneth won't want to drive all the way with his pregnant wife when the roads are icy, so try to be rational."

"I'm sorry I mentioned it. I should have known you wouldn't share my feelings. You never did."

David made no reply. Three years ago, when there had been so much to say, he had decided to keep it all to himself and carry the burden alone. Words had been inadequate to describe what had broken inside him when Susan had delivered their child three months before she was due. She had been half unconscious with pain and angst and so hadn't seen what he had seen: the tiny creature, just a handful, a perfect human being in every detail. A still-born child. His boy. And before he had been able to touch the blood-smeared body, they had taken it away as reverence seemed to demand.

Dominic was the name he and Susan had agreed upon after they had seen in the ultrasound scan that their baby was a boy. Dominic, my boy, he had thought, calling out the name in a soundless cry, knowing that he couldn't grieve properly for a child that was nameless. Then and there, something inside David had given way, the mask of social graces had been torn from his mien and he had begun to insult the midwife—for someone had to take the blame; someone had to be punished. Over the next days, he had controlled himself to avoid torturing Susan with questions about everything she had done in the past weeks and months. His thoughts ran in a treadmill as he kept asking himself if anything unsettling had happened to Susan during her pregnancy, if she had eaten too much or too little, if they had made love too often. There had to be an explanation as to why his boy was dead. Screening his misery with palliative commonplace remarks to Susan, he had got over the worst. It was not as she thought, that he hadn't understood her. She was the one who hadn't probed deeper and so had never learnt about his true feelings. Susan, although physically alright, hadn't been able to conceive again and that had become the focus of her grief. All she wanted was a new baby to replace the dead one which she had never seen. The more David spared her the confrontation with her loss, the more he felt bereaved himself.

"I'm sorry I said that," Susan broke the silence. Her make-up was fixed, the tears that had been brimming in her eyes had flowed back into her system.

"You can stay at home," David said to show his good will, "but I'll go." He was not sure why he sought the pain instead of avoiding it. Jessica knew how much he still cared for her. She would watch him suffer with her usual indifference and thus add to his mortification.

Susan touched his arm. "I'll come, too. It was just a momentary crisis."

Lucky her. There was no end to his own crisis. He missed Jessica, but seeing her didn't help because he missed her even more when he was with her.

Everything was arranged. Nurit had prepared a vegetarian five-course meal and went on to toss the salad. Roger lifted the lids of several pots and pans. "It smells delicious."

Nurit acknowledged his approval with a proud smile.

In the dining room, Edgar, the man-servant, was arranging the china on the long, oval mahogany table. Originally, thirty people should have been sitting at the table tonight—Roger favored round numbers. Unfortunately, Alan had a cold, which was a pity. He was unbeatable for covering awkward silences in the conversation, and his presence was enough to put Jessica in a better mood. Clara and Kenneth had decided to stay at home. Tracy, his secretary, had called to say that she would come alone since her husband had broken a leg during their skiing holiday. So they were reduced to twenty-six.

"I think you can light the candles now," he said to Edgar and went through to the living room. He chose Mozart and Vivaldi and inserted the CDs into the player. Everything was perfect except that Jessica was missing. Her lack of care for other people's feelings was symptomatic, especially when the feelings were his—as if instead of flesh and blood he was made of rock and granite. Of course, that was how he saw himself—a fortress of a man, tall, strong and athletic. Jessica, however, was a blind mirror. He had no idea what she saw in him. Did she desire him? Probably, or she wouldn't sleep with him three times a week. It was strange, when he came to think of it—so regular, leaving no room for improvisation. Stranger even that he had become so accustomed to her timetable that he never approached her off-schedule. Did she take as little notice of his existence as she made him believe? Sometimes he felt like the invisible man.

Roger pressed the play button so that the sound of lightly played strings could soothe his nerves. She had promised to stay at home today, hadn't she? Most irritatingly, he was once more prepared to forgive her for letting him down. If that was what love made of him, a soft, indulgent weakling, then he would have preferred never to have met Jessica. She was impervious to reason and unfazed by his untiring attempts to teach her a basic sense of decency. He bent down and picked up one of the drawing pins she had dropped on the carpet. Clumsy as a child, she was. But he wouldn't let her spoil his party.

The doorbell rang. Oh my God, the first guests—and Jessica

wasn't back yet. Splendid. Edgar went to open the door. It was Jessica. Roger felt a vehement desire to see her abashed, if only to conceal his relief that she was back safe.

"What the hell is going on inside your head, Jess?" he blurted out by way of greeting as she rushed inside and hurled her coat in the general direction of the coat rack. He had no time to lecture her because the bell rang once more. Edgar went to the door again, picking up Jessica's coat on the way.

"I'll change into something decent," Jessica said unflappably. "Don't be stroppy, Roger. I won't take a minute."

She hadn't even cared to say she was sorry. How could he forgive her when she showed no remorse? God, what a mule she was. Recalling his duties as a host, Roger put on a stiff smile and prepared to greet his guests without his wife by his side.

She came down fifteen minutes later, wearing a figure-hugging, black dress and looking absolutely brilliant. She accepted a glass of mineral water from Edgar and began to exchange social niceties. Roger knew she was not a party person and would soon run out of small-talk, so he decided it was time to sit down at the table. Victualling people was the best way to keep them occupied and satisfied.

As a matter of fact, he was very fond of parties—especially the ones he hosted. He enjoyed bringing together people who hadn't met before, introducing them with well-chosen words to give them a common ground, seeing how new bonds were forged, watching, rearranging—in short, pulling the strings. Only Jessica seemed forever immune to his subtle manipulations.

After the dinner, when they had retreated to the living room, she sat on a two-seater by a sash window, which she pushed up every now and then to let in some fresh air. She looked thoughtful, as if in rapt contemplation, but he knew that she was bored to death. He had hoped that she would mix with Susan and David. It was not easy to find someone in her social background whom one could invite. In Roger's eyes, they all lacked class; except

Alan Widmark and the Powells. David had worked as a choreographer on off-Broadway shows in New York before he moved to London two years ago. His wife Susan was a terrific natural-blonde, the perfect eye-catcher for the male guests. At the moment she was chatting with Tracy, who had been in New York for a holiday last year. An odd sight: the tall, slim, fair dancer and the short, sturdy, dark secretary.

Jessica had begun to yawn. It wasn't simple to entertain her. Actually, it was impossible. She had been an only child and had grown into a solitary adult. Maybe it had completely escaped her that she was married now.

David went to sit beside her and began talking eagerly, but Jessica remained monosyllabic. Then Victoria, Roger's sister-in-law, tried to draw her into a conversation. It lasted all of ten seconds. Roger had to do something before everybody noticed her bad manners.

He went over to the sofa and sat down at the place Victoria had vacated. "Jess, my love. What's the matter with you? Why don't you mix?" His tone sounded watery to himself, which probably resulted from his unremitting effort to be nice and polite all evening although his fury about her late arrival hadn't simmered down entirely.

"It's past eleven. I should have been in bed long ago," she complained. "We've got a rehearsal tomorrow."

"It can't be that daunting to stay awake an hour or two longer just once a year. You can't blame me for having birthdays, you know."

She stood up and he followed. "Have your birthday and let me go to bed. I'm sure nobody's going to miss me."

He was completely taken aback. "Don't you see how selfish you are?" he blurted out more loudly than he had intended. "I won't allow you to go off to bed. You had better try and show some interest in—"

"Stop bossing me around," Jessica cut in sharply. Roger was

painfully aware of the silence that followed her outburst.

"I'm not bloody bossing you around," he hissed. "I'm just asking you to be a bit more hospitable. You can't possibly go to bed as long as we have guests."

"Then send the guests away," she retorted.

For a moment, Roger was speechless. "Jessica!"

"I'm fed up with it all. You're always patronizing me. Can't you just let me live my life the way I want to live it?"

"Well, how about me then? Do you give a damn how I want to live? I'm a person with rights and desires, too, believe it or not, and I want a wife, not a dance maniac unable to feel affection. If only you—"

"Oh, stop bleatin' about. No matter what I do, you always get shirty with me."

"And no matter what I say, you always have to demonstrate how stolid you are. Did you ever try to agree with anything I told you?"

"Why should I?" she spat. "You're such a boring old crank."

Before he knew what he was doing, his hand lashed out and hit her violently across the face. There was no way to make it undone. Jessica shrieked, covered her cheek with a protecting hand, turned and ran out of the room.

He dashed after her and caught her on the landing of the first floor. "Jess, I'm so terribly sorry." He reached for her shoulder, but she shook off his hand and pushed open the bedroom door.

"Go away, leave me alone. Go to your precious guests," she said between sobs.

"But I didn't . . . I never . . . Good God, there's blood on your lips."

She touched her mouth with trembling fingers. Her face turned so white that even the marks of the slap vanished.

"Please forgive me, my love. I didn't want to hurt you. I'm so dreadfully sorry. I promise this will never happen again."

She ignored his contrite apology and backed away when he

stepped forward, proffering his handkerchief.

"I'll take care of her," said David, who had come upstairs. He was cradling the small bucket of ice water for the champagne bottle. "I must cool her face or the bruise will show—the last thing we need so shortly before the opening night," he said practically.

Jessica, coming round from her shock, snatched the bucket from David and yelled that she could cool her cheek alone. "Go to blazes! I don't need anyone to take care of me."

Roger decided to let them have it out between themselves. He was tired of rows and arguments, tired of trying to domesticate Jessica. He shuffled downstairs. Edgar was handing out coats and Roger forced himself to say goodbye to his guests with a formal smile, just as he had welcomed them.

"Don't let it spoil your birthday," Victoria said. "She only got what she deserved."

The hall emptied quickly. A few minutes later, David came down. Heedless of Roger's questions about Jessica, he grabbed his coat and left without a word.

Roger looked for Susan and found her upstairs on the landing, crouching as if she were in pain. Her face was ashen.

In the nocturnal silence, the ringing of the doorbell sounded like a fire siren. Alan's feverish dreams came to a sudden halt, and through layers of headache, he struggled to consciousness. The doorbell rang again. It was not the one-tone ring of the front door bell but the two-tone chime at his flat door, so it had to be someone with a key for The Caesar. Ginger and Fred, the parrots, had woken up. He heard them screech in the living room. Ginger, the one of the pair he had managed to teach a few words, croaked, "*Hasta la vista*, baby."

Alan didn't bother to get up. Everybody knew that he never locked his flat—and indeed, after a third warning ring, faltering steps came along the corridor. Alan squinted short-sightedly at his alarm clock. One in the morning. He sat up slowly and immediately had to sneeze. This encouraged whomever it was who was waiting in front of his bedroom door to come in. Alan switched on the lamp on the bedside table and closed his swollen eyes for a second.

It was Susan. She ran across the carpet and flung herself into his arms.

"Gee, Sue, what happened?"

"I hate her," she wept against his shoulder. "She has ruined my life. She's a selfish, unfeeling bitch. I wish she were dead."

Alan, still not quite awake, patted her absent-mindedly. "Shhh," he said at intervals, like he did with little Cindy when she got hurt. Susan wept helplessly until she had exhausted herself. He held her torpid frame away from him. "What happened, for God's sake?"

"I can't . . . it's too much."

He broke the question down into smaller units. "You were at the party, weren't you?"

"Yes."

"How did you come here?"

"I don't know. I think I took a taxi. No, wait—it was Roger's secretary who drove me."

"And where's David?"

Wrong question. Susan started crying again. Alan was not good at shaking or slapping hysterical women, so he just waited drowsily until she had regained some composure. He saw the red light on his bedside phone flash three times. From midnight to seven in the morning, his extension was automatically switched through to the answerphone in Eileen's office downstairs.

"I think David is trying to find you," he told Susan. "We should call him back."

"I will never ever speak to him again in my whole life. Nor with Jessica or anyone else." She helped herself to a Kleenex. "I wish I were dead."

"You can have Cindy's room for tonight. There are toys everywhere, but I suppose you won't mind."

The light began to flash once more. This time Alan picked up the receiver before the answering machine in the office took over. It was David.

"Is Sue with you?" he asked.

"Yes, she's here."

"I thought so. Did she tell you what happened?"

"Her waterworks were on all the time."

"Actually, it's none of your business. Send her home. Tell her I want to apologize."

"It's David," Alan said over the mouthpiece. "He says he's sorry."

Susan crushed the Kleenex, which was smeared with mascara. "I'm sorry, too. I'll never stop being sorry for the rest of my life."

That was not very helpful. "Is it all right then? Do you want to go home?"

She shrugged. "Some problems can never be solved," she said cryptically.

David was still speaking into Alan's ear, urging him to put Susan in a cab.

"Maybe it would be better to let her sleep here. You can come and fetch her tomorrow," Alan suggested in a final attempt to be diplomatic.

Fortunately, Susan yielded. "Call a cab if David absolutely insists. It's no use arguing with him."

Alan said goodbye to David and dialed the number of Lady Cabs, which Eileen had written down for him on a narrow sheet of paper together with some other useful phone entries.

"Someone will be here in a few minutes. I'll see you to the front door."

"No, don't. You're ill. I'm sorry I disturbed you." Susan sounded apathetic now, which worried him more than her fit had done.

Limply, she rose from his bed. "You're a nice chap. You have no idea what it's like to hate someone. Good night, Alan," she murmured and disappeared so soundlessly that, later the next morning when Alan woke up, he wasn't sure whether the nighttime visit had taken place at all. There was something highly surreal and hallucinagenic about it.

His headache had eased away, and after three cups of tea his throat began to clear. He decided he was fine enough to go down and help Eileen, who would come in today although it was a Sunday. Tomorrow the new courses started and she had to look through applications and arrange classes. Apart from that, there was plenty to be organized for the dress rehearsal and the première. New complications kept popping up; his cold, Simon's crazy plans for Eileen and Susan's nervous breakdown.

As he reached the bottom of the stairs, Eileen came in through the front door. In unison, they froze and stared at the mess on the floor between them. The entry hall poster of *Taming of the Shoe* had been torn into tiny pieces that lay strewn all over.

Chapter Two

"Oh no," Eileen protested, "not another hip replacement."

"You've only had one so far. And we're not talking about hips but about your knee." Simon hoped it wouldn't take all Sunday afternoon to convince her. He sat across the edge of her desk, which was covered with neat piles of mail, forms and lists.

She shook her head, and her fine, mouse-brown hair swung from side to side.

"Dr. Shelley said my case was too complicated to justify the risk of an artificial knee implant," she reminded him, unnecessarily since Simon worked with Dr. Shelley five days a week.

"That was because you had immunosuppression complications with your hip prosthesis. But that was before Professor Johnson published his new study on allogeneic vascu—"

"Oh, stop it, will you. I hate it when you talk to me in medical terms. I hate all those cold words. They hurt."

"Just as your leg hurts—and it won't stop unless you do something about it." He bent forward and touched her shoulder. "Look, all I want from you at the moment is to accompany me to Professor Johnson's lecture. He's a very sought-after man. He'll be in Europe for only three weeks. I had to use all my influence to get us two seats for his talk."

"You've done what?" Eileen blinked and pushed her gold-rimmed glasses up the bridge of her nose. "You've made all the arrangements before asking me what I think about it? Tell me it's not true." she began to shuffle through some papers nervously.

"Just imagine. You could walk with a cane. You'd have one hand free. Stairs would no longer be an obstacle. You wouldn't depend on—"

"Yes, I get the picture," she interrupted him. "When and where is this talk?"

He was gaining ground. "On Tuesday, in Richmond, at the Richmond Gate Hotel. It's a lovely conference hotel with excellent cuisine. We'll have a great day, believe me."

"You mean this Tuesday? The day after tomorrow? When we have our dress rehearsal? Impossible. The twins are ill." She was referring to Mira and Shireen, the girls who took turns in the box office and helped Eileen out. They weren't really twins, but extreme look-alikes. They had just spent a holiday together in the Dominican Republic and had returned with a bad virus that would keep them off work for at least a week. "Alan won't let me go."

Simon looked out of the window that framed a dull view of the black-and-white house on the other side of Duke's Road, saying casually, "Alan has no objections."

"You've already talked to him?" she gasped. "What is this? A conspiracy?"

"You're too young to spend the rest of your life on those crutch-es." To stress his point, he tapped at the metallic devices that stood leaning against the desk.

Eileen was unconvinced. "It's better than going back into the wheelchair. There's always a great risk in these operations."

He gave her a moment to ponder over it.

"Would you be very disappointed if I said no?" she asked eventually.

Simon tenderly touched her hair. He had met Eileen in the darkest moments of her life when she had been brought to the London Clinic for prolonged post-operative care. He had massaged her countless times. He could draw an X-ray of her by memory, and a map of the scars on her body as well. Whenever he kneaded her tense muscles, he longed to be able to put his hands under her skin and remove all the painful knots. He knew her so well. There was no way she could disappoint him.

"Chances are you'll make a great leap forward. Next thing you know, you'll put on a pair of tap shoes and out-dance Jessica."

Eileen smiled leniently. It was good to see her face brighten up. It made her pretty in an unexpected way.

"I'm tired of hoping, Simon. I feel as if I've parched all my resources. Apart from this, I also don't think that listening to that famous American professor will help me since I won't make heads or tails of what he says. I'll have no idea how it applies to my case."

Simon opened his mouth to answer, but she went on, "Don't say that you'll explain it all to me afterwards. You're a physio and he'll use specialist medical terminology."

"No problem. After his talk, you can ask Johnson personally about your case. I made an appointment with him."

Eileen leaned forward and closed her fingers around Simon's wrists. "You made an appointment? Why haven't you asked him to bring along his instruments so he can give me an operation on the spot?"

Simon wasn't worried. He could see that she was more amused than angry.

"You should have asked me earlier," she groaned.

"To tell the truth, I even considered not asking you at all but rather kidnapping you on Tuesday morning and taking you to Richmond against your will."

She laughed and shook her head. Strands of her soft hair got caught in the side-piece of her glasses and she raked them back.

"I know you won't give in until I say yes. The problem is there'll be a lot of walking involved—from the parking lot to the hotel, from the conference room to the dining room and so forth."

Gotcha, he thought. "Ay, there's the rub . . . You should be able to live without fearing every single step. Don't worry about walking. When you get tired I can always carry you."

Eileen gave a final sigh. "You win. I insist we share the costs."

He suppressed an impulse to hug her. It wasn't easy to hug someone enthusiastically and carefully at the same time.

"No need to discuss finances. You're my guest. I'll fetch you at six-thirty in the morning. There's a breakfast buffet at the hotel. Smart dress."

At that moment, the door to Eileen's office was banged against the wall and Jessica barged in.

"Did you know that the one thing you and Roger have in common is the way you open doors?" Simon observed.

"Oh, shut up and get lost," Jessica flared at him.

It was only now that Simon noticed that Jessica's face looked asymmetric and swollen. He slid from the desk, scratched the side of his head and wondered if he should offer his consolation and advice.

"Don't look at me. Leave us alone," Jessica insisted and began to weep.

Simon closed the door and shrugged off his concern. Eileen would know how to calm Jessica. He heard fragments of loud music and strode along the corridor to the auditorium where they were testing the acoustics. He saw Pamela standing behind the rear row of seats.

"Sounds hollow over here," she shouted toward the stage. Pamela Hay, the former Mrs. Widmark, was a feast for the eyes—thick hair the color of wheat with freckles to match and a body in tight jeans. The day Alan had told him that Pam was leaving him for Martin Shennan—the man who wrote the music for their shows—Simon had begun to pursue her, so far without success.

He approached her from behind and surprised her with a kiss on the shoulder. "Hello, sweet Pam. Still dating that bloke from the band?"

Pam nudged him with an elbow. "I'm going to marry Martin in May. You're not invited."

"Pity. I've recently specialized in Kissing the Bride. You can hire me for weddings."

She grinned. "Go over there," she pointed, "and listen if the bass is strong enough."

Simon saluted and marched to the left corner. Martin switched on the playback for a few seconds.

"Sounds as if the bass isn't plugged in at all," Simon noted.

Alan, who had been posted at the far right side, agreed.

Together they went to the stage where Martin was angrily fumbling with an extension cord. "You're right. I brought the wrong adapter. Shit."

A little to the side, six-year-old Cindy sat quietly playing with bits and pieces of the equipment. Simon picked her up and threw her into the air. "Hey, little beauty queen. Have you got a spare adapter for Martin?" She giggled and he put her back on her feet. She was a beautiful child for sure. She had a heart-shaped face, Pam's big blue eyes with endless eyelashes, and Alan's shining black hair.

Like an expert, she searched among her treasures and came up with something that looked useful to Simon. He gave it to Martin. "Will that help?"

"Grand. Let's try again." He plugged and switched and soon the small theatre reverberated with the pounding bass.

Simon sat down at Cindy's side. "Isn't that way too loud for you?" he shouted over the noise. "You'll ruin the fine hairs in your auditory canal."

Cindy waited with her answer until the music had stopped. "Just as Mummy said. You're always giving people medical advice," she informed him. "When you're not flirting that is,

Mummy also said. And Martin says you're congopiscent. What is congopiscent?"

Simon made a stern face. "Martin shouldn't teach you such words. Concupiscent means, well, er . . ."

"Randy. It means randy," Alan helped out. His voice was hoarse.

Simon stood up before Cindy could ask what randy meant. "You look haggard, old boy. Having trouble with the maintenance payments?"

"No, with the tonsils. It started yesterday with a terrible headache. I couldn't even go to Roger's party. Come, I want to show you something." He took Cindy by the hand and they descended the spiral staircase to the basement, where Alan opened the door of a small storage room. "I've got a surprise for you. I had some time to kill over Christmas. What do you say?"

They went in. Simon was overwhelmed. Alan had painted the walls in creamy peach and had furnished the windowless room with a massage table, a pine desk and chair, a small cupboard and an electric heater. Two uplighters illuminated the scene with their soft glow.

"That's fab. Wonderful. I love it." He hugged Alan so fiercely that he provoked a coughing fit. "Thank you. That's the long-desired ratification of my unofficial status as—what would you call it? Your dancers' leg minder?"

Alan was chuffed. "I thought we could make the situation a bit more official. I want to pay you."

"No way," Simon declined. "I wouldn't accept money from you."

"I'd feel better if I paid you. You spend most of your free time here."

"This is my true calling, mate. I come here for my own amuse-ment. You should see some of the clients I treat at the Clinic. Old, fat, ugly, hairy."

"Stinking," Cindy offered.

Simon ruffled her hair. "I'd have considered re-education as a vet had it not been for your splendid girls, Alan. Don't ever talk about money again, do me a favor."

Cindy hopped on the massage table. "Why is it called a massage table and not a massage bed?" She lay down as if for sleep.

Pamela joined them. "Hey, Cindy, love, are you tired? Shall I take you upstairs?"

Cindy opened her bright eyes. "Can I stay with Dad tonight?"

"No, your Dad's ill. Maybe next week."

Cindy pulled a face and Pam took her hand. "Let's go up and play. Martin says he doesn't need me as a sound operator any longer. We could teach Ginger a new line."

When he was alone with Alan, Simon said, "Pam told me she's going to marry. Does it hurt?"

They leant against the massage table. "Not any longer. There was a time when I wanted to knock Martin down with his own guitar."

"You could have tied him to a loudspeaker and turned the volume to maximum—best thing you can do with a man who steals your wife."

"And my daughter as well. I would have preferred Cindy to grow up in more civilized surroundings, not in that musicians' commune."

"Yeah," Simon nodded, "She'd be far better off with her bisexual father and his dance troupe."

Alan punched Simon's upper arm with his elbow. "You're just the right person to lecture me on my lifestyle."

Ron stuck his head round the door. He was the electrician, a heavy young man with a bald head the shape of a light bulb. "Alan, we haven't got any more spare lamps. I have to replenish the stocks."

"Eileen will give you the money."

Ron's head was withdrawn.

"Did you get anywhere with Eileen?" Alan wanted to know.

"All the way--well, metaphorically speaking. She was wax in my hands. Of course, she went through the motions of protesting and fighting, but not for long."

"I wonder what she'll say when she finds out that the operation costs a fortune and can only be carried out by Professor Johnson and his team in the States. Especially when none of us has the money to pay for it."

"How about a Rescue Eileen Lanigan Charity Performance?"

Alan laughed sadly. "You never think farther than the next step, that's the problem with you. You're raising hopes in Eileen that are very likely to be dashed."

"Don't worry, we'll get the money somehow. There's Roger, for example. He's rich enough to buy the Johnson Institute if he wants to."

The corridor began to fill with chatter. Simon straightened himself. "It's too bad I won't be here for the dress rehearsal. I could lend a hand with the costumes. Your girls will need someone to zip them into those tight leather dresses."

Alan sneezed disapprovingly.

"Ah, that's where you're hiding, Alan." It was David, who studied the cozy room with his steel-gray eyes. "Looks like a brothel if you ask me."

"It's my new consultation room," Simon explained proudly. "Does anyone need my hands on them?"

"Not yet. Wait till after the rehearsal." David turned to Alan with a reproachful look. "Alan, the troupe's a tad decimated today. Laura will be late because she must take her Latin Lover to Heathrow. And Sue has caught your flu. You'd better keep out of everybody's way if you don't want to jeopardize your show."

"I can't put myself in quarantine," Alan replied. "There's too much work, but I promise I won't give out any kisses."

"Yes, you can leave the kissing to me," Simon confirmed. "Where's Luigi going?"

"Rome, I suppose. Hope he'll be back for the première or

Laura won't be able to perform properly."

When David had left, Alan folded his arms and cast a warning glance at Simon. "You had better keep your hands off Laura if you don't want Luigi to start a vendetta."

Simon tried not to show that Alan was looking right through him. A thought struck him. "How did Susan catch your flu? You said you weren't at the party, didn't you?"

Alan cupped his chin. "Well, that's kind of weird. Susan came to see me last night. She was frazzled and said she wanted to die and never ever to speak to anyone again and some such melodramatic things. I didn't know what to make of it."

"Maybe it was just a lovers tiff with David. Wouldn't surprise me." He moved his chin in the direction where David had stood. "He's as charming as a toilet brush."

"What worries me most is that she said she hated Jessica."

"Susan said that? Oh, dear." Simon began to divine why Jessica was so upset. What a mess. He had to be careful what he said now. "Anything else?"

"No. David phoned and ordered me to send Sue home in a cab. Do you have any idea what's behind all this?"

"More than an idea, actually. I can't tell you, though—it's a matter of discretion." He stepped into the corridor. "I must talk to Jessica."

"Wait." Alan grabbed his arm. "What's going on?"

"We'll talk later." He left Alan behind and climbed the main staircase to the hall. The door to Eileen's office stood open. He went in and took his usual seat on the desk.

"Where's Jessica?"

Eileen was tapping something into the computer keyboard. "She has gone to do her warm-up," she said without looking up.

"Why was she crying?"

"No need for you to know."

Simon grasped the back of Eileen's chair and turned her to face him.

"Alan told me that Susan came to cry on his shoulder last night after Roger's party. Taking this plus Jessica's red eyes, I can't help but fear that Susan found out about David's affair with Jessica."

Eileen's dark eyes looked small through the thick glasses. She took them off and rubbed the bridge of her nose. "Susan is the smaller problem."

"Does that mean Roger has found out, too? That's a catastrophe."

"No, Roger's still in the dark. Jessica was close to confessing, but luckily she changed her mind."

"Now you've lost me."

"Roger and Jessica had a row. He slapped her and—"

"He hit her? The brute. I hope she hit him back."

"She ran upstairs and David followed her. That's when things got really messed up."

"In what way?"

Eileen replaced her glasses and turned up her palms in an defensive gesture. "Sorry, Simon. I promised Jessica not to tell anyone. Not even you."

He shook his head. "And Roger? I mean, what's the state of things between him and Jessica at the moment?"

"Armistice. This morning, she forgave him for hitting her and he forgave her for ruining his party. They were so busy forgiving each other that for a moment she considered telling him everything to get his complete absolution."

Simon felt the color drain from his face. "That would have been my certain death."

Eileen patted his leg. "Seducers lead a dangerous life as you should know by now." More seriously she went on, "Please, leave Jessica alone at the moment. She's fed up with men in general and with her lovers in particular."

"And you must be fed up with Jessica's problems. She's always unburdening herself to you."

She smiled her heart-warming smile. "As long as I can pass some of it on to you."

There was a short, companionable silence, then Eileen said, "I'm beginning to look forward to Tuesday. A day away will do me good."

Simon bent down and kissed her hair. "It's going to be quite romantic. Just you and me and droves of surgeons."

Chapter Three

With painful slowness, she awoke—unable to move, unable to localize the body that seemed to consist of paralyzed nothingness. Her eyelids were sticky and her breath shallow. A stifling panic rose. Where was she? Who was she? The only familiar aspect was the confusion itself. She knew vaguely that she had felt it many times before. It would pass. She concentrated on sounds. There was someone beside her, breathing. The shock opened her eyelids. She managed to turn her head to the left. Against the gray night sky framed by a high, narrow window, she could see the outline of a body under a quilted duvet. She tried to scream, but all her dry throat would generate were feeble, ghostly whimpers.

The body beside her reacted, a hand was stretched out and placed on her left shoulder. Instantly, her body materialized.

"Jessica, love," the stranger said in a sleepy, soothing voice. "It's me, Roger. You're having one of your identity crises." The world shifted back into place.

"Better?" Roger yawned.

Jessica sat up and nodded into the darkness. "Hmm. Go back to sleep." She shuddered in the aftermath of the dreadful sensation. Why did it happen to her over and over again? As far back as she could remember, she had been tormented by these momentary losses of memory and body-control. Her mother had been convinced that Jessica suffered from nothing worse than a variant of infantile somnambulism which would subside over the years, and had seen no reason to consult a doctor; but the blackouts returned whenever Jessica was distressed. She had the fixed idea that one day she wouldn't find her way back to reality.

Roger drew her toward him. "Come on, Jess, lie down again. You're getting cold. Was it very bad this time?"

"It's always bad." Spoon-like, she cuddled into his warmth.

"I keep telling you that you need psychotherapy," Roger mumbled and began to breathe regularly. Jessica couldn't sleep with someone so close to her, but she stayed where she was, in her husband's embrace, and squinted into the darkness. She was not surprised it had happened tonight. Her life had begun to disintegrate. She had managed to mess it up completely, hadn't she? She didn't belong here.

She had felt like a child playing house ever since she'd moved in with Roger and his polished furniture, his affected manservant and affectionate housekeeper, his fine wines and first-rate meals. She was a stranger, an intruder. Her home was The Caesar. Well, had been. Not any longer.

David was still in love with her, more desperately than ever. And Susan had found out. There was no way they could work together any longer. The situation had never been exactly relaxed and easy, but now it had become impossible.

The rehearsal the day before had been a nightmare for Jessica. She wished David and Susan would be abducted by a UFO. Thank God Susan hadn't been at the rehearsal, so that Jessica had been able to at least postpone the dreaded confrontation with her. Eileen hadn't been much of a help in this case. She had advised her to call Susan and to put things straight as soon as possible. Stupid idea. What did Eileen know about passion and jealousy? Hold it. That was a nasty thing to think.

Jessica stirred under Roger's heavy arm. Well, her marriage crisis seemed solved for the time being. She didn't know if it would last. She wasn't even sure whether it had been a good idea to forgive him. The slap had been her chance to break away and put the blame on him—but as long as she didn't know where she could go, she was stuck. Hold it once more. Roger was a good husband, dependable and caring. Jessica realized with surprise that she respected him more since he had hit her.

Her alarm clock began to give tiny beeps increasing in volume. She stretched out her arm and tapped the switch. Now was the time for her breathing exercise. Roger, half-awake, began to caress her breasts, and her nipples reacted. With the detached interest of someone who is having an out-of-body experience, Jessica noticed the symptoms of lust. She unbuttoned her nightshirt. Roger cupped her left breast and squeezed the nipple between his fingers.

"Let's make love, shall we?" she whispered to her own surprise and turned around to kiss him. At first he was too overwhelmed to react. Then he quickly slipped out of his pajamas. He was probably afraid she might change her mind. Jessica sat up, let her shirt glide from her shoulders and positioned herself astride his square hips. Normally, Roger preferred to make love in a position where he was on top; only this morning, she knew, he wouldn't dare propose it. For once, he wouldn't try to force his will on her. She bent down and kissed the fur on his chest. Roger's embrace was good, real and reassuring. The darkness added to her feeling of being held and protected, shielded from her inner turmoil. A sinking feeling spread from her throat, all the way down across her belly, and deeper. She ran her fingers through his hair, which was soft for a man of his build, and gently licked his thinning hairline.

"Ah, Jess," he moaned, encircling her waist with his hard fingers and moving her so that he could reach her breasts with his mouth. When his teeth sank into her skin, Jessica gasped with satisfaction.

Like eiderdowns, the gray clouds hung in the dark sky, and the cold air pricked her lungs pleasantly. Jessica sucked in gulps of air that stung like needles of ice and puffed out bluish clouds. She felt so dynamic that she came to the conclusion that sex in the morning was, after all, an excellent substitute for breathing exercises.

She closed the garden gate and banged her mittened hands. To her left, the slope of Primrose Hill rose gently, lit by dozens of lamps. It was a familiar sight that she loved for all the memories it held. She had grown up in this part of London, a fact that she had not revealed to Roger for fear he could guess that nostalgia was one of the reasons why she had accepted his marriage proposal. Not very flattering for a man to conquer a woman's heart that way.

Every day she walked swiftly along Regents Park Road to the corner of Primrose Hill Road and passed her parents' old house. It was empty, the last tenants having moved out years ago. Her parents hadn't wanted to re-let it. The deserted house had come in handy when she had looked for a place to meet David. Too handy. Pragmatic obstacles can be a great help in avoiding major faults. She entered the park and was about to start running when she heard someone call her name.

"Jessica, heel!"

As she turned, she saw a Labrador catch up with its master, who patted it and called it a good dog. "I thought you were talking to me," she said.

The man fixed the lead to the dog's collar and looked up. Friendly eyes in a wrinkled face studied her. "So your name must be Jessica as well."

Jessica began to run on the spot. "Jessica Warner. Lovely morning, isn't it?"

The man looked about him doubtfully. "When you're as old as I am, you're never warm enough. I wish I didn't have to go out in this weather and at this hour. But the dog . . . . My name's Raymond Aldridge."

"I haven't seen you around the park before, Mr. Aldridge. You must have moved into the vicinity only recently."

Mr. Aldridge patted Jessica the dog, who pranced about as if to mimic Jessica the jogger. "No, been living here for years. I just don't go out very often anymore, but this week I have to because my daughter left her dog with me while she's in hospital."

"Nothing serious I hope," Jessica said feelingly.

"Appendicitis. She'll be back on her feet in a few days. This tracksuit of yours looks nice. Never seen anything so shiny."

"Red's my favorite color," Jessica said. "It's been a pleasure talking to you. I'm sure we'll meet again tomorrow."

"Looking forward to it."

The old man and the dog walked away, and Jessica smiled at their disappearing shapes then began to run. She circled the hill, her feet pounding the grass, her head becoming lighter. Her private troubles seemed small now. Susan would certainly forgive David his adultery, obsolete as it was. If David had taken umbrage at her refusal to renew their affair it was his problem, not hers, Jessica decided and slowed her steps as she left the park at the corner of Albert Terrace. She crossed the street and returned home.

Showered, dressed and refreshed, she entered the dining room in the conservatory. She stooped to kiss Roger on the head and drew back her chair. Suddenly it occurred to her that something was wrong. Roger was not reading the Financial Times, he was not eating, he just sat staring at her with a face that looked as if cast in iron. What had she done, for God's sake?

"Read it," he said and with his index finger pointed at her plate.

Jessica looked down and saw a letter, folded twice. Her hands began to tremble although she had no idea what she had to fear from a piece of paper. She unfolded it slowly. Blocked by anxiety, she couldn't decipher the words at first.

"Read it aloud," ordered Roger.

"'Jessica had two . . . lovers.'" She swallowed dryly.

"Go on."

"'One was David Powell, the other Simon Jenkinson.'" Jessica sank into the chair, her eyes fixed on the neat block letters.

Roger said, "Tell me it's not true."

Jessica's throat and lips were dry. She took her glass of milk and drank. Roger's fist whacked on the table. Jessica choked and coughed, the milk lapping up the side of her glass. Quickly, she dried her chin with a napkin. Her mind had gone blank and she couldn't come up with anything to say.

"Tell me it's not true," he repeated with authority, pushing himself up with his fists against the tabletop and towering above her. Jessica jerked up and her chair toppled over.

"Roger," she gasped and backed away, hands over her face. "Don't hit me."

Two steps and she was against the window. He hadn't moved. He approached slowly, right hand extended like a whip ready to lash out.

"You promised," she winced. "You said you wouldn't hit me again."

His voice rose. "So, it is true."

She nodded behind her palms. He took her roughly by the shoulders and motioned her back to the table, raised the chair from the floor and pressed her down on it. To her growing unease, he remained upright,tall and menacing.

"Jessica, I must know the truth. I can't stand being cuckolded." There was an unsteady streak in his voice. "Tell me about David. Were you so impressed by his dancing skills that you had to end up in bed with him?"

He looked so defeated in his anger that she began to realize how deeply she had hurt him. Their lovemaking this morning only added to the strain, rendering both of them exposed and prone to humiliation.

"It was nothing, really. A silly mistake." She avoided his gaze and looked at her hands, which lay clenched into fists in her lap.

"When did it start?"

"He began to pursue me the day he joined the troupe. I was annoyed. He behaved properly as long as there were others around, but the moment we were alone he would become pushy. I tried to ignore him but he wouldn't give in. It was flattering in a way. In the end, I yielded. I wish I hadn't." She lowered her head further. Roger grabbed her chin and forced it up.

"Look at me, Jessica. How long did it last?"

"Not quite a year."

Roger kicked his chair so hard it banged against the mahogany sideboard. "A year? A silly mistake that lasted a year?"

Jessica threw her arms around herself. "I'm so terribly sorry. You know how difficult it is for me to break with habits."

Roger laughed bitterly. "Who would know better? Oh, Jess."

"David has never stopped loving me, and at the party, after you . . . ." She fell silent. Better not to remind him.

Roger had retrieved his chair and sat slumped, weary, shaking his head. "After I slapped you. I see. He was the knight in shining armor galloping on a white horse, ready to defend his queen."

Jessica looked up. "He thought it was his chance to win me back. I did my best to get rid of him. You must believe me. I never loved David. It was just . . . I don't know what it was."

"Another silly mistake? You're so young, Jess, so difficult to control." Roger lowered his head and dug his fingertips into his scalp.

"Susan overheard what I said to David. Do you know what I think?" She held up the letter like a defensive shield, something to distract Roger's attention from her adultery. "I think it was Susan who wrote this." She had destroyed Susan's marriage and now Susan wanted to destroy hers. Eileen had been right as always. Jessica should have called Susan. Too late now. In hindsight, there were so many things she could have done better.

Small things like switching off the heater that had caused the fire in the old studio; the fire that was responsible for Eileen's accident. Big things like falling in love with Alan before she was old enough to fathom the significance of her feelings. Now she had to fear that Alan would learn about her affairs. She couldn't stand the idea that he'd think badly of her.

Roger had been rummaging in his own grief. "Don't you understand what you've done to me? What if Susan starts spreading the news?"

There they were again, trying to keep up appearances. "I'm sure she won't," she said without conviction.

"Who else knows about your . . . your lovers?"

"Just Eileen." She knew he wouldn't care. In his eyes Eileen counted as a minor life-form. "And Simon." She dropped the name guardedly, not trusting Roger when he was irate. The ensuing silence was even more disturbing. Jessica watched the fried eggs congealing in the dish and the toast getting cold and hard. What a waste—not just the toast and the egg. Everything. The time people spend caring for each other, the misplaced feelings and devotions, the very nature of love.

Suddenly she wanted to run away, to leave the room, the house, London, England. She wanted to board the next plane to Auckland, throw herself into her mother's arms and cry. "I've made such a mess of my life, Mum," she wanted to say. "I've built it on lies and half-truths. I've betrayed my husband and my lover and even myself through denying myself the man I love. I don't want to see any of them again. I don't even want to see my best friend any more. Her disfigured face is a constant reproach. Her crippled legs are a reminder of how healthy and selfish I am. The stomping of her crutches is a physical pain I can feel all through my body. I want to quit, to cut the net I've got myself entangled in, to tear apart the bonds of friendship, love and other burdens. I want to be free of commitments. Then, I'm sure, I'll never wake up to another identity crisis." Oh, to have a planet all for herself, a larger-than-life stage where she could dance herself into oblivion.

Jessica took another sip of the milk, cold now, to steady herself.

Roger was pacing the room. "Simon. Simon of all men. That you fell for that lecherous bastard . . . . What a disgrace. How could you lower yourself to this?"

She bit her lips to conceal an involuntary smile. The affair with Simon was the one thing she refused to regret. It had been a most refreshing and uncomplicated experience. He was no solemn, worshipping lover as David had been. David had always asked her after their lovemaking whether she had enjoyed it. Pathetic! She had felt watched, unable to let herself go under the scrutiny of his glare, compelled to fake orgasms in order to avoid a discussion of what had gone wrong.

Simon had been too busy enjoying himself to care whether she liked his technique or not. When she had heard him come for the first time she had thought he was having an epileptic fit. God, how they had laughed. He was unceremonious and open to ideas, no matter how impracticable they were, making her feel like a zoo animal that was being released into the wilderness.

"So what about Simon? When? How long?" Roger insisted.

"Last autumn. It lasted no longer than a few weeks. He's absolutely discreet, so you don't have to worry."

She couldn't fool Roger. "How does Susan know then? . . . Assuming that she wrote the letter."

"I think I said something to David when he wouldn't stop pestering me on Saturday night. Since Susan was eavesdropping she must have heard it."

Roger circled the table. His hand smacked down on the back of the chair. "Were there others? More lovers? More silly mistakes?" He was behind her now. The muscles in her back grew tense.

"No." It was the truth. The clock on the mantelpiece began to chime. Nine sharp. She was famished after her run in the cold. "What will you do now? Throw me out?" In a way, she hoped he would because that would make for a clean cut.

"No, I'm not a man of rash actions. . . and I still love you." He pressed his hands firmly on her shoulders as though he wanted to keep her from rising and running, far, far away. "God knows why. You've trampled upon my feelings from the day we met, but I'll give you another chance."

How generous, how bloody noble of him. Now she'd have to prove herself worthy of his magnanimity.

"It's a most unsuitable moment to make sudden changes," he went on, "with your première coming up and all. We'll sleep on it."

Sleep on it. As if she were a house he was considering buying or selling.

"We'll sort it out sensibly. I'm not going to be divorced a third time."

Jessica knew he was waiting for a final word from her. "Thank you," she murmured, uncertain as to whether she was truly grateful. She felt disgusted by his condescending patience. When he had gone, she crumpled the letter into a neat little ball and flicked it into the fire.

Chapter Four

"No. Oh, my God . . . aah . . . Jesus . . . . Noooooooo!" Simon arched his back and then collapsed onto a cushion of ginger curls.

Laura panted and laughed. "Don't ever dare to have an orgasm so close to my ear again!"

"Let's try another position, then."

Laura freed her hair and stood up, which caused the waterbed to wobble softly. "Take your fingers off my . . . . Hey, stop that. I'm hungry."

"All I want is to spoil you with a massage. It's a special technique with essential oils."

Laura, beautiful in her nudity, went to ferret about in the kitchen. "I mustn't be late today. We're shooting the video clip."

"I know, but it's not even noon. There's plenty of time for a quick one." He followed her.

"I'd rather have a quick meal. Your fridge is empty except for two eggs."

"Free-range eggs," he specified. "We've had an opulent breakfast. Nothing's left." He nibbled at her earlobe and grasped her buttocks. He loved dancers and their stunning bodies.

She closed the fridge and indicated the fruit bowl. "All you have is oranges. I'm starving." She fingered the refrigerator magnet, a miniature kitchen clock with hands the shape of cutlery.

Simon opened the deep freeze and yanked out a package of fettucini in sugo. "I usually eat at the Clinic. At home I live mostly on Marks and Spencer ready meals. Sorry—I know you've been spoilt by Luigi and his refined *cucina italiana*."

Laura eyed the package with mistrust, removed the lid and had a closer look at the contents. "That doesn't agree with me. You can have it." She probed inside the freezer and brought forward rice with chicken tikka. "That will do. Heat it up for me. I'll go and dress in the meantime."

With a defeated shrug, Simon pushed their meals into the microwave and went to put on some clothes as well. Five minutes later the timer dinged and they sat down in molded plastic chairs at the round bistro table in Simon's crammed kitchen. He began to shovel pasta into his mouth.

"Simon, stop eating like that," Laura admonished him.

"Anything wrong with the way I'm eating?" he munched and took a swig from his glass.

"Reminds me of my father. He's a taxidermist. He stuffs dead animals."

Simon swallowed, grinned and tried to civilize his manners.

Listlessly, Laura forked her rice. "Luigi will be back tomorrow. All you and I had was a one-night stand. You were so good." She sighed and seemed to evaluate what was better: a man who could cook or a man who could satisfy her.

"You mean better than your splendid Latin Lover? That's all the blandishment I need."

"I can only hope Luigi never finds out—otherwise he'd kill you. He's a passionate man."

"For me, passion is not about killing. Shall I show you?"

Her answer was a kick on his shin—oh, those muscular dancer legs.

"No, for you, passion is about taking as many women to bed

as possible. It's an Olympic discipline."

"Would you be very surprised to learn that you have been my farewell performance to promiscuity?"

Laura lifted her eyebrows one by one. "I'm not sure if I'm flattered."

"A connoisseur always saves the best bit till last."

"That sounds as if you keep a list. Must be a long one, what with all the beautiful gals in our troupe."

"Ah, no, most of them are too young for me." He licked the rest of the sauce from his plate. "And Susan is off limits because she's glued to David."

Laura obviously enjoyed taking stock. "And Jessica's entirely fixated on dancing—the most one-dimensional character I've ever met. Maybe she hasn't even noticed yet that there are two sexes."

Simon hid his grin behind a napkin. "Where does she put Roger then, as a species I mean?"

Laura curled and recurled a lock of her hair. "To me he looks as if he's impotent so she probably hasn't got to put him anywhere."

"Or his dick, for that matter. You must have been around if you can tell a man's potency level by his looks." Simon put his shin out of reach.

"Roger is so stiff it looks as if he has to compensate for something." Laura glanced at her watch. "Blast it. I knew I'd be late. Let's go."

"Alan won't tear your head off," he said as he put their dishes on the draining board and stuffed the oranges into a plastic bag.

"It's David I'm afraid of." Laura looked down her front and buttoned her overcoat. "He always tries to degrade me."

Simon put on his anorak. "He made you understudy for Jessica. That means a great deal."

Laura rolled her eyes upwards. "Forget it. Jessica will never under any imaginable circumstance not appear on stage. She had the Aztec two-step during the last two performances of *Tap As*

You Like It, speeding to get to the loo whenever she came off-stage. But there she was, dancing away like the devil. Understudy for Jessica—tell me a better one."

"You sound bitter," Simon said as they descended the stairs.

"I'm not bitter. I simply can't stand the way David treats me. When he had me rehearse Jessica's part, he kept interrupting me every two seconds, making the choreography easier for me because he found I wasn't up to it. 'Laura, dear, you've missed out on the syncopation again, haven't you?' He'd never dare speak in such tones to Jessica. Treats her like a goddess, he does. He's an asshole."

"But a handsome asshole, to be sure." Simon knew he had made a mistake the moment the words were out.

Laura gave him the sharpest look she could bring into her soft eyes. "He thinks he's God's gift to mankind, and his rehearsals are a military drill."

They stepped out into the bleak winter day and turned up their collars. Simon put his arm on Laura's shoulder as they walked. The bag with the oranges dangled around his knees. "Why don't you just tell him you want to be treated with more respect?"

"When you say it, it sounds so easy. What's your secret?"

"Maybe it's just that I'm a very straightforward person and that I handle others as if they were, too. I never look for hidden messages." He kissed her cheek, which was red from the cold. "You're such a lovely and talented girl. You should be more self-confident. Listen, everybody has a weak spot. Find the weak spot in David and you'll have him down on his knees in no time."

"Any offers what his weak spot might be?"

They passed the BMJ bookshop, Simon's favorite hangout, where he had recently bought a book about rejection sensitivity. One of the case studies was about a sociopath with an astounding resemblance to David. "Just think how he always tries to impress you with quotes, which he gets wrong most of the time. He's a sparrow with fluffed-up feathers because he thinks it makes him look like an eagle. Question his authority, contradict him, show him you're superior to him, and his boosted ego will deflate just like that." He filled his cheeks with air and let it out through his pursed lips, producing a farting sound.

"Can't you ever see the serious side of things? David was in a terrible mood yesterday although we all worked hard and gave twice our best. He's used to working with professionals. He's got no patience for amateurs. It's going to be worse today because of the filming. Of course he's nervous, what with all the responsibility he has. Why can't he admit it instead of making everybody feel miserable?"

"Everybody except Jessica, you mean."

They had reached The Caesar. Laura halted her steps and frowned. "Come to think of it, he even made some disparaging remarks to her yesterday."

The more everybody and everything buzzed around her, the more Eileen became quiet and withdrawn, because she had no means to compensate for agitation by stomping and pacing around. She sat placidly as people from the film team came and went and bothered her with their quixotic demands. Genially, she handed out advice and information and explained the use of the copy machine. She smoothed out the odd skirmish, and between forays worked at her computer or answered phone calls. She was checking the balance sheets when Alan came in carrying a tray. "Simon has given out strict orders that everyone gets an extra dose of vitamin C today. He's squeezing the oranges himself. Don't ask how my kitchen looks."

Without looking up, Eileen took a glass from the tray and downed it thirstily. "Just what I needed."

"You're a busy woman today, you are. I'm sorry for that. I'll be glad myself when all that razzmatazz is over."

A cardboard box appeared in the door frame, followed by

Martin Shennan's bearded face. He plopped it on the desk. "Finally," he puffed. "I feared they wouldn't be ready in time." He parted the top of the box, produced a CD and waved it happily. "Ta-da! Three hundred of them for the post-performance sales. You'll have to find a nice place to display them. They'll sell like Elle McPherson's knickers."

"That's what you said about your first album," Alan replied evenly, "except that they were Cindy Crawford's knickers, if I remember correctly."

"Yeah, but this time we'll have the clip. We should have thought of that earlier. It was Pam's idea." As always when he mentioned Pamela to Alan, an apologetic look crossed his face. "And we also have your brilliant cover painting." He held the CD so close to Alan's eyes, he had to squint so hard his contact lenses almost fell out.

"Take it away. I've seen it, y'know."

To please Martin, Eileen took the CD. The cover was a print of the poster for the show. It had lost most of its wild expressionism in this reduced size. *The Shenanigans* was printed on top, and below, under the brushstrokes that represented Jessica's swirling feet, *Taming of the Shoe—The Soundtrack*. "That'll get you into the charts, I bet."

"You can keep it," Martin said generously and patted the pockets of his leather jacket. "Here's the delivery note. You must sign it. I've been wondering if we should print the poster on tee-shirts, too. How's the shooting going?"

Alan was still balancing the tray. "Don't ask me, I'm no expert. It's a kind of organized chaos. At least, I hope someone is in fact organizing it. Here, have a glass of freshly squeezed—"

"Ugh. Can't stand the stuff. Let's peep into the theatre. I want to see what awaits me tomorrow when they film the scenes with the boys and me. Guess where . . . . In a shoe shop. I can't wait to see the finished clip. What an exciting day."

What a day indeed. Once more Eileen attempted to work, but

the next disturbance followed instantly.

"Did you get your share?" Simon asked and moved a stack of registration forms aside at the corner of the desk. Half-sitting, half-standing he smiled down at Eileen.

"Yes, thanks." She swung around in her chair. "You've come to remind me of my workout I guess."

"Yep. Three sharp. The gym is waiting."

"Not today. I've got too much to do, with the twins being on sick leave and—"

"No excuses." Simon took her hands and gently pulled her toward him so that he could steady her as she got up. "One hour every day except weekends," he recited. "No exceptions granted. Refusal is futile." He handed her the crutches.

Eileen sighed. "You slavedriver. How about tomorrow when we're in Richmond?"

Grinning smugly, Simon played his trump card. From the rear trouser pocket of his jeans, he extracted a small, folded booklet. "This is the brochure of the Richmond Gate Hotel—and on page fourteen, what do you see?" He turned it around for her.

"'Cedars Health and Leisure Club,'" she read obediently. "There's no escape it seems. Let me see what they offer. Resistance gym, spa pool . . . ."

"Steam room, beauty treatments," Simon added.

Eileen laughed. She couldn't help it. "I assume those treatments are for you. I'm beyond beauty ideal—on the wrong side, unfortunately."

Simon smiled the special, tender smile he reserved for her. It never failed to warm her heart. He put the brochure on her desk. "Let's waste no more of your time. We'll have the gym to ourselves today, and I want to watch you to see if you've made any progress."

She knew she hadn't. "I'm happy if I can preserve the status quo. I can't possibly put on more weights or increase the number of repetitions. It's like pushing against a wall."

They walked to the lift and rode up to the first floor, where Simon opened the door to the changing room for her. "Let me take care of that problem. Sometimes all that's required to improve training effects is a slight change so that you can activate new muscle sections. You'll see."

Eileen sat down on the bench and clumsily began to strip to her underwear. Simon watched her thoughtfully. "I wish I had healing hands."

"You have," Eileen assured him and put on her training gear.

The gym was a small room crammed with a conglomeration of machines Alan had bought at the sell-out of a health spa two years ago. With the obligatory floor-to-ceiling mirror on one wall, it looked like a maze of chrome and leather. Simon helped Eileen to sit on the bike. Like most disabled people, she was touchy about being helped; but she was ready to make an exception for Simon because she had diagnosed him as a severe case of helper's syndrome.

To warm up, she had to cycle with resistance set to neutral for ten minutes. Simon used the time to adjust the weights on the machines she would use. He was such a good-looking bloke.

They were the beauty and the beast in reversed roles--more like the beau and the cripple. He was not the classical Adonis, though. Simon had a roundish face with small black eyes and low, straight eyebrows, thin lips and a reliable chin. He was neither tall nor athletic. His hands, that was true, were in a class of their own. She had learned to appreciate them.

Her first experience with massage treatment had been nothing less than torture. Tina, the masseuse, had dug her horny hands mercilessly into her thin thighs. Eileen was reduced to tears in minutes and begged to be spared the treatment. Dr. Shelley insisted that it was important for her recovery. Jessica took the initiative and convinced Dr. Shelley that the massage did more damage than good to Eileen, so she was handed over to Simon. It was a day Eileen would never forget. The sun had come out and shone into the treatment room, making her feel all the more naked and helpless. She was petrified when she saw Simon come in. A man. It would be worse. Had she been able to walk, she would have jumped off the table and run away.

To her surprise, he took her by the shoulders and helped her to sit up. "Better to say hello eye to eye, don't you think? I'm Simon, also known as London's most sensitive hands."

"Hello," she mumbled weakly and looked at his hands. Fine bones, smooth skin, long manicured fingers. There was hope.

"Tina is rude, isn't she? She's always in a hurry. I'm not going to hurt you, trust me. We'll take our time. Lie down and relax."

Within minutes, she was crying again; not with agony this time but with sheer pleasure. It was the moment when, after months of misery, she had finally stopped wishing she hadn't survived the accident, and she fell in love with Simon. For five years now she had been torn between gratefulness and despair. She was grateful for having a friend like him, but desperate whenever it struck her how futile it was to crave more.

"Don't slow down. Go on pedaling," Simon called over.

"I was thinking of our first encounter."

Simon looked at her. "You've changed a lot since then. You were so skinny I could feel the DNA of your muscle cells. I won't stop working on you until I have you fully reconstituted."

He had finished his round of the equipment and rolled up the sleeves of his white shirt. Eileen was overcome by a desire to kiss the fine white flesh of his inner forearms.

"Are you ready?" he asked her and put his hands over hers on the handlebars.

"For whatever you want me to do."

He closed his fingers around her wrists. "Eileen, you surprise me," he said in a deep voice. "I've never done it in a gym before, you know. Well, I suppose those machines could be used for some really startling positions."

She freed her right hand and slapped him playfully. Simon

kissed her palm. "Sorry, dear. I shouldn't make jokes about it. Let's start with the crunches."

Eileen took off her sweater, lay down on the long bench, bent her knees, clasped her hands behind her neck and curled her torso upwards. Simon pushed up her tank top to check her muscle contractions. With his warm, dry hand on her stomach, she exhaled and slowly lowered back down.

". . . nineteen, twenty." Simon counted her contractions. "Good. Now the twisted crunches." His hand moved across her flat abdomen. "Your left external obliques are weak compared to the right obliques. Make it two twists to the left after each twist to the right. That should balance you." He stood up and banged into Alan who had approached from behind.

"They won't let me watch the filming any longer," Alan snorted. "As if my sneezes could be heard above the music—and it's going to be synchronized anyway."

Simon nudged Alan. "That's cruel, mate—you're the mastermind behind it all and they don't let you watch. How's everyone doing?"

They went to sit on the weightlifting bench.

"Much better than I thought. At first, they were intimidated by the cameras and mikes, but now they're like fish in water. But I'm worried about Jessica because she's disconcerted and chaotic. She should be completely in her element, shouldn't she? It was a dream of hers to be filmed."

Eileen had finished her set of crunches and sat up. "She's having a private crisis. How does it show?"

"First, she put on the wrong dress," Alan itemized. "Then one of the screws on her shoes came loose because she had forgotten to fix it. The last catastrophe I saw before the director threw me out was that she almost kicked in the lens of a camera when they were shooting a close-up of her feet."

Eileen was worried. She had tried in vain to talk to Jessica in her dressing room. Jessica had been dismissive and monosyllabic. Was she still concerned about David or had she had another row with Roger? Eileen moved to the lat machine.

"We'll try a new variant here," Simon told her. "Grip the bar underhand and pull it down in front of you instead of behind."

Eileen tried. Simon stood up, went over to her and pressed his hand softly into the nape of her neck to correct her posture. She pulled the bar once more toward her chest.

"Tuck in your chin." He cupped her jaw with his hand. It was a gesture of great tenderness, but the spell of intimacy had already been broken by Alan's appearance. After two repetitions Simon let go of her.

"How's David?" Eileen asked Alan. "Is he very nervous?"

"That's another oddity. He's kind of nice. No snide remarks."

"He is indeed," Simon confirmed. "When I brought Laura in ten minutes late, he waved it off and said the schedule was being altered by those troublesome film people every five seconds."

"Laura?" Alan asked with a warning growl.

"We met in front of the stage door," Simon said lightly. Eileen knew from the way he grinned that he was lying. She pulled harder and quicker.

"David even touched me," Alan went on. "He patted me on the shoulder."

"I can't get over it," Simon gasped. "He was always afraid to catch a gay bug from you."

"It's not funny," Alan said and blew his nose. "I think he's behaving unnaturally. It must have something to do with Jessica. I told you how Susan came to see me after the party and said she wanted Jessica to be dead. Something has happened and I wish I knew what."

Simon and Alan turned their heads to Eileen, who pretended full concentration on her exercise. Alan shrugged and stood up. "I'll go and get some of your work done for you, Eileen."

She let go of the bar. "Don't. You'll mess up my tables and forms again."

"But I may answer the phone, may I? I know how it's done. You wait until it rings, lift the receiver—"

"Oh, buzz off."

Alan half laughed, half hiccuped and left. Simon went over to Eileen, sat astride the bench behind her and began to knead her shoulders. She shrugged off his hands, not knowing where her sudden bad temper came from. Was it because of Laura? Not very likely. As long as Simon just philandered and didn't start a firm relationship with another woman she'd never be seriously jealous.

"I think I'm nervous about tomorrow. One way or another I'll have to make a decision."

"We'll decide together," Simon promised.

Eileen, pacified, smiled at him over her shoulder. He kissed the ugly scar on her cheek. Simon had no problems touching her in places that others even avoided looking at.

It was late, eight by her watch, when Eileen decided to call it a day. She switched off the computer, removed her glasses and, like a tired child, rubbed her eyes with the backs of her hands. That's the price you pay for being indispensable, she thought as she taped a list to the computer monitor. The list consisted of do's and don'ts for the next day when she would be in Richmond. The don'ts were vital because Alan was no computer whiz and she preferred him to keep his hands off the keyboard.

The silence was soothing. Wisely, Alan had turned the room directly above her office into the gym so that she wouldn't be disturbed by the sound of hopping feet from the studios. Jazz dance was on tonight, as well as breakdancing and two ballet classes, but no sound came through.

The film crew and the dance troupe had all left together in high spirits for some pub to have a combined post-filming and pre-première celebration. Even Jessica, who usually declined attending these social ventures, had joined them. Eileen could only guess that she had been reluctant to go home and face another dispute with Roger. All the questions Eileen wanted to ask Jessica would have to wait until the day after tomorrow.

David had excused himself. No pub tour for him. Ostensibly, he wanted to go home and look after Susan. Eileen suspected he was avoiding Jessica. Sometimes Eileen wondered if she should call herself lucky for leading such an uneventful private life. She stretched her arms and rhythmically moved her shoulders up and down. It didn't help much; her tiredness grew by the minute. No pub tour for Eileen, either. They hadn't asked her because it was generally known that the constant pain in her left leg wore her down quickly and that all she longed for in the evening was a bed. A grumbling sound from her stomach made her aware of another problem. The last thing she had eaten had been a tuna sandwich for lunch. Now she finished the glass of protein shake Simon had prepared for her before he left. Strawberry flavor, it was too sweet to slake her thirst.

Hunger and weariness, Eileen thought with grim humor, the ultimate challenge for someone who has to walk home on crutches. The boarding house where she had a room was at Cartwright Gardens two streets away—five minutes for a lazy ambler, two for someone with Jessica's vigorous pace, twenty for Eileen, who had to place her feet carefully, her mind controlling every move. Had Simon brought her the news about Professor Johnson now, she'd have willingly agreed to have her busted knees, hips and all the other painful parts of her body replaced, never mind the risks.

Ten past eight. Maybe she should take the lift to the second floor, vandalize Alan's fridge and go to sleep in Cindy's room. He'd have no objections. Another resort was the wheelchair that stood in a store room near the hall. She could wheel herself home and leave the crutches behind. Tired as she was, even making the decision proved too great an effort. She was granting herself a few minutes of unrestrained self-pity when Helen came in, a youthful-looking woman of sixty-odd years with wiry gray hair and a nose as red as a beacon. Her job was to take care of the costumes, shoes and props. Dressed in a thick padded jacket, she was ready to leave.

"I say, luv," she said brightly, as if working overtime were her idea of invigoration. "Chaos has been defined anew today. The costumes were scattered and hidden in the strangest places." She searched her pockets and brought forward a crumpled sheet. "Thanks to your list I could check if I'd found everything. You must print out a new one. I used this one to cross out the items I put back in place."

Eileen took the sheet from her, smoothed out the creases and wrote "Print" across it with a red felt pen. She then saw that something still seemed to be missing. "You haven't ticked off . . . Oh, it's Jessica's practice shoes. Well, I suppose it's because they were at their usual place anyway."

"No, they weren't. I wanted to ask you if Jessica had taken them home with her."

"Not as far as I know. It's highly unlikely."

"Surely Roger wouldn't let her practice on his parquet floor, would he?" Helen scoffed. "Well, she won't need the shoes for the dress rehearsal tomorrow."

"She uses them for her warm-up. She'll be upset if the shoes don't turn up in time."

Unconcerned, Helen waved it off. "She's a bit obstinate, isn't she? Grand airs like a prima ballerina. A sound thrashing would help to put the world straight for her. If she's so particular about her practice shoes, she's got to take better care of them."

"Normally she does. Alan said she was a bit distraught today."

"Everybody was. Except myself of course. How about you? You look worn-out," Helen said with unusual motherliness.

"You could do me a favor and fetch me the wheelchair from the store room."

"Rubbish," Helen said resolutely. "I'll give you a lift home. Not much of a detour for me. Come, luv, let me help you with your coat. My Mini is parked behind the house."

Chapter Five

On Tuesday morning, Edgar Keelan drove to work by bus as usual, reading the Daily Telegraph as the vehicle trundled along like a ship in a steady breeze. When he got off in Regents Park Road, the heavy night sky began its slow transformation to the leaden gray of a cold, overcast winter morning. Upright and brisk, like a man who feared neither twilight nor stiff winds, Edgar stalked down the road. The moment a gap occurred in the flow of traffic, he crossed the street. He pushed open the gate to the Villa Cathleen, mounted the steps to the front door, opened it with a smooth turn of his key and closed it noiselessly. He then shed his coat and put it on a hanger, collected the paper and the morning mail, quickly leafed through the envelopes on his way to the dining room to see if—rarely though it happened—a letter for Mrs. Warner was among them, placed paper and mail in a neat stack next to Mr. Warner's plate on the dining table, and went on into the kitchen, noticing with a satisfied glance at the wall clock that it was eight sharp.

"*Boker tov,* Ed," said Nurit, who came in through the door that led to the laundry room. She was carrying a basket with ironed shirts. "You keep an eye on the pan, do you, as I take theez upstairs?" Her diction was heavily accented and sounded as if she were rolling pebbles in her mouth.

The bacon sizzled aromatically. Edgar arranged butter and jam on a tray. Nurit returned, shaking her head. "Mrs. Jessica, she sleep in the guest bedroom last night." She cracked two eggs on top of the bacon. "The door eez open and the sheets crumpled. Strange. And there eez a broken glass in the rubbish bin. You know what I think, Ed?"

Edgar was a man without opinions and therefore not interested in other people's views. He took an apple from the fruit bowl and began to peel it proficiently.

Nurit filled a basket with toast. "I theenk they 'ave been quarrelling again and she carried it too far. Oh, sure, it waz simply a matter of time. I theenk he threw her out of their bedroom. Mrs. Jessica, she eez an ungrateful creature. She has all the luxury a woman can want, she has, and Mr. Warner, he eez a fine gentleman." Nurit looked hurt. "He eez, right?"

The peel came off in one spiral. Edgar cut the apple in half, removed the core of each in one smooth, circular cut and took a hefty bite.

Nurit accepted this as affirmation. "Mr. Warner, he always falls for the wrong women. Mrs. Cathleen was not better. A puppet she waz—nice looks but no brains, no character, no nothing. Do you know what he needs?" She tilted the pan and the bacon slid onto a plate.

Quietly, Edgar poured milk into a glass and put it in the microwave.

"He needs a woman who knows where her place eez," Nurit went on as she poured boiling water from the kettle into a teapot. "She eez not too young and she has a good, firm body with a full bosom. Ah, not the flat-breasted type he fancies. Do you see?"

Vividly. Nurit had just given a compelling description of herself. The microwave beeped. Edgar put the glass of milk on the tray, checked with a quick glance if the breakfast was complete, and carried it into the dining room where he put it on the sideboard. Perfect timing, as always. Mr. Warner was coming downstairs. Edgar poured the tea for his employer and retreated into the kitchen. Eight-thirty. In the next minute, the front door would slam shut and Mrs. Warner would stomp up the stairs to shower before she came to join her husband. She knew how to organize her day, that was one thing Edgar could say in her favor.

Nurit had laid the kitchen table for their breakfast. "Ah, I want to know what zee row yesterday morning waz about. But you, you not let me leesten, *bushah wecherpah*. So furious he waz, Mr. Warner. Such a temperament he has."

Edgar buttered his toast and filtered out the avalanche of Nurit's jabber. Nurit, used to his lack of interest, continued her soliloquy in Hebrew. Among the ticking of the clock, the clanging of cutlery and the humming of the dishwasher, Edgar waited for the sound of the front door. When it didn't come, he began to feel uneasy and went into the dining room where he found Mr. Warner eating alone.

"Is Mrs. Warner not having breakfast at her usual time today?" Edgar asked. An innocent enough question.

Mr. Warner slapped the paper on the table. "What does she think she's doing?" he burst out. "She has every reason to try and show her good will, given how lenient I was. Do you know when she came home last night?"

"No, sir."

"Half-past midnight. I was scared to death with concern. I was already considering calling the police when she turned up at last. The troupe went on a night-club excursion. Of course, Jessica never thought of calling me to say she'd be late."

Edgar tried to withdraw, but Mr. Warner pinned him to the ground with a new outburst. "When I think what a fuss she made when I wanted her to stay up a little longer on my birthday, and then she comes home at half past midnight, slightly tipsy, too." Mr.

Warner stood up. "I'm not going to wait for her." He plonked down his napkin. "You can clear the table."

"Very well, sir."

"On the other hand . . ." Mr. Warner turned around, ". . . she wouldn't change her morning routine, would she? Maybe something has happened to her."

"I'm sure Mrs. Jessica wouldn't run for longer than an hour on an empty stomach. When did she leave?"

"I have no idea. The last time I saw her was when we went to bed." He kneaded the handle of the door. "She slept in the guest bedroom last night. She isn't still asleep, is she?"

"No, sir. Nurit just told me the door was open." Edgar came to a conclusion. "Since she went to sleep late, I surmise she also awoke late. That might explain the delay. She must, however, have left for her jogging round before I came in or I would have heard her."

Mr. Warner looked at the grandfather clock. "Five to nine. She should be back any minute now," he said. He seemed torn between rage and worry.

"You could go and look for her if that would help to put your mind at rest."

The moment Mr. Warner had left, Nurit emerged from the kitchen. "I hope he geeves her what she deserves when he finds her."

He issued a resolute jolt with the index finger.

"You parasite."

No response.

"You ungrateful creature."

He pressed harder. Still no reaction.

"You dumb, incompetent sponger. You wouldn't treat Eileen like this. Oh no, you wouldn't dare. She's your queen—but I am the one who bought you and who's paying for your software and printer cartridges." Alan pressed the *Enter* button twice for good measure.

File cannot be accessed, the computer blinked for no discernible reason.

"Listen, you silly thing, all I want you to do is to open the bloody file. I'm not going to interfere with it. No new entries or deletions. Just a short look, that's all." Alan pressed another selection of buttons.

File cannot be accessed, the computer maintained.

"You are repeating yourself, you stupid apparatus. I'm not giving up this time. Eileen always makes backups." He leafed through the disks. "Here it is. 'Employees, pupils and suppliers.' Now take this." He entered the disk into drive A and tried to look up the file names in the menu.

No valid command.

"This is my last warning. Open the file or I'll activate your self-destruction sequence. I hope you've got one."

Drive A does not exist.

Alan held his head. "What? Have you gone completely mental now? Drive A's over there, where it has always been. I should have known you're a nihilist."

The phone rang. "Is Jessica there?" It was Roger's crotchety voice.

"Where there?"

"At the theatre."

The theatre doesn't exist, Alan was tempted to say. "No, of course not. It's quite early. The preparations for the dress rehearsal won't start before two."

"Are you sure she's not there? She could be in one of the studios."

Alan sighed. "I'll go and look. But what makes you think she's here?"

"She didn't return from her jogging round, so I walked all around Primrose Hill. There was no trace of her. When I came back, I saw that her car was missing."

"That's because she left it here last night. You see, we all ended up in a club in Soho. Long before the rest of us disbanded, Jessica took a cab home, which was better anyway because she had drunk two Manhattans and she's not used to it."

"Where's Eileen? Maybe she knows where Jessica is."

"Eileen's not in today. Simon took her to a conference with a famous surgeon from the States. They'll be in Richmond all day. Didn't Jessica tell you about it?"

"Why should she? I'm only her husband."

Roger hung up. Alan began to feel worried. He searched the house, as promised. Jessica was nowhere. Maybe she would turn up any minute in a taxi to retrieve her car.

Resignedly, Alan fumbled with the computer keyboard. Like magic, the list of supplier addresses he had wanted appeared on-screen.

An hour later he rang Roger back.

"Jessica hasn't come to the theatre, Roger. Has she returned home in the meantime?"

"No, she has not. I'm getting really nervous."

So was Alan. There was a tingling feeling in his belly. "I'll make some inquiries from here. I'll call you the moment I've found her. Would you do the same, please?"

"Actually, I'm not going to wait for her any longer. I've got several appointments in my office. If Jessica hasn't turned up by two o'clock, I'll go to the police and report her missing. God, this woman is my ruin."

Alan considered whom to call. Where was Jessica most likely to be? Her family lived in New Zealand. She had no close friends in London except Eileen, Simon and himself. How about Susan? Had Jessica gone to see her to settle their dispute? It was a possibility.

Susan answered the phone in a throaty voice.

"Hello, Sue. It's Alan. How's your cold?"

"Better. And yours?"

"As good as dead. The virus doesn't seem to be of the persevering type."

"I'll come to the rehearsal today, then I'll see if I'm fit enough to perform."

"Fine, but that's not why I'm calling. Have you seen Jessica this morning?"

"Jessica? No, why?" She sounded alarmed.

"Roger's looking for her. He's worried because she didn't return from her jogging round."

"Oh." There was a pause. "Oh, dear. Did he mention how things are between them at the moment?"

"No, he didn't. What do you think is going on?"

"Something dreadful, and it's my fault. I was so angry and hurt I had to find a valve and I . . . . Oh, shit. I didn't think about the consequences."

"What the hell did you do?"

"I . . . I don't . . . no, I can't talk about it over the phone. See you at the rehearsal then. I'll have to take the bus, as David has the car."

"Don't you come together?"

Another pause. When she spoke again, she sounded as if she were fighting back tears. "He's staying with a friend for a while. I miss him so."

"I'm sorry. I know how it feels to be deserted. Why don't you come an hour earlier so that we can talk before the crowd comes in."

"Thank you. I feel terribly lonely at home."

"Do you have the address where David is now?"

"Yes. Hang on a sec."

Alan's brain clicked and ticked. Jessica and David. A strange liaison, but not unthinkable. It would explain their peculiar behavior the other day and Susan's hysterical fit after the party. Things happen at parties. But wouldn't Roger know about it? And could it be possible that Jessica had run away with David? In that case, he'd probably have to stage the show without his two leads. No, he decided. Jessica would never rate a man higher than her dancing.

After Susan had given him the address and phone number of David's friend Norman Patmore, Alan tried the number. Nobody answered. He swung the chair round to the computer screen.

"I wish Eileen were here, old pal. Don't you, too?"

At lunchtime, Alan called the Warner's house and talked to Edgar, who had made inquiries in all London hospitals. Since Jessica had no ID on her—Edgar had checked and found that nothing was missing except her jogging attire—there was a possibility that she was unconscious or having emergency surgery and no one could ask her who was to be informed. Furthermore, Edgar had sent Nurit out to ask neighbors and passersby if they had seen Jessica—but that too had come to nothing.

Alan thanked Edgar. He found it a bit odd that the butler showed more initiative to search for Jessica than her husband did. Before he went upstairs, he activated the answering machine and looked out of the window to see if Jessica's Renault was still there. It stood where she had left it last night. She had a parking permit for the area, so it wasn't in danger of being clamped or pulled away.

His appetite was put off. Ghastly scenes popped up unasked for as he mounted the stairs. Jessica in the hands of kidnappers. Jessica crying for help. Jessica raped. Jessica strangled. Alan had to do something to keep himself from behaving like a Jewish mother.

"*Hasta la vista*, baby," Ginger received him.

"Hi, guys." He raised a hand to the volière. That made him think of something. He would paint. What had brought the association? Volière—cage. Yes, of course. He had painted his best portrait when he had been in an awfully bad temper after the casting meeting for *Taming of the Shoe*. Jessica would be Katharina and David, Petruchio—that much was clear. Alan had suggested Laura as Bianca, but David preferred Claudia for the part. Laura, although downcast, was too diffident to stand her ground. With false generosity, David made her understudy for the part of Katharina. The truth was that none of the girls was even remotely skilled enough to replace Jessica, so the choice was arbitrary. David conducted himself so impertinently during the meeting that Alan had decided to talk to him in private afterwards.

"David, I think you have a problem," he said. "Do you want to talk about it?"

"I've got no problem at all," David snapped, "and if I had one I wouldn't want to discuss it with you, of all people."

"Then why are you behaving as if you had one?"

"The hobby psychologist talking."

"I'm just offering my help."

"If you absolutely have to play Mister Sunshine, then go and comfort Laura."

"I've already done so."

"You always get your priorities right, don't you?"

"I think you should apologize to her. It'll make you feel better."

"When I need your advice, I'll rattle your cage," David dismissed him.

Alan, in a red rage, spent two hours wielding the brush. The result was a brilliant painting of Jessica in a wild dance. Alan was decently surprised by his own talent. He couldn't have painted a better poster for the show on purpose than through this lucky hit.

"I'll rattle your cage," David had said. Cage—volière. And David had got it wrong. The correct insult was "I'll rattle your chain." Pretentious moron.

A painting session could help him now to counterbalance his distress about Jessica's mysterious disappearance. He went over to his small artist's studio where a huge, primed canvas stood on the easel, waiting for a moment of inspiration. Poisonous green and watery blue, those were the colors that equaled his mood. He put on his overall, filled a glass with turpentine and another with thinner, unscrewed the tubes of oil paint and pressed generous splodges of green, yellow, blue, black and white on the palette. A mermaid whirling in an eddy, he decided, was a promising motif. His technique was not learnt or skillful, but it led to quick results. Painting was dancing with the hand, and whatever he painted had to be twirling or spinning. Only once had he tried to paint a still-life, and it had looked like a bouquet ruffled by a tornado.

In sweeping swings of his arm, he applied the colors with a broad brush. The rhythm of the motion entranced him. The two-dimensional surface of the canvas transformed into an ocean of inconceivable depth. Undercurrents forced the water into gyrations; bubbles of white foam crowned it. A mermaid rose, scales glittering on her tail, fair hair floating around her like pale seaweed. She stretched her arms and bent her body with delight as she spun in the whirl and danced the dance of seaborne buoyancy.

Alan surfaced from his meditation, sank the brushes into the turpentine and stepped back to evaluate his work. With bewilderment, he recognized the nymph's features. She resembled Susan. His subconscious had apparently not stopped worrying about how she felt now that David had moved out. She would be in a similar state as he had been after Pam had left him. "You're a wonderful father but a lousy husband," she had said, but had taken Cindy with her, nevertheless, to live in Martin's commune. Alan recalled with painful clarity how his rage had been followed by a brew of bereavement and humiliation.

The brooding shifted his perspective. As he stared at the mermaid, her cheerful expression transformed into a grimace of despair, and her hands, it seemed to him now, were not raised in exultation but in a cry for help.

Alan shed the overall, cleaned his hands and closed the studio behind him. He was not alone. Someone was clattering in the kitchen. Had Susan already come? Or was it Jessica? Jessica. His heartbeat went up expectantly as he hastened into the kitchen, where he ran into Susan. Water dripped from her hair, and for a moment he thought she was the mermaid brought to life.

Susan gave a start. "Alan. You've finished your painting? I didn't want to interrupt your work. When you paint you're like Jessica when she dances. I made us some tea."

He took the tray she had prepared and carried it to the couch table. "How come your hair is wet?"

"I forgot to wash it at home. I hope you don't mind that I used your bathroom."

"No, of course not." He turned her around and pressed her wet curls with the towel she had draped over her shoulders.

"Alan."

"Uhm-hm."

"Let's make love."

He dropped the towel. "What?"

She pivoted. She was so tall that her emerald eyes were level with his.

"I want to make love. Now. Please, Alan." She placed her hands on his chest.

"That's impossible."

"Don't you find me attractive?"

"You're a knock-out, Sue, but I haven't made love to a woman since Pam left me. I'm more inclined toward men at present," he said cautiously. It was tricky to turn her down at this time of distress.

"You're still working both ways, aren't you?" she pleaded. "I am very versatile. You'd enjoy it."

Softly, he removed her hands. "You wouldn't want to betray David, would you?"

She gave a short, snappy laugh and slumped on the sofa.

"Or is that exactly what you want?" he asked and sat down at

her side. "To hurt David for . . . . Well, for whatever he did to you."
Shyly, he stroked her wet hair.

"I'm sorry, Alan. I'm kind of hysterical. I thought I could hurt
both of them if I slept with you. You haven't deserved to be used
like this. Are you angry?"

"Not at all. What do you mean by 'both of them'?"

"David and Jessica, of course."

"So it's true that they're having an affair."

"They had one, but it's history. It lasted for almost a year and
I didn't notice. I must've been blind."

"I see." He didn't see anything, in fact, and was getting more
confused by the minute. "Why should it hurt Jessica if you seduced
me?"

"You don't know? You really don't?" Susan covered her lips
with her fingers. "Alan, you're so innocent. Did you never see that
Jessica was in love with you? She was smitten with you from the
first day she saw you."

"Come on, she was a child of eight then."

"I wasn't much older, twelve I think, when I saw David in a
show and was lost. I only started to take dancing lessons at the
school where he taught because I hoped it would bring me closer
to him. I practiced like mad to achieve access to his class for
advanced students. Quite a parallel, when you think of it. You were
Jessica's first dancing teacher." She put a hand on his thigh. "I
was as helpless at showing my feelings as Jessica. No word or
hint. I waited for David to make the first step."

Alan processed the information carefully. "Are you telling me
that for more than fourteen years Jessica has been waiting for me
to . . . . That's ridiculous. Did she tell you all this?"

"No. I heard how she told David at the party. The doomed
party," she added glumly.

"Then my theory that Jessica has absconded with David is
obsolete."

"He'll be here this afternoon, don't worry." She looked at her watch. "Any minute now. I'm not sure if I'm up to it—to seeing him, I mean. Maybe I had better stay up here. They don't need me on the show. I've got no solo and I'm the eldest. I feel like a matron among all those youngsters."

Alan patted her hand. "You look as much like a matron as a butterfly looks like a Concorde. The background group would lose a lot of its effect without you." Actually, the last thing he wanted was for Susan to remain alone in his flat. She might see the painting. "I insist you come down with me." He filled their cups. "But first, let's drink."

Susan dipped a sugar cube in her tea and licked it. "I said some silly things when I came to you the other night. I hope you haven't taken them seriously. I also did something terrible." She crushed the sugar between her teeth. "It was in the heat of the moment."

"I know. You tore up the poster."

"I'm sorry for that, but what I was actually going to confess is that I wrote a letter."

"A letter? To whom?"

"Roger."

"To let him know about Jessica's betrayal?"

She nodded. "It was an anonymous letter."

"Holy shit." His brain swerved into a lane he would have rather ignored. Had Jessica disappeared because Roger, unpredictable, irascible, choleric, had made her disappear?

"I feel so guilty. If Roger did something to Jessica, it would be my fault."

He looked for a way out. "Maybe he didn't believe what you wrote. What were the exact words?"

"'Jessica had two lovers. One was David Powell, the other. . . .'"

Alan frowned. "Who? Who was the other one?" he urged.

"Simon."

Alan needed both hands to steady his cup. "Simon? Does he never know where to stop?"

"He knows precisely where to stop," she said. "His target group must not be too young, too old, too unattractive or too married, like me for instance."

"Or too male like me. He's absolutely straight, you know."

"You mean, you tried to . . . ." Susan giggled in a way so young and relaxed that Alan could see her grief melt away.

"I did." Fondly, he kissed her damp head. "Only to learn that he'd rather do it with my ex-wife."

She boxed his thigh. "Just as you'd rather do it with Simon than with me. I'll never get over it." Suddenly, she was serious again. "And Jessica would rather have you than David or any other man in the world. It's a miracle the set-up worked for so long."

David peeped into the girls' dressing room.

"You must change your dress," he said to Laura, who was pulling up her net stockings.

She lifted her head in surprise. "Me? Why?"

"You'll dance the lead. Jessica isn't coming today," David explained. "Alan's hopping around like a mad cow, asking everyone if they've seen her this morning. Have you?"

Laura, still puzzled, shook her head and looked at the others.

"Me neither," Claudia said. Susan looked away.

"What happened?" Emily asked.

David turned up his palms. "No idea, really—so we'll have to make do with you as Katharina, Laura. Victor will dance the Petruchio. It's no use if I dance with you. I would outclass you."

Laura thought of Simon's advice to question his authority. She stood erect and looked firmly into his eyes. "Isn't it Alan's job to decide that? After all, he's the producer."

"Alan is not in a state to make decisions. Not as long as Jessica is missing."

Chapter Six

A paunchy man in his thirties had come in to report an accident.

"I swear to God, ma'am, I was driving very, very slowly," he jabbered. "It was his fucking fault. There was more damage to my car than to the ramshackle thing he calls his bike. And it was he who begged, 'No police, no police,' in that whining voice of his. He was Pakistani or something, judging from his accent. My car was practically standing when it happened. I thought it better to come in and report it. I don't want to be charged with hit-and-run. My car's out there," he pointed toward the glass door with a podgy finger. "You can see the scratch. He was bleeding, too. Out of the nose I think. Not really injured, God beware. I asked him for his name and he said something that sounded like Swahili to me, then back he was on his bike and resumed his slalom between the standing cars. The traffic lights had turned red, you see. Actually, he should be made to pay for the scratch on my car. I was just so diverted by the blood and his Arabian insults I didn't react fast enough."

WPC Kathryn Fuller, fresh from Hendon Training Center, listened attentively and converted the twisted report into neat sentences, which she wrote into the small yellow leaflet that contained the questionnaire for accident reports. Don't write what they say, she had been taught, write what they think they are saying.

"Which street was it, sir?"

"Oh, I forgot. Somewhere near Euston Station it was."

With her pencil, Kathryn tapped at the map of Camden on the wall. "Show me."

Paunchy ran a yellowish fingernail over the map. "Here, I think. And he was coming from there. Cycled straight ahead without looking left or right. He was lucky I was driving so slowly."

The blue-framed glass door to Albany Street Station banged open, and a tall man rushed to the desk. "My wife has disappeared," he said out of breath. "This very morning."

"Yes, sir. Please take a seat over there and wait your turn." Kathryn nodded toward the three-seated bench by the door. The man took a step backwards and remained standing as if in protest.

She turned once more to her first client. "I can smell alcohol on your breath. Have you had a drink before or after the accident?"

"Just a pint for lunch."

She explained to him that he'd have to blow into the tube of the breathalyzer. "Don't hold onto the device, sir, I'll hold it for you." Paunchy tried. A beep indicated that he hadn't done it right.

"No, sir," Kathryn said stoically. "You are sucking when you should be blowing. Steady yourself and try again."

The next attempt failed as well.

"That wasn't long enough. Don't let go of your breath in one short blow. Breathe out steadily for ten seconds. Imagine you're blowing up a balloon."

The tall man stepped forward. "I can't believe it," he exclaimed. "My wife is in heaven-knows-what danger, and you are wasting precious minutes with this nonsense."

Kathryn cleared her throat. She had been told to deal with clients in order of appearance. It seemed, however, that people were unwilling to queue in a police station.

"Keep calm, sir," she said. "I'll ring a colleague and ask him to come down."

"Yeah," Paunchy fell in, winking in her direction. "We've got a blow-job to finish here, right?"

The door was flung open and a bundle of papers was slapped on top of the jumble on the desk. "What the hell is this?"

Detective Inspector Frederick Terry, accustomed to splurges of theological swearing from his superior, hardly looked up from the timetable he was studying. "My report on the Severlock case. It's written all over the front page."

"Good God, spare me your sarcasm. This," Detective Chief Inspector Derek Gould landed the flat of his palm on the sheets, "is the epitome of misguided lyrical energy."

Terry grinned. "I seem to have overdone it with the adjectives again." He leant back in his swivel chair, slipped off his wire-rimmed reading glasses and began gnawing the side-piece.

Gould gave a loud sigh of despair and irritation, a sound he mastered like no one else, and lowered his bulky body onto a chair after checking that no sharp, dirty or fragile object was lying on it.

"It's worse than ever. You'd turn the London Phone Book into a collection of love poems if they let you."

"I always get somewhat sentimental around Christmas," Terry admitted.

Gould picked up the report and read one sentence at random.

"Take this for example. 'A cold drizzle filled the air and, shivering in my Burberry, I brooded in front of Archway tube station until the suspect, whom I now know to be a paragon of virtue, had safely returned to his dull basement flat.' Jesus, Terry, you're not Jane bloody Austen." He shook his head in disgust. Distracted by an object that this movement had brought into his view, he added, "And what in Christ's name is this shoe doing on your desk?"

"It proved helpful as a source of inspiration in the case. You see, the victim's shoelaces were—"

"I read the report." Another sigh, slightly modified to exhibit his growing impatience. "Now that the case is closed, would you mind putting your source of inspiration down on the floor?"

Terry contemplated the suggestion. "The shoe is also very useful as a paperweight. Whenever I open the window there's a draught which muddles up all the files and loose papers on my desk."

"Muddles up! Almighty! What is there to be muddled up? Your desk is beyond chaos. It must have reached a state of higher order because the laws of entropy will not allow it to get messed up any further. Future archaeologists will remove layer after layer hoping to find the Holy Grail." Gould had made his point and got up. "Tidy up a bit, will you? I'll have Mrs. Turner rewrite your report. She has enough common sense to extract the facts from this . . . this Christmas tale you dared hand in as a report."

"Yes, sir." Terry shrugged imperceptibly and tried to turn his attention back to the timetable. He couldn't concentrate, which wasn't Gould's fault. Terry felt blocked. He had spent days comparing statements, checking circumstantial evidence and looking for a motive, but the investigation had come to a dead end. Terry rubbed the bridge of his nose with his thumbs. He knew he was staring too hard at the facts to see if they fell into a pattern. He had got bogged down in details and his brain needed some airing.

The shoe! He'd take it back to Blockley and have a chat with him. Blockley was always enthusiastic about something; a book he'd read, a film he'd seen, a recipe he'd tried, or anything else he had come across lately. His eagerness could be unnerving, but also catching and refreshing at other times. Such a time was now, Terry decided, snatching the shoe and going into the CID room. DS Timothy Blockley was right there, at his desk, flirting nonchalantly with one of the girls from the typing pool.

At this moment, PC Brick barged into the CID room. "I've got a problem," he said to no one in particular. His eyes fell on the inspector. "I've got a problem, sir," he repeated and handed Terry a sheet. "Missing person report," he explained. "A Mr. Warner came to report his wife missing. He's the bothersome type. Kept breathing down my neck as I checked the computer for reports about recent accidents and unidentified corpses. Now he insists on talking with a detective. He's waiting in the corridor. Didn't manage to get rid of him."

That was hard to imagine. Brick was a giant. Terry took the report and gave it a quick read. Dancer, theatre—that was in Blockley's field. He held out the shoe and Blockley took it. "Sir?"

"You can deal with the missing dancer."

Blockley looked pleased, and the girl from the typing pool withdrew hesitantly. Brick held the door for her. "Mr. Warner, you may come in," he shouted, turned to salute and left. Terry leaned against the windowsill and folded his arms. He'd watch the scene and enjoy it. Obnoxious clients could be quite entertaining.

The bereft husband stalked in. Terry judged him to be an affluent man in his late forties, well-groomed, tall and broad-shouldered, with excellent taste and a fine tailor. He held his chin up as if to herald authority.

Blockley offered him a seat. "I'll have a look at the report first." He read what Brick had taken down. "Jessica Warner, née Gresham," he recited, "Twenty-two-years-old, dancer at The Caesar, last seen by you around one o"clock last night. Disappeared this morning when she was on her jogging round, dressed in a red flannel tracksuit over a white polo neck jumper. Angora wool underwear with long underpants, white sport shoes, red scarf and gloves with a woolly hat to match."

"She runs through the park every morning from seven-thirty until eight-thirty," Warner said, as if his wife's dress required an explanation.

"A daily routine, then. Did she have anything else on her? How about a wrist watch?"

Warner, upright, stiff and apparently ill at ease on the wooden chair, shook his head. "None. Oh, there's her wedding ring, of course. Platinum with a small diamond. I should probably also mention that the top of her suit carries her initials in white embroidery."

Blockley rubbed his cheek. "How can you know what she was wearing? The report says you last saw her before you went to bed."

"It's her usual jogging gear. Nurit laid it out for her in the evening. Nothing else that belongs to Jessica is missing. You see, that's why I'm so worried. She's taken nothing with her."

"How about her passport? Driving license?"

"It's all in the rucksack she uses in lieu of a handbag, together with her credit card and keys."

"And who is Nurit?"

"My housekeeper. I also have a man-servant, Edgar Keelan. He called every hospital in London." Warner turned his fists inwards and banged his knuckles against each other.

"All the hospitals? Your servant is a man of astounding stamina. Did you check every other possibility before you came here—family, friends, neighbors, the like?"

Warner got up. "Do you think I'm an idiot? Of course I've checked every possibility."

"Which would be?"

"The Caesar. Full stop. There's no other place in the world where to look for her. When she didn't turn up there for the dress rehearsal, I knew that something must have happened to her."

"Did you contact her family?"

"They live in Auckland, New Zealand. No use looking for her there."

Terry knew that Blockley had sufficient self-respect to survive some measure of disrespectful treatment. How long would it take until he lost patience?

"We'll check train stations and airports and call her family." Blockley scratched his scalp through his thick, brown hair. "Since the troupe is having its dress rehearsal today, I assume the première will be tomorrow. Could it be that your wife got cold feet? An attack of the jitters, an extreme case of stage fright, say?"

"Stage fright? Jessica? She's a dance-aholic." Warner began to pace. Two steps, turn, two steps, turn. The space was restricted. "She could be dead by now. Why don't you start doing something?"

Blockley stood up slowly. He was a head smaller than Warner. "Why don't you stop shouting at me?" he asked with a penetrating glance. "Is that your idea of coping with a crisis? Wouldn't it be better if you cooperated instead of wallowing in misery?"

Warner, dumbfounded by the reprimand, sat down and apologized. "This morning, I walked the round she usually takes. There was no trace of her—and it's hardly a place where you can hide someone . . . a body, I mean. There aren't many trees on Primrose Hill."

Primrose Hill. Terry would rather be there than in his office, tidying up or shifting through files and tables. He pushed himself from the sill and stretched out a hand.

"I'm Detective Inspector Terry. Pleased to meet you, Mr. Warner. I have a strong feeling that this case requires a thorough investigation, and the sooner the better. We don't want traces to become cold, do we?"

Warner looked up in awe. Terry knew that what conferred authority was neither his rank, which wasn't high enough, nor his looks, which were unspectacular, but rather his deep, corrosive voice. Still, a touch of doubt seemed to remain. Warner exhaled a forced laugh. "You mean, you want to handle it?"

"Sure enough. I happen to have a vacant slot in my schedule." Terry turned his back on Warner and winked at Blockley, who looked baffled. "We'll split up the investigation. You, sergeant, will drive to The Caesar and begin inquiries there. The dress rehearsal might still be on. Try not to upset the troupe too much."

Now, Blockley beamed. "No problem, sir."

"I'll see Mr. Warner home."

"I really don't think this is necessary," Warner said. Clearly, this was more attention than he had asked for. "What if Jessica returns? I'd feel a downright fool to have troubled you for nothing."

Terry turned around and smiled. "Don't worry, sir. If your wife returns, we'll all be happy. I'll take two constables with me to search the park and the neighborhood." He hoped Gould wouldn't appear and thwart his escape.

Terry climbed out of Warner's white Mercedes. "Most peculiar that anyone should wish to go jogging at this time of year," he said with a controlled cough and watched as his breath immediately crystallized in the stinging air.

Warner locked the car. "There are hardly any weather conditions that can keep Jessica from doing what she thinks is good for her." He looked around like a nervous bird as he had done incessantly as they drove. Terry assumed he was trying to spot his wife.

Brick parked the panda car at the kerb and bent his long body to squeeze himself out. PC Stapplethorne slammed the other door shut. "How shall we proceed?" he asked. The constables were equipped with descriptions of what Jessica had last been wearing and copies of a photograph from Mr. Warner's wallet.

"One of you take the streets, the other one the park. Show the photo around and ask everyone you meet if they've seen Jessica this morning or at any other time today. In two hours, when it's getting dark, you can start ringing at doors."

"Nurit has done that already," Warner said.

"Sure, but what about the people who were at work?" Terry turned to the house. Neat flowerbeds, hibernating, lined the path. The villa was painted a light blue with contrasts in white around the windows. The wood of the door was white, too, with insets of leaded glass and a brass lion's-paw knocker. It was a quaint building—definitely not as stately a home as you would expect when you knew that Mr. Warner employed a butler. He was either understating his wealth by refusing to live in Mayfair or Chelsea, or he was exaggerating his lifestyle by affording a man-servant.

"Villa Cathleen," Terry read the golden letters above the door.

"Named after my second wife, who was Irish," Warner explained and unlatched the gate. Terry had a closer look at him because he had heard a slight tremolo in his voice.

"Are you all right, sir? You are pale."

Warner clung to the gate. "Maybe I'm in a state of shock. It wouldn't be surprising, would it? I was only worried so far, but now that the police are involved I begin to realize the enormity of it all."

Terry sat down on the brown button-backed leather sofa--the kind of furniture that doesn't allow slumping into it but rather forces you to sit uncomfortably upright. Edgar, the butler, served tea and sandwiches. Nurit, on Warner's request, brought an album with more photos of Jessica.

"These are our most recent photos. They were taken during our winter holiday on Tenerife."

Terry put on his glasses. He needed a photo that showed Jessica alone. He glanced over the pages quickly. There were three pictures that could help to find and identify her. One showed Jessica beneath a Christmas rose in full blossom. Her dress was the same red as the plant. In the second, Jessica was sitting on a black lava stone on the seashore, her hair blown out of her face by the wind. The third was the best. Terry preferred snaps to posing. Jessica had been caught unawares in half-profile. She stood in a barren landscape of brown rocks and the occasional cactus. Her face was that of a perfectly modeled doll, round with large blue eyes, accented by long lashes and eyeliner. The fringe of her blue-black hair, cut into a fashionable zigzag, hung over her eyebrows. Her full lips wore red lipstick and looked like a fresh wound on her pale skin. She was the type of woman who would preserve her childlike appearance far into adulthood.

"Can I have the negative of this one?" The negatives, sorted according to date, were in a small cardboard box which Nurit had brought as well. He found the strip with the right negative, put it into his wallet and produced a leather-bound notebook and pen from his pocket. He suppressed the desire that popped up immediately to doodle away on the neat white sheet. Doodling was his worst vice and sometimes made his notes illegible.

"Let's go through the possibilities. First of all, could Jessica have run away?"

Warner shook his head. "Of course not. I thought I had made that clear."

"How long have you been married?"

"It will be three years in June."

"So your marriage is young, you're very much in love with each other, and that's why you don't think she could have wanted to leave you?"

Warner didn't look at him when he answered. "I wish it were so. Look, I hate being asked questions. It'll make things easier if I tell you everything you need to know about Jessica."

Terry poised his pen and waited.

"I met Jessica three and a half years ago when I was strolling over Primrose Hill on one of those rare perfect summer days. Suddenly, an empty wheelchair came toward me at full speed. I managed to stop it and pushed it uphill to find the proprietor. There were two young women having a picnic in the grass, and I asked them if the vehicle was theirs. Jessica sprang up and thanked me, her mouth smeared with fruit juice. She looked lovely. She said they hadn't noticed the wheelchair had gone off on its own. The other woman was Eileen Lanigan, Alan's secretary. Alan Caesar Widmark is the owner of The Caesar, where Jessica dances."

"She's handicapped?"

"Eileen? Yes, she is. A mishap occurred—at least that's what they generally call it, quite inappropriately, if you ask me. She sprang or fell out of a window when a fire broke out in The Caesar five years ago."

Warner stood up and began to pace up and down as he had done at the police station. "She's also Jessica's best friend."

"Have you already talked to her about Jessica's disappearance?"

"No, she's away today, so Alan told me—in Richmond—a conference or something."

"Maybe Jessica is with her," Terry suggested.

"In that case, Eileen would have called Alan and told him. She's conscientious and reliable."

Terry was not happy about what he had to say now since it would increase Warner's nervousness. "They could have had an accident. How would Eileen get to Richmond? By tube?"

Lines appeared on Warner's forehead. "Simon is driving, I think."

"Simon?"

"He's a physiotherapist. Works at the London Clinic. In his spare time he treats Alan's dancers. You think the three of them could have had an accident before Eileen was able to inform Alan that Jessica's with them? I don't know. Jessica in a red tracksuit at a conference. How can we find out?"

Terry had already reached for his mobile phone to call in. "Do you know the make of Simon's car?"

"No, I'm sorry."

As Terry asked for a check whether there had been an accident that morning somewhere between central London and Richmond with two women and a man in a car, he watched Mr. Warner who was nervously rolling up his tie. Why was he so talkative when Terry had the impression that he was in fact a very reticent character?

Terry shut the phone. "No accident. That possibility is ruled out then. So you met Jessica on Primrose Hill while she was having a picnic with her best friend."

"They asked me to join them. We ate and chatted. I felt younger by the minute. A few days later I went to see Jessica in her flat. It was untidy. I wouldn't say Jessica was sluttish, just not practiced as a housewife. She told me that before Eileen's mishap she used to share the flat with her, and Eileen had been the one who had tidied up. Jessica was young, only nineteen. She needed someone to look after her. There was something about her, an energy she radiated, combined with a helpless and childish attitude toward the practical aspects of life. She fascinated me and appealed to my protective instincts. I fell deeply in love with her. When I proposed to her and she said yes, I couldn't believe my luck. What I didn't know, however, was that she would come in a threepack, that I would also marry Eileen and tap dance."

"You don't like Eileen?"

"Well, it's difficult not to like her, she's such a poor little thing—but I was jealous. You see, jealousy is a big problem for me. I destroyed two marriages with my obsessive mistrust, and I'm determined not to let it happen again."

"Jealousy makes as much sense as throwing away what you've got for fear of losing it when you keep it."

"Are you sure you've chosen the right profession? It took my behavioral therapist two years and far more words to knock this message into my big ol' head. In fact, without the backing the psychological treatment gave me, my marriage to Jessica would have turned into a nightmare."

"Because you were jealous of your wife's best friend?" Terry asked more cynically than he had intended.

Warner laughed with acerbity. "I'm talking about tap dance, good man. Jessica once told me that dancing was better than having sex."

"Did you have other reasons for being jealous?" After all, Jessica was young and beautiful.

"Of course not." Warner looked out of the window now, as if to avoid Terry's stare. "I told you, it's pathological. It wasn't easy for me to adopt a more objective attitude. I'm glad to say that I've learned to discipline myself."

Terry chose a cucumber sandwich from the tray. "Your wife puts all her energy into her dancing, doesn't she?" he said before he took a bite.

"Time, energy, passion—there's hardly anything left for other occupations. She's very single-minded and, as far as I know, she's always been like this. When she was five years old, her parents had to take her with them to a tap dance show because the baby-sitter had cancelled the appointment. Jess told me she was completely thunderstruck and from that day onward kept saying that she wanted only one thing in life and that was to become a dancer. So her mother sent her to ballet class. Jessica hated it because this was not the kind of dancing she had had in mind. She found out there was a new dancing studio which had tap classes. The day of the opening she was there, at The Caesar. Alan had to call her mother and persuade her to let Jessica register, otherwise the girl would have camped on the doorstep—and she was only eight then."

Terry smiled. "Very grown-up for her age." He had been a good deal older when he had finally found the courage to tell his parents that he would no longer live up to their expectations. "Did Jessica get her way?"

"They agreed on a compromise. Jessica was allowed to register for Alan's tap dance class on the condition that she continued to learn classical ballet which, in her mother's eyes, was the real thing. Four years later, Jessica was sent off to boarding school. They had ballet classes there, but no tap dance. Jessica ran away several times until her parents gave in and allowed her to return to London. When Jessica was sixteen, her family emigrated to New Zealand. She refused to go with them. She stayed in London, all on her own—another very grown-up thing to do. She moved in with Eileen and earned her living as a dance instructor. It's been a straight lifestyle. Tap dance is everything to her."

For the first time, Warner looked directly into Terry's eyes. "You see now why she wouldn't run away. She's been working like mad for the new show, and she'd never let Alan down. There must be another explanation. We should look for the most likely thing to have happened. She could have fallen and harmed herself." His face turned ashen. "Good God."

"What's the matter?"

"I was just wondering how she'd react to a serious injury to her legs. She often says that she'd rather be dead than live a life like Eileen's. She could have committed suicide after an accident on her jogging round."

It was a ridiculous assumption, but Terry didn't say so. His thoughts took a different direction. "We take so much for granted, don't we?" he said. "We walk as if it were the most natural thing on earth. It's only when we meet someone less fortunate that we become aware of our vulnerability."

Roger wiped that away. "What a load of pathetic gobbledegook. Yes, of course, Eileen herself says she's grateful for every step she can make. You see, she's out of the wheelchair now—and apart from that, she's a person with lots of interests. She reads books, she learns languages. She can live like that, but Jessica couldn't. Jessica is her legs. That's the point."

"You mean you're married to a pair of legs."

"Don't try to be witty, Inspector, I can't stand it."

Terry feared he had interrupted Warner too harshly. "Tell me about your holiday on Tenerife."

"I have a firm that deals with real estate, with a branch in Puerto-de-la-Cruz. My firm makes seventy percent of its turnover with house sales on the Canary Islands. I've got a house there where I stay for several weeks every December. I had a hard time persuading Jessica to come with me this winter. She didn't want to leave London and her beloved studio. It was the prospect of being spared the family reunions at Christmas that made her change her mind—my family, I mean. The flight from New Zealand being so long, Jessica's parents never came to London after their emigration, not even for our wedding. Jessica didn't mind, though. Do you know the Canaries?"

"I've never been there. They are called the islands of everlasting springtime, aren't they?"

"They are lovely. A paradise. Unfortunately, in Jessica's eyes, the paradise turned into a private hell of hers. Right from the moment we boarded the plane she was complaining. She was in a terrible frame of mind all the time, and in the warm breeze of Tenerife, our relationship became chilly and immobile."

"Did she miss her daily routine?"

"Sure thing. She needs a wooden floor to practice, but all the rooms in my house in Puerto have stone floors. She wanted to go jogging, but the paths are stony with lots of loose pebbles and she was afraid of hurting her feet. I took her to the Playa San Marco, a lovely spot, and she complained about the black sand, the shingle beach and the menacing waves of the Atlantic ocean. She drowned me in an endless litany of lamentations."

"That sounds to me as if she were determined not to enjoy herself. We always perceive the world in the way we are inclined to see it."

"It became absurd after a few days," Warner acknowledged. "She found fault with everything, the half-finished houses you see everywhere, the cacti, the 'oppressive' slope of the Teide mountain, as she described it. She said it was the most ghastly environment she had ever seen, and that the air was so boring and tepid, so odorless that you felt no difference between breathing in and breathing out. Have you ever heard anything more ridiculous?"

Mr. Warner had spoiled his wife thoroughly. "It takes two to tango. How did you react? Did you give her a good piece of your mind?"

"No, I didn't. So far, all we had was an emotional landslide and I didn't want it to turn into an avalanche. I suppressed my anger and frustration, even though I was beginning to wonder if I had been mentally competent when I had married Jessica. On our way home from the airport, when we were back in good old frosty London, she insisted I drop her at the studio from where she returned five hours later, smiling and in a perfect mood. She didn't even notice my frayed temper. I had no idea I had such endurance. Jessica really brought out the best in me." He said it with unveiled bitterness. "I've lost her," he added mystically.

"When did your suppressed resentment bubble up again?"

Warner looked alarmed. "What makes you think that it did?"

"You said you had lost her."

"You are not my bleeding marriage counselor," he hissed. Forcing himself to calm down, he went on. "Our domestic problems have nothing to do with Jessica's disappearance. You shouldn't waste your time asking me silly questions and behaving like an agony aunt. Go and find Jessica, for heaven's sake."

Terry saw it fit to raise his voice then thought better of it. "Tell me more about her," he said calmly. "Or would you prefer to delay our conversation until I have talked to your servants?"

Roger gave a dry laugh. "You're as pig-headed as Jessica. Well, you'll learn about it anyway. Edgar is very discreet, but Nurit is awfully chatty. In fact, my emotions did bubble up when Jessica disappointed me once too often. I had asked her to stay at home on my fiftieth birthday, just this one day, and she promised she would. She slowly worked herself into a state. First, she got angry because Nurit wouldn't let her help with the party preparations, and later she ruined a carpet. I began to fear she was looking for a pretext to get away. Jessica hates parties and everything to do with them. When Alan called and said he couldn't come because he was in bed with a temperature, Jessica sulked for a while and then, without a word of explanation, put on her coat, said she'd be back in time, and was gone. It was so typical of her—and of course she wasn't back in time. I had to call Alan, and he went to find Jessica and remind her of the party. She didn't even apologize when she returned."

"Did you let it pass?"

"I did. I drank too much that evening to help swallow my distress, but it only made things worse. Jessica's lack of social skills infuriated me. We had an argument in front of everyone. God, what a painful scene. When Jessica wouldn't move an inch and insisted that it was all my fault, I got so enraged I . . . ." He paused and lowered his voice. "I hit her. A slap. The first time I have ever raised a hand against a woman. I was deadly ashamed. Did you ever hit a woman you loved?"

"No, never. Lack of opportunity, you might say. I suppose it hurt you more than her."

"Absolutely. She ran upstairs and I followed her and apologized like mad, but she was adamant and wouldn't listen to me. I went downstairs again and got rid of the guests. When I came to our bedroom, Jessica was already asleep. The next morning, to my great relief, she was calm and reasonable and forgave me."

"When was your birthday?" Terry inquired and considered taking a second sandwich.

"On Saturday."

"Three days ago. You don't think the slap drove Jessica away, do you?"

"No," Warner responded almost inaudibly. "I don't know a lot about Jessica, to tell the truth. She never opened her heart to me. I was wrong when I said I've lost her. I've never really found her." He sat down at last. "Where has she gone? It's driving me mad."

Terry let his eyes wander around the room—the fine furniture, the silk carpets, the oil paintings and lampshades of stained glass, the porcelain with gilded rims. "She could have been kidnapped."

Warner nodded serenely. "I assure you, I'm prepared to pay any sum to get her back. Shouldn't you put a listening device on my phone in case there's a call from a kidnapper?"

"We'll have a trace put on it by BT," Terry promised. "I'm sure you know that, as a rule, kidnappers insist that the police be kept out."

Warner rose again and went over to the window to stare at the street. "They could be watching my house. When they see the panda car they might decide to kill Jessica." He tapped his knuckles against the marble sill. "I should have waited until tomorrow. I called you in too early. Damn."

The man was a nervous wreck. Terry tried to divert him. "Who knew about your wife's jogging routine?"

"Goodness, everybody. And anybody could have watched her and studied her movements."

"Do you know if your wife has any enemies?"

"Enemies? No, of course not."

"Someone who envies her success?"

"No, certainly not. Everybody knows how hard she works and how much they depend on her. Without her, the troupe would be . . . Oh, you should have seen the standing ovation she had every night with their first big show. They know they owe their success to her."

"How about yourself—do you have any enemies?"

Warner frowned. "There are always people who don't like you, but I can't fathom anyone who could be labeled my enemy. I can think of no one who could do such an awful thing to me." The light from outside was fading, and he began to switch on lamps around the room.

"Maybe we can find something among your wife's personal belongings that could give us a hint of what might have happened to her."

"She doesn't have any personal belongings. She moved into my house with just two suitcases, containing her clothes and some documents."

"No fond childhood memories? Albums with photographs of her family? Books or CDs? Letters held together with a ribbon?"

"She doesn't get many letters. Sometimes her mother writes. She reads the letter once and throws it away."

"She must have a reliable memory."

Warner stopped in the act of drawing a curtain. "What a fool I am." He slapped his forehead. "I've simply not thought of it. She does not have a reliable memory, not at all. She's prone to blackouts, especially when she's in emotional distress. It happens in the early hours. She wakes up with a kind of temporal amnesia. These episodes date back to her early childhood. I told her to see a therapist, but she wouldn't."

"How do you notice when it happens?"

"She panics and makes sounds like a frightened child."

"What brings her round?"

"The best thing is a familiar voice. She had a blackout yesterday. I spoke to her and she came back to reality immediately. When she's alone, as she was last night, and there's no one to help her, then it can last for an hour or longer."

Terry waited for Warner to come forward with the answer to the question that stood unspoken between them. Why had Jessica been alone last night?

Warner drew the last curtain slowly. The burgundy brocade reflected the lights softly.

"You see, Jessica came home late last night and went to sleep in the guest bedroom," he said. "She had drunk something, which wasn't good for her. The alcohol could have caused a blackout of greater intensity this morning."

"Would she be likely to get up and leave the house in that state?"

"She does all kinds of things when there's nobody to bring her back. She told me she had her worst series of blackouts after Eileen's accident. That was before I met her. She lived alone then in the flat she had shared with Eileen, and she was terribly distressed because of the fire and all. Every morning she would wake up completely disoriented and wander around the rooms in a desperate search for her identity. Then she knew what to do and wrote notes telling herself who she was. She hung them on walls and put them everywhere so that she would find one quickly. But last night . . . She has never slept in the guest bedroom before. Maybe she got up and looked for something or someone. She found the tracksuit in the bathroom and put it on. She left and . . . God knows where she went in her confusion. I shouldn't have let her sleep in the guest room. I just didn't think of it."

"Don't work yourself up into a state over it, sir. No use feeling guilty about something that's a mere hypothesis."

The melodious chime of the doorbell startled Warner. Even Terry felt excited and stood up. It could be Jessica.

The butler came in. "Inspector, one of your constables wants to talk to you."

"Thank you. Excuse me for a minute, Mr. Warner."

Brick was filling the front door. "We've found something," he said. "It was in the first litter bin on the right when you enter the park on the corner of Primrose Hill Road."

Stapplethorne lifted the back of the panda. Inside, between the drug field-testing kit and a pair of workboots, there was a semi-transparent, yellow plastic bag. Brick pointed his torch at the bag, which contained one or two pieces of clothing. Terry parted the neck of the bag and saw that the clothes were of a shining red.

Chapter Seven

Susan's beauty waned deplorably when she was crying, when lines of pain creased her forehead and unbecoming red blotches highlighted her ivory skin, when mascara mingled with her tears and colored them a grainy black. David had seen her cry so often he no longer noticed these mutilations. Instead of compassion, he felt a time-honored but worn-out uneasiness.

Leaning against the jamb of the girls' dressing room, he watched Susan fighting with her zip, tearing at her costume, sobbing and drawing up mucus. What had he done? Susan's performance during the first dance had been wanting but he hadn't remarked on it—and yet, as soon as the music had stopped, she had stormed down the stairs and he had been obliged to follow her. It was more a social reflex than genuine compassion. He couldn't let her leave the dress rehearsal without an explanation.

Through the stairwell, he could hear the music for Laura's first solo and her fervent though ineffectual attempts to dance the part with Jessica's stance and conviction. He could feel in his own feet that she was not absolutely synchronous with the music. Jessica was always so perfectly at one with the rhythm that it seemed as if she herself sparked it off the stage.

He waited for Susan to say something—not that it would make any difference. Like ice floes, they had drifted apart slowly, and by now the gap between Susan and him had become so wide they had to shout at each other to make themselves heard, though still not understood. Soon he would be out of her sight, and she out of his.

"You're not coming back, then?" David asked, finally.

Susan pulled at the sleeve until the dress fell sideways, exposing her high breasts.

"You're the one who's not coming back," she said pugnaciously.

"I was talking about the show."

"The show's over and done with for me. Leave me alone. Go upstairs. You're supposed to feign at least some basic interest in the rehearsal."

He said nothing. He'd let Susan vent her anger on him. It would do him good—make him feel rightfully hurt.

"You don't care about the show any longer," Susan went on truculently. Her flow of tears had subsided. "That's why you wanted Victor to dance the lead."

"Laura isn't up to my standard."

She cast him an angry look. "She will rise to the occasion. It's bad policy to replace two leads; you might ruin the show. You have no compelling reason to refuse to dance with Laura. It's unfair to everyone, especially Alan. It's his show."

"I see. You're worried about dear Alan. I've often wondered what's going on between you and him."

The dress fell to the floor. "Don't be silly. He's just a friend." Susan stooped to unlace her shoes and David could see the tattoo on her left shoulder blade. He had chosen the motif himself: a small, pastel-colored water-lily. When he had asked Jessica if she would like to have her ankle tattooed with a rose she had mocked, yes, sure, if he had his butt branded.

"Just a friend, is he? Then why do you talk to him more often than to me? There's hardly a problem, no matter how intimate, you don't carry to him. It's always him. Or don't you discuss anything at all? Is it merely a pretext?"

"That's ridiculous and you know it." She stepped out of the shoes, threw back her head and sent her curls flying. There had been a time, before Susan had lost their child, when this movement had aroused a warm, pushing feeling of desire in his throat. Until her miscarriage, she had been perfection for him. It was perfection he craved—flawlessness, reliability. Jessica had represented all these values for him . . . but she, too, had let him down.

He picked up the costume, a move to cover how poor his act of mistrust was. "You went to see Alan in the middle of the night, didn't you?"

"I was desperate. I didn't know where else to go after the party. You had left without me."

"And so you went to cry on Alan's shoulder," he persisted. "If I hadn't called and told him to send you home immediately, you would have stayed on and he'd have comforted you, then kissed you and later—"

"Stop it. I'm not going to listen to any more of this crap. He had a cold."

"And you had it the next day. Intense exposure to his virus, I suppose."

Susan grabbed the short screwdriver that lay on her make-up table and stabbed the wood with all her force. The tool left a cross-shaped mark.

"How dare you accuse me of having an affair with Alan? You have betrayed me." She was yelling now in a screeching voice, which made it easy for him to justify his lack of respect for her. "Who do you think you are? Just look at yourself. You're past your prime. Is this why you're backing out of the show? Because you feel you can't compete with the young ones any longer?" Like a soldier putting on his battle dress, she thrust her legs into her trousers.

"That's completely off the mark." He took a step back, felt it was a mistake because he could no longer lean against the door jamb now, and held his arms akimbo.

Susan slipped her jumper over her head. When she saw he was withdrawing, she shot a last arrow. "You're still in love with her. Admit that you are."

"Do we have to go down that road again?"

"You don't want to dance with anyone else. For Jessica, only for her, did you want to be the Petruchio. Not for me or Laura—"

"For God's sake, Sue."

"—or any other woman in the world. Is that because Jessica is a shrew and you thought you could tame her? Or has she made you her serf?"

His hands cramped into claws. Again, he was aware of Laura's footfall. Not regular enough. He longed to hear Jessica dance. When she danced he could recognize her blindfolded. The precision of her footwork was unrivalled, especially among these amateurs. He had dreamt of moving her on from here to real fame, the West End first, then Radio City Music Hall in New York.

A picture nudged into his mind—the delicate outline of Jessica's feet, how shapely they were, how strong and yet soft the insteps had felt to his lips. It was true. He had been her slave from the minute he met her and now he was about to sacrifice everything for her: his marriage, his career, his pride. Love, he had learned in the purgatory of despised devotion, was deeper than hatred, fierce and ardent. It was the most relentless of all feelings.

The argument was over for him. He turned to leave. The music had changed. Heavy steps, like those of a tribal dance, were pounding on the planks of the stage, like an echo of his throbbing phantom pain.

"David."

With repugnance, he felt Susan's fingertips graze his back.

"I'm sorry," she said. "I know you were humiliated as much as I was."

He halted, paralyzed. She wouldn't dare speak it out, would she?

"It's foolish of me to think your feelings for Jessica haven't changed. You're more likely to loathe than to love her after she told you that—"

"No!" David turned and grasped Susan's forearms. "Don't even begin to think about it."

He let go of her when he saw his horror mirrored in her eyes. What he saw was his severed self, the part of him that had been Jessica's lover—and it throbbed and burned worse than ever.

A heartbeat later he had regained self-control. He would somehow manage to get through the crisis in a civilized manner. Placidly he said, "It doesn't matter any longer," surprised at how simple the truth was.

Give Blockley a theatre to investigate in and he'll be happy, like a burglar with a brand-new set of skeleton keys. That had been the idea behind it, hadn't it? As Detective Sergeant Timothy Blockley steered his old Vauxhall along Euston Road, he felt both peeved and amused, for he had again fallen for one of Inspector Terry's ruses. Just because the inspector was at odds with his work and needed a subterfuge to get out of his office, it didn't mean that he, Blockley, had to join this pointless investigation. What would he write in his report? Went to dress rehearsal, had a good time, ferreted about backstage to find missing dancer? Jessica Warner had only disappeared a few hours ago. Sending out two PCs to search Primrose Hill would have been more than enough. In fact, Blockley was certain this Jessica person would soon turn up again. In his eyes, Warner's vociferous behavior had been a hysterical overreaction, nothing more. Much as Blockley enjoyed working under Terry—for he was nice and never pulled rank—he was a bit concerned that the inspector's eccentric modus operandi might rub off on him.

The bright sign of The Caesar came into view as he rounded the corner. Too late for vacillations—he'd make the best of it. He backed into a parking space behind a red Renault, took out the copy of the missing person report and compared the license numbers. The car was Jessica's. He went over. Through the frosted windows, a huge, dark shape contrasted with the beige leather of the rear seat. He scratched at the ice with his thumbnail and peered inside. What could have passed for a human body turned out to be a navy blue plaid. Unless Jessica returned or was found within twenty-four hours, a forensic team would go over the car. Blockley doubted they would find anything worth their time.

He turned around to the theatre and saw a woman, tall and blond, charging out through the swing doors and then stalking toward Euston Road. She didn't look at him; her eyes were opaque with reflections from her own thoughts—dreary thoughts, judging by the tightness of her lips. He blocked her way and produced his ID. "Can I have a word with you?"

She recoiled in sudden consternation as if she had run against an invisible wall.

"What is your name?"

She dithered. "Susan. Susan Powell."

"It's about Jessica Warner. She's been reported missing."

"Oh no," she blurted out. "I don't want to talk about Jessica. I don't even want to hear her name again. As far as I'm concerned, Jessica is dead."

"Dead as in deceased, late?"

"No, dead as in no longer of significance. I'm not responsible for Roger's reaction to—" She broke off. "Forget it. Now let me go."

He wasn't exactly detaining her, was he?

"Goodbye, Mrs. Powell, and take care."

She was already scudding away as if driven by tail wind.

Inside The Caesar, Blockley leaned against the wooden counter of the closed box office to study the poster on the opposite wall. Roger Warner had called his wife a dance-aholic, and that was exactly how she looked on the painting—intoxicated by dance. *Jessica Warner & David Powell*, he read and deduced that the male lead was Susan Powell's husband. Were there grounds for jealousy? Jealousy could explain why Susan had reacted so harshly on hearing Jessica's name.

A stand on the wall next to the box office window offered a selection of leaflets. He picked one for *Taming of the Shoe* and unfolded it. A photo of Jessica dominated the first page. Another showed David Powell, who was praised as a renowned choreographer and dancer with an impressive background of successful shows in New York. The show was staged with a troupe of amateurs, pupils of the advanced tap classes, plus some of the teachers. The youngest member of the troupe was fourteen. A CD with the soundtrack was advertised on the back of the leaflet.

Blockley pocketed it for his private collection, then strolled to the high, double-winged door of the theatre from which he could hear a roaring rhythm which exploded into his ears the moment he swung open one wing of the door to slide inside. The auditorium was dark, rows of mostly empty chairs reflecting the red and blue lights that illuminated the stage where the dancers, three girls dressed in red bra-tops and miniskirts and three boys wearing black, leather trousers and sparse tops with studs, tap-danced energetically to a medieval tune which had been fused with a hard rock rhythm. The set-up had the feel of a fetish party.

Blockley found himself tapping his right foot and twitching his shoulders to the music. He made out about a dozen people, most of them standing, watching the show with the posture of pundits. A man with a dark, straggly beard tiptoed behind the back row as if to test the acoustics.

The music changed, the dancers withdrew and a girl dressed in a fluffy affair of white silk came gliding downstage. A spot of milky light followed her. Her naked feet touched the ground with feather-like softness. Blockley stood transfixed. This would be the Bianca of Shakespeare's play, he assumed. Long, straight, dark-blond hair flew like a gently blown curtain with every movement of her head.

When the drums set in again, another girl, or rather a woman, stomped onto the set. Her aggressive footwork in heavy-plated shoes perfectly contrasted the blond girl's timid footfall. This had to be Katharina, originally Jessica's part. In the red dress and with her glossy black hair, Jessica would have looked better than this ginger-haired one. The two women on stage were joined by a man, and once more music, lighting and choreography changed.

Bathed in red and yellow spots, they danced around each other, with the blond soon retreating and leaving the stage to Katharina and—as Blockley guessed—Petruchio, although the muscular, dark-haired man who danced the part bore no resemblance to David Powell's photograph in the leaflet. Maybe another understudy. When the number was over and the two dancers stood panting, Blockley joined in the applause of the other bystanders and then slipped out to find someone he could interview.

The corridor led to a lift and a flight of stairs that was built around it. A door on the right was labeled Office. He knocked, tried the door and found the room empty.

The office was cozy, with beech furniture, potted plants and files in assorted colors. The desk, though stacked with sheets and magazines, was orderly. The inspector ought to see this.

Blockley went to the lift, which looked new—like everything else inside. The Caesar was an old skin with new innards. Blockley decided to go downstairs. He found a long corridor, bright with spots and pine paneling, lined with doors, each painted a different color. He opened the red door and breathed in the atmosphere. How exciting it must be to get ready for a performance, to dress and titivate oneself with thumping heart, sweaty palms and butterflies in the belly.

To his disappointment, the room was bare of personal touches. There was a mirror surrounded by light-bulbs and in front of it, accurately aligned, two make-up pots and brushes, a box of Kleenex and a tin of shoe polish, but none of the paraphernalia one

would expect, such as photos, paper clippings or dried flowers.
Blockley looked into drawers. There was a dispenser with wads
of cotton wool, a red-handled screwdriver, a manicure set and a
notepad with a stub. In the midst of his rummaging, he was
addressed by a harsh voice.

"What are you doing in Jessica's dressing room and who are
you?"

"Detective Sergeant Blockley," he said automatically and
swiveled round. An elderly woman was eyeing him with mistrust.
Her gray hair was cut so short it stood up in bristles.

"Do you have a search warrant?" she asked sharply.

"Er . . . no."

Suddenly her face broke into a smile. "I've always wanted to
ask that question. I must have got an overdose of cop shows.
Never mind. Are you here about Jessica?"

"Yes, ma'am."

The woman dumped a bundle of clothes on the floor. "My
name's Helen Blythe-Warren, the Girl Friday of the troupe. Look."
His eyes followed her fingers to an empty shoe rack. "This is the
exact place where Jessica usually puts her practice shoes. They
are very special, handmade. A talisman, you could say. Last night
when I cleared up I couldn't find them. Jessica was already gone.
Now that she seems to have disappeared, I wonder if she took
them with her because she knew she wouldn't be coming back."

She took a roll of yellow semi-transparent plastic bags from
her apron, tore off one bag, rustled it open and stuffed in the
clothes she had tossed down. "Dirty laundry," she explained.
Blockley gave Jessica's room a parting look and followed Mrs.
Blythe-Warren.

"That's all I can tell you, I'm afraid," she said in the next room,
turning to a mobile hanger and taking down a gray dress that had
been artfully torn to rags.

"Fourth act," Blockley observed. "Petruchio takes Katharina
to his house and tames her."

"Right, luv. And I must take this up so that Laura can change her costume. Have you already talked to Alan?"

"Alan Widmark? No, I've only just come."

"I'll tell him you're here. You can wait for him in the office."

Blockley thanked her. In the office, comfortably slouched in the upholstered visitors' chair, he wrote into his notebook what he had found out so far. A little later, the door opened and a girl of six or seven years joined him.

"Dad'll come in a minute. Are you from Scotland Yard?"

Blockley closed his notebook and smiled at the child. When he saw that she looked displeased, he put on a more serious air and replied, "No, I'm from the local police station." He showed her his warrant card. "Detective Sergeant Timothy Blockley. And who are you?"

"I'm Cindy. Are you looking for Jessica? They're all looking for her, you know, and Dad's upset and Mummy says I can't stay with him overnight, although his cold is much better. That's unfair, ennit?" She looked at him as if she were expecting him to do something about it.

"Well, that's a scandal, really," he said. "So your Mum and Dad don't live together."

"Of course not, they're divorced. And when Mummy marries Martin, I'll throw the rice for them. Loads of rice." She looked him up and down. "Have you got handcuffs?"

"I haven't come to make an arrest and so I left them in the car." He was sorry to let her down again.

"I've got some, but they're only of plastic and you can unlock them without a key because there's a knob you can press to get free. They're no good." She began to suck the tips of her black hair. "Here's Dad," she announced.

"Sorry I made you wait."

Blockley turned and moved to get up.

"I'm Alan Widmark. Oh, do stay seated." Widmark slumped into the swivel chair behind the desk, and Cindy immediately went to sit on his lap. With a warm smile, which only partly masked his concern, Alan Widmark asked Blockley if he would like a cup of tea. Blockley declined.

"You've already met Cindy, my daughter." Stroking the girl's hair, he went on, "I'm surprised that the police are already sending someone round."

"Mr. Warner convinced us that his wife wouldn't abandon the show."

"This is absolutely true. The theatre is her home, her life, the core of her existence. For her, running away would be tantamount to committing suicide."

Blockley saw the implication of his own words unfold on Widmark's face.

"Cindy, love, go and watch the rehearsal." He gently put her on her feet.

"Simon said it's too loud for me."

"And this is too delicate."

Cindy sighed and left.

"She's nice," Blockley remarked. "She interrogated me very effectively."

Widmark grinned, which made him look young enough to be Cindy's elder brother.

"Would Jessica have a reason to kill herself? Is she the type for it?" Blockley asked.

"I doubt it. Jessica is . . . sort of self-centered. She's obsessed by staying healthy and . . . ."

"And suicide is a very unhealthy act."

Widmark fumbled with the computer mouse. "It's not in line with her character. But you never know. She's an introverted person and she has had private problems lately. So . . . ."

Blockley felt he had to say something reassuring. "She left no suicide note or farewell letter."

"She wouldn't. Jessica doesn't write letters. She told me once that she hadn't written a single letter in her whole life."

"Very introverted, indeed. Can you imagine what else might have happened?"

"I've got no idea—that's what makes it so unbearable. Susan has a theory, but it's not more than a wild, unfounded accusation."

"Susan Powell? I met her when I came."

"She left the show. I'm worried about her."

"Trouble with her husband?" Blockley ventured. "David, I presume. I peeped into the rehearsal. He wasn't dancing the lead."

"No, he kind of backed out."

"As a consequence of Jessica's disappearance?"

"Yes. Look, it's all very complicated and what I know is fragmentary. Half-truths can be misleading. Strange as it may sound, for we've been working together for fourteen years, I don't know much about what Jessica feels, what moves her, worries her. I have difficulties believing that she's developed an erotic fixation for—" He stopped abruptly and stared absent-mindedly at Blockley's notebook. "She's like a daughter to me. Jessica and Cindy could pass for sisters. Black hair, blue eyes, heart-shaped face." He looked up again, puzzled. "What was I going to say? Yes, there's something cooking, definitely. But I don't think I've got the right to tell you because it's very private. You'd better talk to Susan."

Jessica, Susan, David. Two women, one man. "Is Jessica having an affair with David?"

Alan considered the question for a long time. "They had one, but it's over. I only learned about it today, and it was quite a shock for me."

"Does Mr. Warner know it?"

"Y-yes . . . . Because of a letter Susan wrote him two days ago. Please, do talk to her. I have no right to give away other people's secrets."

Blockley decided to leave it at that. He could always come back to Alan if Susan remained as tight-lipped as she had been on their first encounter. Maybe there was someone else to interview.

"Does Jessica have any close friends?"

"Yes, Eileen, my secretary. Eileen Lanigan. She's not in today, and she's not at home either."

"As her friend, Jessica might have a key for Eileen's place."

"Of course. You mean, Jessica could be hiding there?" Alan grasped the receiver. "Eileen lives in a boarding house. I'll call the landlady," he said over the mouthpiece.

"Hello, Mrs. Horn. It's Alan. Could you do me a favor and see if there's someone in Eileen's room? Yes, I know she's in Richmond. It's Jessica I'm looking for. Thank you . . . . Yes? I see, thanks anyway. Could you ask Eileen to call me when she's back? Thanks." He replaced the receiver and shrugged defeatedly. "Jessica has to be somewhere. I've asked everyone. No one has seen her since last night. Has anyone been sent out to search Primrose Hill?"

The *crème de la crème* of criminology. "Sure enough. We've, em, split up the investigation, you know. It could be helpful if we had the addresses of the people who work for you."

Widmark ruffled his hair. "Of course. It's just that . . . . Well, I'll try." He turned to the computer desk and pressed a key. The monitor lit up. "Where's the address file?" he mumbled under his breath. "Ah, there it is. He did it. Good boy. Now print. Hey, I said print. Oh, sorry." He switched on the printer and smiled apologetically at Blockley. "What now? No paper? I've just refilled . . . . Oops, wrong cassette."

Blockley waited patiently at first, then began to tap the tip of his pen on his notebook. "Look, can I help you?" he finally asked.

"Yes, please. You see, I'm not made for modern information technology. If I tried cybersex I'd end up castrated."

Cindy decided that instead of returning to the rehearsal she'd go downstairs and play in Jessica's dressing room. She would put on a pair of Jessica's shoes and pretend she was the star of the show. That would be great fun—and she would put on lipstick, too.

In Jessica's room, Cindy found David sitting on the desk. Bad luck. He'd try to talk to her, like he always did, and ask her strange questions. He'd hug her, too. She didn't like the way he hugged her. It didn't feel okay, somehow. Mummy had said not to let people touch her in ways she didn't like. But how could she stop him? How would she explain? David would ask why she let Simon and Martin hug her. She could tell him it was because Martin's beard tickled so funnily, and that was why she liked it.

But she'd never tell him that she liked Simon's hugs almost as much as Daddy's, and that she would marry him when she was big. That was her secret. She'd marry Simon, he of the magic hands, as they called him. She found his sense of humor his best trait—and he always made her feel special, calling her beauty queen and such.

That was none of David's business, of course. She'd better keep away from him. His hugs were always too hard. They hurt. That was it. If he tried to hug her again she'd tell him it hurt. If she had the courage to say it, that was.

David was looking up now, seeing her. Too late to turn around.

"Cindy? What're you doin' down here?" His voice was as hard as his hugs.

"Playin'." And what was he doing down here? He should be in the wings watching the show. That was a phrase she liked. "In the wings" sounded better than "backstage."

"Cindy, if you were a flower, what would you like to be?"

Cindy reached for Jessica's lipstick and unscrewed it. Jessica had allowed her to use it. "I don't want to be a flower at all," she said stubbornly. "I want to be a bird. A hawk."

David made an impatient sound. "Yes, but if a magician came and wanted to turn you into a flower and you had to make a choice, which flower would you choose?"

"None at all. I'd fly away and leave the silly magician behind." She hoped he wouldn't ask her more strange questions.

"You're just like Jessica," he said morosely and reached out for her. Cindy stepped back.

"I don't want you to hug me. It hurts," she said, trying not to blush.

"Sorry. I promise it won't hurt this time."

"Why do you always wanna hug me?" Asking for reasons often made grown-ups give up whatever they were about to do.

He gave her a sad look. "Because I lost a child."

Now, that was the stupidest thing she'd ever heard. "You can't lose a child. It's not like a doll you mislay." To impress him, she added, "There's a police detective in Eileen's office. He talked to me, he did."

David's inanimate face began to move. His brows narrowed. "What's he come for?"

"Top secret." That was a phrase Helen had taught her. Sounded mighty good—and it was a nice exit line, too. Her lips smeared with lipstick, she left to see if the detective was still around.

Andrew Sedgewick, the forensics technician, stood in front of Terry's desk and gawked with his fishbowl eyes over his glasses, which he kept pushing up. Immediately, they would slide back to the tip of his short nose. Terry had never seen Andrew look through—only over—them, as if they were a support for his gaze.

"It's impossible to detect fingerprints on polythene with the equipment I've got," Andrew explained. "I assume the bag hasn't been used before, since there are no remains of other materials inside. On the suit, I found no traces of blood, semen or dirt."

"Anything that indicates it was forcefully torn from Jessica?" Terry asked.

"No, the seams are intact, not even stretched. The fabric is homogeneous. A hair we found inside the top matches the sample you brought from Jessica Warner's hairbrush. Tomorrow I'll look for fibers of other origin."

"We're talking about Jessica's jogging suit," Terry informed Blockley, who had joined them a minute before. "It was found in a bin on Primrose Hill, in this plastic bag. The suit has her initials, and Roger, as well as his two servants, identified it. Where the bag comes from, we don't know. Nurit, the housekeeper, assured me that they had 'no yellow bags of theez or any other size' anywhere for any conceivable purpose. She was very exhaustive on the subject."

"I've seen one at The Caesar," Blockley said. "They come from a roll and are used for dirty laundry."

"A roll, yes, there's perforation at both ends. Perfect match, I'd say." Andrew pushed up his glasses. "As to the fragments the housekeeper found, they belong to a small balloon glass and they're stained with cognac. From the size and shape of the fragments, I'd say the glass hadn't been dropped to the ground or smashed against a wall, but crushed."

"Crushed by a hand? Then there should be blood on it."

"It's very thin glass. The fingerprints on it match those of the husband, Roger Warner. The skin on a man's palm is thick enough to crush such a glass without getting cut."

"You should have seen Mr. Warner's face when Brick took his fingerprints," Terry said to Blockley. "Thank you, Andrew."

Andrew collected the sealed evidence bag which contained the yellow plastic bag and left. Blockley sat down. He had brought two cups of tea and two sandwiches. "Tuna or Salmon?" he asked Terry.

"Neither, thank you." He began to shift papers on his desk until he found three Cadbury cream bars in the in-tray. He unwrapped one and dipped it into his tea. "I'm made up of bad habits. Sorry." He licked the half-molten mass. "Well, then, let's exchange notes." He handed Blockley his notebook. As soon as the sergeant opened it, a grin began to play at the corners of his mouth.

"Oh no, have I done it again?" Terry leant over. Daggers dripping with blood and flowers growing out of brick walls were doodled around his spidery handwriting. Terry shook his head. "I wasn't even aware I had done it again. It was easier to give up smoking. I hope you can read it nevertheless."

"No problem at all, sir."

Shamefaced, Terry looked at Blockley's neat shorthand.

"Well," Terry said after a while, closing the book and returning it to Blockley. "You've dug up some interesting facts. Jessica had an affair with David Powell. Two days before Jessica's disappearance Susan Powell wrote to Roger, informing him of his wife's adultery. Jessica's favorite pair of shoes has been missing since last night—shoes once more. If I put a pair of tap shoes on my desk, Gould will think I'm a fetishist."

Blockley hitched up his trousers and crossed his legs. "I wonder if you can walk into any given set of persons and tell them about a crime and—whoops—they start behaving guiltily and accusing each other. I had the impression that Susan was on the point of telling me that Roger had killed Jessica. We've really got a case here, haven't we?"

"I'm not sure yet," Terry said conciliatorily. "Jessica could be trying to solve her problems by running away. The method worked when she didn't want to go to boarding school any longer."

He finished the first chocolate bar and began to tear the wrapper off the next. "I did something similar when I was a boy. My mother used to make me play the piano for her visitors; aunts with hairy nostrils or scary old men from the neighborhood. She went to extremes to please these people. She made me put on a suit, one of those mock grown-up-looking things, and a starched shirt with cufflinks and a bow tie. With my hair parted and greased, I looked more simian than human. After I had played, they would all grab and kiss me." The memory sent shivers down his spine. "I tried everything to escape the ordeal. I feigned cramps, I coughed miserably. My mother was relentless. One day I locked the piano and mislaid the key. It turned out that my mother had a spare key. In my exasperation, I saw only one way out. I decided to run away and, to be prepared, packed a bag which I hid under my bed. The next time my mother announced that we had guests and laid out the suit for me, I made off through the back door. That would teach her not to bother me again."

"You think that's what Jessica's doing? Hiding somewhere? That she hopes if she's back in time for the opening night, every-thing—affairs and what other trouble she's caused—will be for-given and forgotten?"

"She's got some infantile traits, hasn't she?"

"She took nothing with her."

"Maybe she had a bag ready and hidden. We'll have her bank accounts checked to see if she's had any extra expenses lately." Terry squinted at the third bar. Soon the tea would be too cold for a dip.

"Shall I get you a fresh cuppa?"

Terry flushed. "Oh, thanks, but . . . em, no. What's your theo-ry?"

Blockley looked unhappy. "The facts fall perfectly into place when we assume Jessica has committed suicide—that she took her shoes and a plastic bag home with her last night because she planned to kill herself. Alan Widmark told me she joined them on a pub tour, but her mood was dreary and she drank alcohol, which is not in line with her healthy lifestyle. She must have had the shoes in her handbag, if it's large enough."

"It's a red leather rucksack." Terry indicated its size with his hands.

"I suppose that sometime last night she left the house, dumped the bag with the suit into a bin—which could be her equivalent of a farewell letter—and, carrying the only earthly pos-session she cared about, her practice shoes, looked for a place to hide and die. The cold alone would do. She could have taken sleep-ing pills to make it easier."

"Why should she want to commit suicide? Because her affair

had been disclosed? From what Roger told me, I would characterize her as a person who doesn't care what others think of her."

Blockley played with his empty Styrofoam cup. "I'll go and see Susan Powell tomorrow. I think it's important to know exactly what she wrote to Roger and why she did it."

"It's a nice little irony, isn't it? Roger has been so busy suppressing his jealousy, which he thought unjustified, that he didn't realize his wife was indeed unfaithful."

"Or else he was hiding the fact that he knew it."

Terry finished his tea. "I can easily imagine him jaundiced with jealousy and killing Jessica in the heat of the moment. Nurit Berman, the cook, heard them quarrel yesterday morning. Susan Powell's anonymous letter must have been in the morning mail. When Jessica didn't come home in time in the evening, Roger had hours in which to work himself up into a state. One rebellious remark from Jessica could have blown the fuse."

"First, he crushed the glass from which he had been drinking—then he went for Jessica's throat," Blockley plotted. "Afterward he had all night to remove the evidence of his deed."

"The flaw is that he's too clever to hide the corpse without letting anything else disappear to cover his deed."

"And the missing shoes don't fit into the picture, either."

"Same for the tracksuit in the bag. It doesn't quite make sense. The suit could be a diversion, but Roger wouldn't take Jessica's shoes from the theatre, for fear of being seen. He's not likely to be around there. In fact, he hates tap dance."

"I saw Jessica's understudy dance. It was dazzling. If Jessica's even better, how come she's still with that troupe of amateurs?"

"She's not really pursuing a career, it seems."

Blockley reached into the inner pocket of his blazer and produced a leaflet. "They're trying to push this show as professionally as they can. They've produced a CD and a video clip is coming up."

Terry turned the leaflet in his hands. "And now it's all in danger of falling apart because Jessica is missing."

"And David isn't dancing on the opening night either. Even Susan backed out."

"Susan could have killed Jessica out of jealousy," Terry said and unwrapped the third chocolate bar. He was a lucky man insofar as he never put on weight, no matter what or how much he ate. Only his teeth had suffered from prolonged chocolate abuse.

"I'll talk to her tomorrow morning. I hope she'll be more approachable this time. She said something about not being 'responsible for Roger's reaction to—' and then she stopped and blushed. She looked like an ad for a guilty conscience."

"She must have been referring to the letter she wrote to Roger, according to Alan. I'll go to The Caesar tomorrow and talk to him, and also to Eileen Lanigan, of course. She can certainly tell me more about Jessica's alleged affairs and her blackouts." Terry smoothed out the wrapper of the bar against his desk. "Has it struck you that people who look weak are often much stronger inside than those who display mountains of strength? Like Jessica, who appears so healthy and self-centered, and yet seems to have skipped several stages of character development. Or Roger, who seeps authority with every gesture, and yet allows himself to fall for a selfish woman. I wonder what kind of person David is. Success requires either strength or recklessness."

"I couldn't talk to him after the rehearsal," Blockley apologized. "He had set off without commenting on the rehearsal. He's got a reputation for being arrogant and conceited."

"He's probably another case of weakness in disguise. And Alan? What's your impression of him?"

"He's in his mid-thirties, younger-looking and handsome. Honest, but not very talkative. The perfect darling. You'll like him, sir."

Was there a mocking streak in Blockley's tone? Terry had never been sure how much was known about his private life. He cleared his throat and handed Blockley the leaflet back.

"There remains one last theory—that Jessica was attacked, raped, murdered or whatever by a stranger who chose her at random."

"And who knew how to hide a body."

"Except that Jessica doesn't belong in the victim category. She'd have kicked, screamed, counter-attacked. Someone would have noticed. Let's leave it at that. When you've finished talking with Susan Powell tomorrow, we could meet at Roger's house and take a walk around Primrose Hill. I want to get the feel of the place." Which was his favorite excuse for taking walks.

Blockley got up. "I almost forgot. Alan gave me two tickets for the première. Would you like to come with me?"

Terry squirmed and put on a forced smile. Two months ago he had seen the Royal Ballet. That was what he called a great night out. "Well, I . . ."

Innocently, Blockley added, "Just to get the feel of The Caesar, sir."

Chapter Eight

Eileen stood at the high window that overlooked the walled garden of the Richmond Gate Hotel. Nothing stirred out there. In the dark, the leafless trees looked like charred, blurred skeletons—blurred because Eileen was short-sighted. She leaned her crutches against the sill, pressed her hands on the ledge and rested her forehead against the cold pane. Now she could see a phantom. It was her alter-ego, the other Eileen, the one who hadn't made the wrong decision, who was healthy and pretty. Pre-mishap Eileen. She was flitting across the lawn, her feet bare, her hair long. When she stepped into a rectangle of light that fell on the lawn from one of the ground-floor windows, the restaurant maybe, she pirouetted so wildly that she looked as if she had hopped right out of one of Alan's paintings.

Normally, Eileen would have chased the image away, but right this afternoon Professor Johnson had said that positive mental imagery was an important constituent of physical wellness. It was one of the comments that had filled her with a sense of trust in a situation that, to her judgement, was more than chancy. After he had studied the CT scans and other documents Simon had brought along, Johnson told her that he would like to try a new, improved method on her. Well, not yet proved to be improved. So new, in fact, it wasn't more than a computer simulation of flesh-and-blood surgery. In her case, three complicated operations were necessary—on her knee, hip and back, consecutively. After that she would go through a long, mostly painful, recovery process during a stay of at least four months at his institute. The good news was that it would not call for any expenses on her part. The complexity of her fractures made her a unique, compelling case. At the offer of free treatment, she became suspicious. Was he looking for a guinea pig?

"All my patients are guinea pigs," Johnson conceded. "Whether they pay for the privilege or not. It's in the nature of experimental surgery—consider the first heart transplants."

Consider the *Titanic*, Eileen thought. The pane was as cold as an iceberg. Pre-mishap Eileen was still dancing her silent dance on the cold lawn, leaving no footprints, but causing a gleam of hope to light up Eileen's eyes. Hope, so airy and uplifting, was the magic word. Risk, uncanny and downbearing, was its counterweight. To which side would the seesaw of fate swing for her?

"I don't know what to do." Those were the first words she had spoken since dinner. She had been silent all evening, and Simon had accepted her mood in his usual way—one of the many things that endeared him to her—laid-back and at ease with himself and the world. His presence alone made her feel more competent and complete, as if a part of him seeped into her and transformed her.

She hadn't protested when he announced that he had booked a room for them long in advance and intended to stay overnight. There were two pairs of pajamas in his suitcase, two toothbrushes and a bottle of massage oil. It could have been romantic had she not been so preoccupied with the Professor's prognosis. Simon ran her a bath, helped her in and out of the tub, massaged her, and still she found nothing to say, was even too immersed to notice his gentle ministrations. Her mind was crammed with ugly words—surgery, corset-plaster, immunosuppression—and even scarier images—scalpels slitting her skin, chainsaws slicing up her bones. She was getting so tortured by her imagination that she couldn't bring herself round to seeing the picture Professor Johnson had painted for her: a renewed Eileen, swiftly walking with an elegant cane, free of chronic pain and muscle cramps.

While Simon was in the bathroom, she slipped into the smaller of the two pajamas, chose one side of the bed and pretended to be asleep. A few minutes later, Simon crept in on the other side and switched off the lights. Sleep wouldn't come. As soon as she heard Simon breathe regularly, Eileen ventured to get up and walked over to the window. There she stood, gazing at pre-mishap Eileen, the silent dancer, until she had disappeared into the far shadows. Eileen returned to the four-poster bed.

"I really don't know what to do," she told the pillow as she sank into it.

"Don't worry," Simon, whom she had thought to be soundly sleeping, answered drowsily. "There's a very wise, experienced decision-maker in your head. It's called the subconscious. It has already come to a conclusion. When you stop thinking about the pros and cons, and weighing the chances and risks, then the answer will percolate to the surface of your mind. And it will be the right decision." He moved closer.

"Well said, big Yeti," she laughed and warmed her forehead on his cheek. She was astonished how soft his stubble was, like fluff. "I've just discovered why all women are crazy about you. You don't get scratchy when you haven't shaved."

"That makes it seventeen."

She could feel his cheek move as he spoke. "Seventeen what?"

"Reasons you have found why all women are crazy about me."

"That's nonsense."

"No, it's true. I've been counting them ever since we met. Number one was that I've got very regular, white teeth. Number two—"

"Okay, you're right." She felt embarrassed, especially since they were sharing a bed tonight. She'd rather not talk about his physical features.

Simon propped himself up on his left elbow and looked down at her. All she could see of him in the darkness was his outline and the whites of his eyes. "And I also know why you keep saying these things. Because you are in love with me, Eileen," he said in his soft, gentle tone.

A hot, helpless feeling spread from her solar plexus. Her fingertips began to buzz. She pressed her head deeper into the pillow, away from the mouth she loved so much. When his lips were almost touching hers, she turned her head; he moved it back, tenderly but firmly. A mild panic rose, as she knew he was going to kiss her. He tasted fresh, too good to be true. When Simon began to unbutton her pajama top she stopped him with both her hands. "No, Simon. We can't . . . . We're friends."

"Would you prefer to do it with a foe?" he asked, his lips grazing hers as he spoke.

"I don't want to do it at all." She pressed the duvet firmly against her chest. It was a lie. She wanted it, wanted it so much, too much. But it was impossible—couldn't he see that she wasn't in the mood? And even if . . . .

He ignored her protests and snatched away the duvet. His hand moved to her stomach and pushed up the pajama top. In an attempt to cooperate, Eileen lifted her chin and closed her eyes. When he kissed the hollow of her throat she waited for her body to respond, but she felt as dead as the skeleton trees in the garden. She tried to evoke her feelings of the other day in the gym and saw that she had changed too much. She was not only post-mishap Eileen but also post-talking-to-Professor-Johnson Eileen, too concerned about the future to enjoy the present.

"Please, stop it."

"We could try it the other way round," he proposed. "You could seduce me, how's that?" Simon plopped back on his pillow.

"It's silly." Eileen sat up and readjusted her top. She was angry because now that she was closer than ever to getting what she had long desired, she realized that she had banned the idea of making love with Simon so firmly into the realm of illusion that it was out of reach. She couldn't make out his expression. Was he dejected? Or rather amused? She tried to explain her refusal of his generous proposal.

"Why should you want to drive a jalopy when you can have all those Porsches and Rolls-Royces like Jessica and Laura?"

"Collector's pride, maybe."

She could hear him smile. How she loved the warmth of his voice. She extended a hand and put it on his lips. Nothing she could say would make the situation any better, but she tried.

"The last time I had sex was more than five years ago. I'm practically a virgin."

"Great. I've never had a virgin before."

She widened her eyes in surprise. The shallow bit of light that came in through the window didn't help her to read his expression. "You're kidding."

"I've always avoided virgins. Women tend to attach special emotions to their first lover, and I didn't want to be the target of those emotions."

"You're right, I did attach special emotions to Colin." She looked out of the window, directing a wan smile at the equally wan sky. "We split up three months after the fire. He couldn't stand to see me suffering any longer." Some people give you strength, others suck it from you. When Colin had left her with a thousand excuses and regrets, she had felt a sad relief because she had come to hate seeing herself through his eyes. In his presence, all she had wanted had been to die in his arms. This wouldn't have agreed with Johnson's theory of positive mental imagery.

Simon sat up, placed his warm palm on the sensitive stretch of skin and nerves between her shoulder blades and kissed the side of her throat. She was tempted to remark that maybe the true reason for his success with women was his stamina. Number eighteen if his count were right.

"You never mentioned Colin before."

"I think I suppressed the memory. The years we had together were in another universe, another time-space-continuum." When Simon's hand moved down her spine Eileen tried to divert him. "It wasn't such a good idea to stay overnight," she remarked. "We'll both be late for work tomorrow."

"I'll take you directly to the theatre, and then I'll drive on to the clinic."

"I will have to change my clothes."

"Your dress is lovely. Nothing wrong with it."

"I'll need fresh underwear."

"I bought a set."

"I had no idea you're such an organized person. Did you know the right size?"

"Baby, I know your size so well I could knit underwear for you." His mouth was at her earlobe. "Darling Eileen, try to relax. There's nothing you have to fear. I won't hurt you. I know the exact angle to which you can spread your legs without dislocating your hips."

"Is that your most efficient opening line?"

She was beginning to feel exhausted. Five years of longing destroyed in a few seconds—like a long distance runner who gave up inches short of the finishing tape; like the crew of Apollo 13 unable to land on the moon. Her dreams had been running in orbits, not really expecting a moon to exist—not for her, not for post-mishap Eileen.

"You simply don't twig it. I can't stand the idea of you making love to me out of pity." She lowered her voice because the truth hurt. "I don't want to think that you would sacrifice yourself just to please me."

Simon switched on the bedside lamp. The sudden light made her close her eyes to protective slits. He took her by the shoulders.

"Eileen, I do understand. You're not like other women. Sure, there's not a single woman who's not preoccupied with her looks, but your self-depreciation is pathological. Your picture of yourself has been shattered, and you are still trying to glue the fragments together. What you need is a completely new image of yourself as a woman."

"Did you hold that speech spontaneously or was it rehearsed?"

"A bit of both. I rehearsed ten different versions and then spontaneously decided which one to use."

She smiled despite herself. "And by making love to me you want to polish up my image, or what?"

"Well, I thought love was the cure. It seems we have to step back and take a longer run-up. It doesn't help you a bit if I love you when you can't love yourself."

Her eyes stung and, between her half-closed lids, tears were squeezed out.

"I love you, Eileen." He closed his arms around her.

She wanted to disappear inside him, to melt into his familiar smell. She never wanted to stop touching him. "Simon." His pajama top was soaked with her tears. "What do you mean by taking a longer run-up?"

"A therapy I invented especially for you." He carried her into the bathroom where he switched on the light with his elbow and let Eileen down on a stool in front of the huge wall mirror. The sudden change of scenario confused her, and when he undressed her she remained as limp as a puppet.

"What I want you to do is to make a declaration of love to yourself," he began to explain, "To every single part of your body. Start with your feet and work your way up. Then go inside. Don't forget a single bit. Liver, kidney, blood—anything. And it must be unconditional. Don't say, 'Left cheek, I love you despite the scar,' or, 'My mouth, I love you because your smile is so lovely.' Make no positive or negative comments whatsoever. That's what I mean by unconditional."

She looked at her reflection. She couldn't even see herself

properly without her glasses. "That's idiotic. I can't do it."

"I insist. I won't let you out of the bathroom until you've done it. And speak aloud. You won't mean it in the beginning. Let it develop its own dynamic."

"What kind of mantra is this? What's it supposed to be good for?"

"You'll see." He left and closed the door.

For a moment, she hated him. Her crutches were in the bedroom, and her only chance to get back to bed without asking him to carry her was to creep over the hard tiles. Had she known it would end with this farce, she'd rather have allowed him to go on with his seduction routine. Well, if Simon was daft enough to suggest this therapy then she couldn't make too much of a fool of herself by carrying it out. Get it over with, she told herself, the sooner the better.

"My feet, I love you," she almost shouted so that Simon could hear her. "Each of my toes, I love you." She went on with calves, shanks, knees, her voice getting lower, her tone warmer. You can't say "I love you" without feeling at least a tinge of tenderness. When she reached her belly she felt a new sensation, a kind of gratefulness for being alive. She began to touch her body parts as she assured them of her love and went on, addressing every aspect of her physique up to her scalp and hair. She fell into a tailspin of pleasure, and a new intimacy with her body arose. When she began to concentrate on her innards, she closed her eyes to visualize her heart, lungs and right kidney—she also sent a loving thought to the left kidney she'd lost. It was amazing how much there was to be loved; glands, tendons, neurons, muscle cells, hormones, an entire cosmos of structures, magically animated. There was something else there, something finer and more ethereal than blood. Her hands automatically moved toward the source of this life energy. She could feel its pulsation under the soft skin of her belly. She had been co-existing with this marvel without ever becoming aware of it. Her fingertips brushed against her wiry pubic hair. "I love you, you crazy little thing," she said and cupped her sex.

She had completed the exercise and smiled at her fuzzy mirror reflection. It's me, she thought, it's really me. She would no longer stay in her inner exile, the doomed planet of mishap. And there was Simon, like a supernova in a universe devoid of stars, Simon who loved her as unconditionally as only he could love.

She just had to think of the way Simon's eyes lit up when they arrived in Sevenoaks on their bi-weekly visit to his brother's house and he stooped to take Peter, his retarded boy, out of the wheelchair, pressing his lanky body lovingly against his chest. Or how he smiled with undisguised pride when Barbara Jenkinson, his brother's wife, called to tell him that Peter had learned to say a new word. And the kid was all of sixteen years old. Simon was so different from Colin, so steadfast despite his mercurial character.

She got up and stood with trembling legs until Simon came in a few seconds later, cradled her in his arms and carried her to the bedroom. Her flesh had awoken, and she sensed a sweet lassitude as he lowered her gently to the bed.

"I'll have the surgery."

Outside, in the cold winter night, the other Eileen lifted and swirled through the air like a fairy on a snowflake.

Chapter Nine

Her mind was adrift, her body non-existent. All she knew was that she was waking up, although it seemed to take hours while her consciousness came and went. Her eyes finally opened to the grayness of dawn. Her breathing was slow and inefficient, her lungs constricted. Who was she? She hadn't a clue. She stared at a damp patch on the otherwise featureless ceiling. Where was she? Her brain was a hallway with all the doors closed, inhabited by vague shadows; nameless, moving nowhere.

She managed a deeper breath into the void that was her chest. She tried to call for help but was unable to find her voice. Her body felt strait-jacketed, both from the outside and the inside. Slowly, she turned her head, which was propped up on a thick pillow, to her left, toward the light that came through a square, undraped window that looked out onto a dull view of flat roofs and chimneys. Disappointed, she let her eyes travel around the room in search of a familiar sight. Apart from the bed on which she was lying—a brass bedstead with a firm mattress—there was a wardrobe on the opposite wall and an empty bookshelf, both of a wood so bleached with age that she couldn't make out its grain. The only door, its varnish cracked and decayed to a dirty yellow, was closed, locking out the world. A heavy silence filled the space between the walls with their peeling paper, whose pattern had faded beyond recognition.

She noticed the smell of mildew. How could she be in a room that smelled rotten? There was nothing in it that bespoke of a person's presence, unless someone was happy to share his world with dust. There were faint, overlapping footprints in the dust on the floor where she—and someone else?—must have walked to the bed. With disgust, she saw a used condom lying by the leg of a chair . . . or was it a sausage peel? The chair, painted to match the door, stood by itself, fulfilling no apparent purpose. Turning her head fully to the right, she saw rings in the dust on the bedside table, as if a glass which had recently stood there had been taken up several times and put down again in slightly different positions.

No, this was not a room in which she or anyone else could wake up under common circumstances in a normal, day-to-day life. Something had to be terribly wrong here, the worst being not the eerie atmosphere of this place but the fact that, remotely, it was to her eyes what a worn-down path is for the feet—a way often walked, a sight often seen. When? Where? The overwhelming stench of humidity confused her so much she couldn't come up with any tangible memory.

The coverlet was a mismatch, for one because it was there at all, and also because it wasn't a faded duvet or threadbare sheet but a goosedown comforter, thick and warm and covered in crisp white linen that gave off a fresh smell. She buried her nose in it to distract herself from the olfactory discomfort the mildew caused.

What was happening to her? Who was she?

She concentrated on her hands as they slowly came to life, removed them from under the coverlet and lifted them. They were as heavy as lead but they looked intact, small and slim. When she tried to wriggle her fingers, she found that they were numb. It would pass. The question was whose fingers they were. She let them sink back and discovered that the surface of the coverlet was cold. So was the air. Awfully cold. Why? Why was it so cold in this room? Why was she in this room that was unheated and obviously uninhabited?

She looked out of the window again over the chimneys onto flat roofs, and it was as if she had awoken to this view many times before. She lowered her gaze to the central heating under the sill. Its presence alone made the room feel even colder. In front of it stood a gas stove, not larger than Dad's briefcase . . . . Her heartbeat went up. She was at home, at home. This ghastly place was her very own room! A murmur of relief mixed with her forced breathing. She had a name again, Jessica Gresham.

Of course her room would be empty on her last day in this house. Recalling that she would have to say goodbye to her parents for a long time today, she was not at all surprised that she had had a blackout again. Dad and Mum were bound for New Zealand this afternoon. Their belongings had been shipped in a container weeks ago. After breakfast Dad would drive her to Islington, where she would live with Eileen Lanigan. He would kiss her demurely and Mum would scold him for being so sentimental. After all, they weren't leaving the bloody solar system, she would say and hug Jessica with her firm arms and . . . wait a minute. If this was still going to happen why could she remember it as if it had already happened?

Jessica grabbed the bedclothes and forced herself to concentrate on the things that really should trouble her: what it would be like to share a flat with Eileen Lanigan who was ten years older; whether she would have to make many compromises and allowances; would she feel in the way when Eileen's boyfriend— Colin or Calvin—came to see her? Jessica had met him once or twice, an average-looking, shy, young man. He was a good match for Eileen, who was nice but not exactly an eyecatcher. Jessica frowned. She could feel the lines on her forehead like little spasms of thought. Something was totally wrong with the mental image she had of Eileen. There was a scar on Eileen's cheek that looked oddly familiar. Past and present began to draw apart, the overlap became thinner, the time line disentangled. She remembered moving in with Eileen, the fire at The Caesar, her marriage to Roger, making love with David.

Oh, my God, David.

Jessica jerked back onto the pillow in sudden knowing shock and covered her mouth with her hands. Her parents leaving England, that had been years ago. She couldn't possibly be here, in the old house, the place of her adultery, her secret meetings, lying in the very bed where she and David used to make love, under the coverlet David had bought, calling it "the down for our love nest."

She sat up again and pushed away the bedclothes. Adrenaline circulated her system. She would run out into the cold winter morning and return to reality. But something blocked her . . . she couldn't stand up . . . her legs . . . they wouldn't move. They didn't seem to belong to her. Well, they hadn't come alive yet, she soothed herself. A blackout had this effect sometimes. She angrily folded back the goosedown comforter to the left all the way down—and then she saw that there was no way for her to get out of here.

Ten seconds passed as she drew in quivers of breath until she was on the verge of exploding. Then she began to scream.

Police Constable Stapplethorne estimated that the temperature had dropped by two or three degrees. He pouted and tried to form rings with his billowing breath. There weren't many people around in the park in this vile weather. His colleagues, who had swarmed out among the houses of Primrose Village, were busier, that was sure. A young woman with Afro curls hurried in his direction. For the seventh time this morning, Stapplethorne showed Jessica Warner's photo, asked his set of questions and drew another blank. He switched off the pencil-torch and walked a few paces to keep warm. The real trouble was that he had forgotten his cigarettes.

"Morning, Officer. Giving up smoking?"

Stapplethorne looked at the old man who had entered the park and was unleashing his dog. "Sorry?"

"I saw you puff at the end of your torch." The old man rolled up the leash and shoved it into a pocket of his coat. "Pretty cold these days. I'll need two cups of steaming tea with rum to warm me up when I'm back home."

"That's the trouble when you own a dog," Stapplethorne sympathized. "There's no hiding from bad weather. I've got a dog myself, a Mastiff. Yours is a Lab, isn't it?" He bent down to pat the dog which was sniffing at his trouser legs.

"She's not mine, she belongs to my daughter." The old man hitched up his scarf over his chin. "I saw another policeman in Rothwell Street. What's up?"

"We're trying to find someone who has seen this woman." Stapplethorne flashed his torch at Jessica's photo. The old man gave it a narrow-eyed look and bent his head.

"She looks like someone I've seen before. I'm not sure who it could . . ."

"She runs through the park every morning."

The man raised a pair of bushy eyebrows. "Wait a second. I think . . ."

"Her name's Jessica Warner."

"Now I remember. I met her on Monday morning. A nice young lady in a red tracksuit. We exchanged a few words. I didn't recognize her on this photo because she had on a woolly hat when I saw her."

"How about yesterday, Tuesday morning? Did you see her again?"

The wrinkly face broke into a huge smile that revealed two

irregular rows of discolored teeth. "Yes, sure I saw her." His smile sank. "Good God. Has anything happened to her?"

"She's missing. Where and when did you meet her yesterday?"

"Meet is the wrong term. I saw her from a distance. Same time as today, I'd say, around a quarter to eight. I was somewhere over there." They strolled to the gap in the cast iron railing that enclosed the park. The dog, irritated that the walk should terminate so quickly, barked its protest.

The old man pointed down the road. "I was about to leave the park when I saw her coming along Regents Park Road."

"And you're sure it was Jessica Warner? It was still dark."

"She was wearing this shining tracksuit of hers. She hadn't seen me yet, and I thought I'd wait a few seconds for her to draw level. I stooped to put Jessica—my dog's called Jessica, too, you see, that's how Mrs. Warner and I got into a conversation on Monday—where was I? I put Jessica on the leash and she got entangled. When I looked up again, the young lady wasn't there any longer."

"You mean, she had vanished?"

"At first I thought she had crossed the street, but then I saw that a car had stopped to pick her up."

"And you saw her get in?"

"Not quite. I only saw her legs being tugged in. Then the door was closed and the car drove away. Good heavens, she hasn't been kidnapped, has she?"

Inspector Terry was in his late forties. His hair was dark blond streaked with gray. Fine lines ran all over his face and across his nose, which was a modicum too large and not exactly straight. His deep-set eyes were dark, wrinkles radiating out from them when he smiled. As they shook hands, Alan felt a slight electricity and noticed a small movement of the inspectors lips, a tightening followed by another, more timid smile.

He liked the low-key, unobtrusive way in which Inspector Terry asked questions, and—although he was reluctant to give away what he considered to be secrets—he caught himself telling him all he knew about Susan's anonymous letter.

"As I told your sergeant," he finished his account, "I don't like to spread rumors. I'm not totally convinced that Jessica really had those affairs with David or Simon."

Terry nodded understandingly. "It's a messy situation for you, isn't it? I hope your secretary can shed some light on Jessica's latest moves. Mr. Warner said Eileen Lanigan was the only person whom Jessica trusted."

"She's her best friend, but she isn't in yet. I was already beginning to fear that she had disappeared, too, because she failed to call me back last night—but she rang me early this morning and said that she was still in Richmond and would come in around nine." Alan saw Terry scribble frantically in his notebook. Had he said anything of importance? "Actually, I'm glad I have a chance to talk to you before you meet her. The news about Jessica will knock the wind out of Eileen and she . . . she's not the kind of person you'd rashly expose to a shock."

"I heard she's handicapped."

"Yes, and I'd like you to know how it happened."

Terry looked at him with unveiled interest. Thus encouraged, Alan went on. "There was a fire, five years ago. When it broke out I was on my way back from a skiing holiday in Aspen with my family, so I didn't see the fire—only the ruin it left of my old studio."

"Where was that?"

"Right here, in the same building. The ground floor and first floor housed the dance studios which we shared with two other dance companies. The office was on the second floor, where I now have my flat."

"You live there with your family?"

"No, I'm divorced."

"Sorry for interrupting. So you arrived at the airport—"

"I was standing at the luggage carousel when my name came through the loudspeakers. 'Mr. Alan Widmark, please come to the information desk.' Gives you the creeps when this happens. The message was that there had been a fire in my studio. An hour later I was here. Everything was covered in soot. It stank. But the sight of the destroyed building didn't really hurt. It was replaceable. Of course, there were memories connected with it, but that's what memories are for."

"To preserve the transitory things," Terry mused.

"The real tragedy was what happened to Eileen. She was in the office that day, going through the routine of preparing the beginning of the lessons after the holidays. Nobody was here to warn her. She noticed the fire when the smell of smoke crept through under the door. She found the corridor in flames. The heat burnt her lungs. She banged the door shut and opened the window to get fresh air. The fire brigade had already been notified by a neighbor."

"The fire station is just around the corner in Euston Road," Terry said.

"It was a question of seconds and help would have arrived, but Eileen panicked when the draught from the window caused the fire to spread over the carpet into her office. She climbed out of the window, lost her grip on the frame and fell."

"Three storeys deep? What did she land on?"

"Her left side."

"I mean the ground."

"Asphalt. The odds were against her surviving it. Her left side was smashed, several vital organs crushed. Later, at home, I was unable to do anything practical like turning up the heating or unpacking suitcases. Pam did it all. She also dealt with the police, wrote to the insurance company and informed a handful of real estate agents that we needed new rooms. We held classes at an interim studio for a year until the renovation of this building was completed."

Alan smoothed out the edges of a sheet the printer had crumpled when he had tried to print out an order form. "Eileen was all bandages when I saw her the next day. She was comatose and remained in that merciful state for several weeks. I happened to be there when she came round. She looked at me with her dark eyes and said, 'I'm falling, Alan, I can't stop falling.' I'll never forget that."

A smile deepened the wrinkles around Terry's eyes. "What you're trying to tell me is that I should handle her with kid gloves, right?"

"Yes, especially since she's so close to Jessica. You see, when it was clear to what degree Eileen was crippled and how little hope there was for her to lead a normal life, Jessica started a private campaign. She would not allow Eileen to give up. She found ways to motivate her during the painful first year of rehabilitation. Jessica was young and energetic and sometimes too enthusiastic in her expectations, but Eileen could take it. I had an elevator and ramps built in for Eileen's wheelchair so that she could work for me again."

"It was good of you not to give her up."

"She's not just an employee but also a friend. The arrangement worked perfectly. Her father drove her to the studio in the mornings, and I took her home as soon as she showed signs of fatigue. The big moment came three years after the fire when she made her first careful steps. Last year she abandoned the wheelchair for good and began to walk on crutches. She no longer lives with her parents but in a boarding-house nearby. On the emotional side, it was Jessica who helped her to achieve all this. I was there for the practical things and Simon for her physical well-being."

"Roger mentioned him. A physiotherapist, isn't he?"

"Exactly. Eileen was moved to the London Clinic a few months after the mishap. Simon works there, he was her personal trainer. After Eileen had been discharged, he went to give her a massage every day after work. That way, he gradually became a part of the troupe."

Alan heard the clang of the front door, then the stomping of Eileen's crutches. "She's coming," he told Terry in a stage whisper. The steps halted outside. There was a prolonged silence. Terry looked at his notebook, frowned and snapped it shut.

"What's she doing?" Alan asked. Finally, Eileen limped in, followed by Simon. In her vermilion, silk dress, she looked nothing like the description of the poor cripple he had given Terry. There was a sensuality about her, a new femininity. Her hair was voluminous, her lips had the fullness and shine that's caused by a passionate kiss. Alan felt guilty for having to destroy this excellent morning for her. Simon, in a dark suit and tie, had the dapper look of a successful businessman. He carried their coats over his right arm. His left hand was caressing Eileen's neck. Alan understood, but couldn't believe it. This time Simon had definitely gone too far.

Inspector Terry stood up, introduced himself and offered Eileen his chair. She sat down, perplexed, like a visitor in her own office, and propped her crutches against the desk.

"I've come to talk to you because Jessica Warner has been reported missing by her husband," Terry informed her. Obviously, he preferred the direct approach—which was probably better than preparing the ground with a phrase like, "I'm afraid I have very bad news." Alan watched Eileen's expression. Blankness made way to a display of emotions that forced her muscles in competing directions. Even her pupils seemed uncertain whether to contract or dilate.

"But . . . ." She looked at Alan for help.

Simon, having hung up the coats, perched himself on the corner of the desk. "But she'd never run away," he finished Eileen's thought. "Jessica wouldn't do that. She knows she's the linchpin of the show."

"When did she disappear?" Eileen asked. Simon put his hands

over hers, which were trembling.

"Yesterday, sometime between one and eight in the morning."

"You must have had a hell of a day," Eileen said to Alan. "What happened after you all went to the pub on Monday?"

"Jessica stayed with us until midnight, then she drove home in a taxi."

"And when she got home," Terry continued, "She had a short controversy with her husband and went to sleep in the guest room. That's why Roger couldn't tell us at what time she left the house. I'd like to talk to you in private because you are Jessica's best friend and know about the problems she has had lately."

"Yes, of course," Eileen said, flustered.

"You can talk in my flat where you won't be disturbed," Alan offered. Eileen reached for her crutches, stood up and for a moment looked as if the only thing supporting her was Simon's reassuring smile. Then Terry opened the door and Eileen followed him.

"I can't believe this is really happening." Simon looked at his watch. "I'd better be going. My first massage is scheduled in half an hour." He hesitated. "What are you doing now, Alan? With the show I mean?"

"Laura and Victor will dance the leads."

"Victor will need a strap for his knee. Did he have problems during the dress rehearsal?"

"He grit his teeth."

"I'll be here in time tonight." He went to get his coat.

"Simon, there's something—"

"Oh, come on, Alan. Eileen's old enough to—"

"That's not what I wanted to talk about. I feel I should warn you that Roger knows about you and Jessica."

Simon turned around. "Oh dear. I thought I could rely on Jessica's discretion. I can't believe she told anyone but Eileen about us."

"It was Susan who gave you away."

"Everything's going helter-skelter into chaos. I'll stay clear of Roger until Jessica is back." Their eyes met. "You don't think Roger did something to her, do you?"

"He's not exactly what I'd call a balanced character."

Simon dumped his coat on the desk. "That's a grisly idea. I never expected a love affair to have such dire consequences."

Alan could no longer hold back his resentment. "You stupid git. Jessica of all women! One might think you haven't got enough intelligence to power a doorbell."

"It's my improvidence, dear, leading me astray sometimes."

"You call it improvidence, I call it depravity."

"If I didn't know you better, I'd say you're giving me a homily." Simon cocked his head and Alan was painfully aware of his good looks and the cedar groves smell of his cologne. To top things, Simon softly placed a hand on Alan's shoulder. He never spilled a drop of macho energy. You couldn't be cross with him.

"I'm sorry. I promise I won't be messing with your girls again."

"What about Eileen?" Alan asked as Simon came around the chair and pressed his thumbs into the sides of his spine. A hot feeling of arousal spread under his skin. Why did Simon have to turn every harmless exchange into a sexual situation? "You'd better stop it."

"Dating Eileen?"

"No, what you're just doing with me."

"Just a massage. You're tense." Simon removed his hands and leant against the desk in front of Alan.

Before he could make a suggestive remark, Alan said, "I don't want to patronize you, but if you're going to hurt Eileen's feelings—"

"Hey, Eileen's got a right to have them hurt like anyone else— but don't worry, Eileen's feelings are safe with me. You know I'm reliable."

"You are, but in unpredictable ways."

Simon patted Alan's shoulder, said he was in a hurry, grabbed his coat and left.

Alone again, Alan gave his mind a break after all the troubles and slipped into a sexual fantasy that started with his being arrested by Inspector Terry.

They went up in the elevator. Miss Lanigan's dark eyes penetrated Terry.

"Is there a special suspicion on the part of the police to make them send a DI?"

The elevator doors parted. Looking out into the short corridor, Terry answered evasively, "It's merely a routine investigation."

The door to the flat wasn't locked. The first thing that caught Terry's eyes as he entered the living room was a huge volière reaching from floor to ceiling, with thick-leafed plants and zigzagging branches on which sat two red-and-green parrots.

"Ginger and Fred," Eileen introduced them. "They had been illegally imported. Alan's uncle, who works in Customs, saved them from dying of thirst."

"They fit in perfectly. This is the most colorful interior design I've ever seen." The settee was scattered with so many orange, red and green scatter cushions that Terry couldn't make out the texture of the upholstery. A bowl of pistachio nuts stood on the couch table. The sweet-sharp smell of oil paint pervaded the flat. He guessed that the vivid paintings on the wall were Alan Widmark's own work.

Eileen sat down and leaned back against the soft cushions. She disappeared like a cherry in a mount of whipped cream. The muscles under her eyes had begun to twitch. He had seen this before, on Michael, during the last days of agony before his merciful death.

"Are you suffering from chronic pain?" he asked.

"Alan told you about the fire, didn't he?" she asked back.

"He wanted to make sure I wouldn't put the thumbscrews on

you."

A smile flashed up and made her look beautiful in an unexpected way. It was her eyes, he decided. Those large, dark eyes under perfectly-formed, full eyebrows.

"Sometimes," she said, "I wish I could make a mirror copy of the right half of my body and replace the left half with it. I used to take lots of painkillers, and they helped less and less and began affect my right kidney. The left one had to be removed after the mishap. When the doctors feared renal failure was imminent and wanted to put me on dialysis, Simon sent me to a homeopath and then to the Pain Relief Clinic at Whittington Hospital. Jessica used to accompany me when I went there. I can't believe she just disappeared."

"Her tracksuit was found in a bin on Primrose Hill, wrapped in a plastic bag. I compared the bag to those in the dressing rooms on the ground floor. It's the same make."

Eileen gasped. "That's scary. Have you met Helen?"

"Sergeant Blockley talked to her yesterday."

"Did she mention Jessica's practice shoes? They were missing on Monday evening—or have they turned up again?"

"She told Blockley about them. No, they haven't been found."

Eileen began to tug so jerkily at her pearl necklace that Terry feared for its stability. "If Jessica took her shoes home, if she herself put her suit in a bag and dumped it in a bin then she might . . . but to what end? Is anything else missing from among her belongings?"

"Nothing, not even her passport, driving license or keys—only the clothes she puts on when she goes jogging. Would you think suicide a possibility?"

"No," she exploded, bending forwards.

"You must know Jessica very well."

"Better than most people know her, including herself." She leant back again, but her body remained tense. He felt slightly unsettled by the way her eyes were riveted on his, as if she were trying to keep them from wandering to her scar. "I was twenty when I began working for Alan," she went on. "Jessica was ten. She was just one of many pupils in the tap class. We didn't get to know each other personally until six years later when Alan asked me to put a note on the info panel that Jessica was looking for a flat-share. I offered her to move in with me. That was a mistake, as I soon found out."

"In what respect?"

"In every respect. Jessica was a nuisance. Egoistic, untidy and not willing to make compromises. I despised her. And that was mutual. No, wait, that's not quite true. Jessica was too concerned about her own precious self to bestow emotions on other people."

This fit perfectly into the picture Roger had given Terry of his wife. A spoiled brat. "Doesn't sound like the beginning of a friendly relationship to me."

"I was already thinking of throwing her out again—but then the fire happened. I spent a long time in hospital and Jessica kept the flat for herself, although she couldn't afford it. I think Alan helped her out. For a long time, she didn't come to see me in hospital. When she came at last, it was to ask how the 'blasted washing machine' worked—her words, not mine. She didn't dare look at me, which made me feel like a leper. I was glad when she left. The only people who helped me at that time were my parents and Alan. Alan was great. He didn't offer the usual cheap comfort, which is the last thing you need when you feel totally wretched. He said I had lost almost everything that makes life worth living, and that I should mourn for it as I would mourn for a dead friend."

"According to Alan, it was Jessica who helped you."

"That was later. One sunny morning in May the nurse put me in a wheelchair and wheeled it to the French window so that I could look at the trees in their full bloom. I wasn't able to move the chair myself. I was a wreck. I wanted to die in peace. I knew Alan was planning to take me back into his office, but it seemed so remote, so unfathomable. On that particular morning, Jessica came to see me for the second time. She was shocked because the doctors were convinced I'd never be able to walk again. She said she couldn't accept the verdict, as she called it, and promised that she'd bring me back on my feet. She kept her promise."

Eileen went on, saying that Jessica had changed considerably. For Jessica, her legs were the most important part of her body and Eileen's fate must have struck her as extremely cruel. From that morning on, she came to see Eileen for two to three hours each day and tried to cheer her up. She insisted that Eileen was moved to the London Clinic, where they had a state-of-the-art physiotherapy division. There she met Simon.

"Jessica and Simon were a nice team of torturers. Eileen do this, Eileen do that. Lift this weight, swim the length of the pool, eat your vitamin supplement, drink the protein broth, wheel your chair, it's only a gentle slope uphill, keep moving." She grinned at Terry. "You can't imagine how strongly this endears people to one another."

Terry could. Helping himself to some pistachios, he absorbed all the intimacy that had evolved in this close circle. Jessica and Simon had become lovers. Then there was the intensity between Simon and Eileen when they had come into Mr. Widmark's office, a palpable physical closeness that had excluded the rest of the world.

"When Jessica married Roger, did it change your relationship to Jessica? Did she have less time for you?"

"On the contrary. That's when we really started to be friends. Before her marriage, Jessica was completely self-contained and didn't need a friend—but that changed with the emotional distress her marriage brought along."

"Roger caused her distress?"

"Plenty. He loves her so, and Jessica can't stand being loved."

Terry was startled. She can't stand being loved. In a single sentence, Eileen had explained why Jessica was so likely to hurt those who cared for her.

"They were fairly happy together," Eileen continued, "as long as Roger didn't expect a display of similar feelings from her. When he no longer saw his fulfillment in adoring Jessica and letting her have her way, things went out of control between them, and very quickly so. How much do you already know about that?"

"Roger told me about their holiday on Tenerife and their quarrel on his birthday."

"Then you're perfectly in the picture. I feel for Roger. He's not the totally altruistic type who thrives in an asymmetrical relationship where all the giving is expected from one partner. When he realized that Jessica didn't in the least enjoy being at the receiving end of his affection, he must have felt used and discarded. It isn't too obscure a demand for a wife to go on a holiday with her spouse. For a normal wife, that is. Jessica, however, is slightly autistic. This is not meant as a diagnosis, it's just the best way to describe how every change in her daily routine unsettles her. The holiday on Tenerife turned into a prolonged crisis, but that didn't give her the right to treat Roger like a doormat."

"You have a critical view of your friend."

"She's someone you love for her strength and despite her shortcomings. Deep inside she's still a little girl, very alone and insecure. And she has those terrible blackouts when she's too wound up. It can be anywhere from minutes to hours until she gets her bearings again."

"Is she able to dress in this state? To walk out into the street?"

"Why? Oh, I see, you think that's how she disappeared. Roger would have noticed, he'd have done something." She frowned. "I forgot, he wasn't there to help her. You said she slept in the guest room."

"What would Jessica have done in the case of having a blackout on Tuesday morning, waking up in the guest room? Would she have called for someone, wandered around looking for Roger?"

"She wouldn't have been able to look for Roger, because during her blackouts she doesn't know whom to look for. She's completely amnesiac—but she would've been looking for someone, anyone, rather than walking out of the house and getting lost."

Terry looked at the three paintings on the opposite wall; a snowstorm, a spinning gyroscope, and five children on a cloud dancing ring-a-ring-o'-roses. He began to feel dizzy.

"Roger's birthday party was a turning point," Eileen said.

"Were you invited?"

"No, smoky air irritates my lungs. On Sunday Jessica told me what had happened. I wonder if Roger mentioned . . ."

"That he hit her? Yes, he told me."

"Jessica said she was so ashamed because she knew she deserved it. I think she's more fond of Roger than she knows. The real trouble that night was David." She rolled the pearls of her necklace between her fingertips. "I'm not sure if I have a right to tell you."

"I know that Jessica had an affair with David—and one with Simon as well."

"How can you know?" she asked sharply. "David wouldn't . . . and Roger wasn't privy to any of this, naturally."

"Alan told me."

"Who could have . . . ?" The penny dropped. "Susan."

"Yes, she went to see Alan yesterday morning."

"And poured out her heart to him as usual."

"I'd like to know more about the Powells."

"If you think it can help you. David joined us two years ago, and he immediately began to chat Jessica up. Not openly, but whenever they were alone. Since he was the choreographer of the show and Jessica the lead, they had a lot of time together. I didn't understand why she started the affair when it meant that there was one more man who loved her too much and who expected things from her she was unable to deliver—passion, devotion and love. It made her life terribly complicated. But once the pattern was set, once she had made a routine of dating David once weekly, she couldn't give up the habit so easily."

"The autistic trait? Well, how long did it last?"

"Nearly a year. She ended the affair last year in April. And Simon—"

"Wait." He was sure that Eileen was withholding an important part of the story. "Why did she end the affair?"

Eileen looked away. For a minute, only the chattering of the parrots filled the room. "It certainly has nothing to do with what's going on at the moment, and she told no one but me."

"I'll keep it to myself."

"You're too curious."

"That's my job."

"Your job is to find Jessica, not to judge her love life."

He was sure she would get up and pace the room like Roger if she could. "I'm not judging, simply collecting facts. The more the better."

"A common criminal could have raped Jessica, or a psychotic killer could . . . I mean, Jessica could be dead for all we know."

"Then it wouldn't make any difference if you told me—"

"Oh, do shut up." Eileen took a deep breath. "Sorry, Inspector."

Terry waited, a tactic that often made people talk, yet didn't work with Eileen. He tried a shot in the blue. "Was she pregnant?"

It earned him a pained smile. "She was, yes. When Jessica was worried because her monthly was a week overdue, I bought a home pregnancy kit for her and helped her to carry out the test. It was positive. She knew that David had to be the father because Roger has had a vasectomy. Jessica didn't want David to know about it for fear he could insist she have the child."

"I suppose she wanted an abortion."

"She said she couldn't have the child, it would be the end of her career—which for her meant the end of everything—not to speak of what this would do to Roger and David. She was honestly afraid Roger could kill David. Or her. Or both. I told her she had to accept the consequences of her doings, and that her career wouldn't be destroyed, just put on hold. It was unrealistic of her to think she could have an abortion with Roger being none the wiser. If she didn't want to raise the child, I would do it for her. Roger and David could do with each other whatever they felt was appropriate."

"That was not the advice she had sought."

Eileen smiled grimly. "No, it wasn't. She said I was an unrealistic idiot, and it was her life that was being destroyed, and that carrying a child was the most dreadful thing she could think of. It would cripple her."

Terry found that a severe lack of tact seemed to be symptomatic for Jessica.

"A few weeks later, Jessica had a miscarriage. Two days of cramps and high temperature and heavy bleedings, then the worst was over. She told Roger that she had an upset stomach."

"And David. What did she tell him?"

"Only that she didn't want to be his lover any longer. David wouldn't give up. He was kind of lurking, waiting for his chance to win her back. It would have unnerved me in Jessica's place. She ignored it, certain that his feelings would calm down. Unfortunately, she was wrong.

At Roger's party, when David saw Roger hit Jessica, he must have thought this was his moment of triumph. He went to console Jessica, he kneeled in front of her and asked her to give him a second chance. He said she was his red rose, his perfect flower, he wouldn't let her go on living with this brutal bastard who maltreated her. A lot of romantic stuff, all wasted on Jessica. She's not susceptible to romance and thought she could give him short shrift, but he wouldn't stop urging her. As a last resort she began to insult him. She said things like, 'I never loved you,' 'You're not the perfect lover you think you are,' 'I never had to feign an orgasm when I was with Simon.' This is how David learned about Jessica's second affair, and Susan, who was listening, heard it too. David was nailed to the carpet, hugging Jessica's legs. Seen from a distance, it's hilarious. Jessica was so upset, she knew no other way out than to burn David in the third degree. She said, 'I didn't want your child and I don't want you.'"

Terry was surprised David hadn't followed Roger's example and slapped her. He tried to imagine what this had done to David. Not only had Jessica rejected his sincere feelings, she had also trampled on their past, their lovemaking and had revealed unmistakably that she had been pregnant.

Eileen continued. "Sometimes you regret something before you do it, but you do it all the same. Jessica had given away her best-kept secret—and not only David knew it now, Susan as well. When Jessica looked up, she saw her standing in the doorway, white as a ghost, trembling. David jumped to his feet and backed out of the room. She shut and locked the door, hoping they would all go away and leave her alone."

"And all that a few days before the première."

Eileen smiled sadly. "Well, David is a perfectionist with a totally professional attitude. I told Jessica so when she feared she had ruined Alan's show."

"And Susan?"

"I don't know how she took it because I haven't seen her since. She was ill."

"Did Jessica talk to you on Monday?"

"It was difficult. There was the film team . . . I had hoped that today . . . God, where is she?"

"I'm surprised she didn't discuss her new problem with you."

"What new problem?"

"Susan wrote a letter to Roger on Sunday. He must have had it on Monday, and thus have learnt about his wife's affairs."

This revelation made Eileen tug so hard at her necklace that the clasp came loose. She stared at the coil of pearls in her lap as if it were responsible for everything.

"Roger's servants told me that Roger had a noisy row with Jessica over breakfast on Monday." Nurit especially had delivered a lot of details—overturned furniture, threats.

Almost inaudibly, Eileen asked, "Do you suspect Roger of having . . . ? You know what I mean."

"All we have is circumstantial evidence consisting of a motive and a perfect occasion."

"I don't want to say that I think Roger incapable of . . . of doing it but . . . how shall I put it? He's an overtly correct individual. If he had killed Jessica he'd immediately have given himself up to the police, and since he hasn't done that, I'm sure he's innocent."

Eileen would make an interesting witness in a cross-examination. "Jessica and Simon, when was that?" Terry asked her.

"It was a short affair, lasting for a few weeks in October last year. They remained friends afterwards. Simon is a ladies' man. He's having affairs all the time. There are never any hard feelings involved when he breaks up with a woman." Terry noticed a change in her voice. It sounded like crystallized honey. "Is that all then?"

"For the moment." Reluctant to leave her, he got up. "Thank you for being so frank."

"I have to thank you, Inspector, for not looking at my scar all the time. It looks nasty, but I was so fed up with surgery I couldn't face another skin-graft operation."

"Actually, I had completely forgotten about it. You have such a beautiful smile."

"Slightly askew, I'm afraid. Goodbye." She stood, leaning on one crutch, and held out her right hand. Her fingers were cold.

On his way out, passing the volière with its rich, leathery foliage, he turned around. Eileen had walked to one of the window bays. She wasn't moving her shoulders, sobbing or trembling; there were only those tears silently streaking down her face. He returned and dabbed her cheek with his handkerchief.

"Was it this window you fell out of?"

"No, the other one, guarded perfectly by the birds now. That's not why I'm crying. I'm so terribly worried about Jessica."

Terry hugged her lightly, his hands softly placed on her back.

With his lips, he touched her hair, which smelled of vanilla. He could feel the heartbeat in her tiny ribcage. It was the closest he had ever come to desiring a woman.

Chapter Ten

Throughout her life, Jessica had always been able to move her feet freely. The horror of this vital part of her body, of her identity even, being forced into a state of inertia was so mortifying that she reacted like a wolf in a trap, fighting, pulling and tearing at the two pairs of handcuffs that tethered her feet to the brass bars of the bedstead—a pointless undertaking. When she gave up with exhaustion, her underwear clung to her skin, cold and sticky with perspiration. Her ankles throbbed with pain where the steel had cut into them. Jessica thought of Eileen. Daggers of pain, that's how she described her agony, daggers of pain all down her left side. Jessica began to weep. It was her fault. She had messed up her own life and everyone else's life. She was a curse, only getting what she deserved.

Just what exactly was it she was getting? Her memory of the past hours—or days? She couldn't tell—was blocked, safely encased in a far-away region of her mind. Her last clear recollection was that of stepping into the winter morning for her jogging routine, a good, healthy feeling, alive, fit, capable of walking wherever she wanted to. How had she ended up in her parents' house?

She passed it every morning, but she never went inside, not since she had quit with David.

Who had tied her to the bed? Vaguely she recalled someone saying that she had to be punished. Why had he taken away her sports shoes and had instead put her practice shoes on her feet? What a ghoulish thing to do, as if to remind her of what her feet were made for.

Jessica wrapped the coverlet firmly around her, lay back on the icy pillows and closed her eyes. She was afraid to plonk out and then awake to a new identity crisis, but she had to find out what had happened, to get calmer, to look for a way to escape from this nightmare. She breathed regularly, but the air was too cold to allow deep relaxing intakes. The chill of the room seeped into her body. She began to tremble uncontrollably when cold and fear mixed. Her stomach was cramped with hunger, her throat dry with thirst. Jessica was beginning to dread that she had been taken to this place to die alone and in misery.

She could take off a shoe and throw it at the window. If the glass broke, someone in the adjacent houses might see it. Not very likely, though. If only the window showed onto the street . . . and with the glass smashed the cold would be dragged in. She could try to scream . . . but she had already screamed at the top of her voice, hadn't she? If no one had heard her then, it was no use trying once more. What if she combined those things, if she broke the window and then screamed as loud as she could? It was worth a try.

He had to wait for an hour before the street was clear. He feared they had come to search the empty house because they were standing in front of its gate, an old man with a dog and two policemen. What were they doing there? Had the old fogey witnessed something? If Jessica called for help, would they hear her? It was unlikely, since the room was on the top floor at the rear of the house. Yet, he should have tested the acoustic situation before. He was anxious to see if Jessica was alright. He had left her alone for more than twenty-four hours. The little gas stove had certainly operated for just a few hours before running out of gas. He had brought six spare bottles of gas on Monday morning. It was high time to reheat the room.

When the policemen had left, he waited five more minutes, then took the bag with the Thermos jug, got out of his car and crossed the street quickly. He made sure no one saw him go up to the front door. Once inside the house, he hurried upstairs.

Jessica sat up as she saw him come in. Her face and fingers were white, her body shaking. "Oh God, it's you," she quivered. "I'm so glad to see you. How did you find me? Please, get me out of here quickly."

It seemed that he had drugged her too strongly and that she hadn't come round completely yet. "I'm not here to free you. Don't you recall it was I who lured you into the house? No? Well, it'll come back. First of all, I'll fix a new bottle to the stove."

Aghast, she stared at him. "You. You?"

"Yes, me—and it was about time, too, that someone took care of your lost little soul."

"What are you talking about?" When he didn't reply, she went on, "Oh no, don't, please, don't do this to me."

Ignoring her pleas, he stooped below the window sill, replaced the gas bottle and ignited the stove. He saw her practice shoes lying on the floor. "Hey, what was that supposed to be good for? Did you hope to be able to slide out of the handcuffs—maybe we should call them footcuffs—when you took off the shoes? I closed the cuffs to the last notch. There's no escape unless you find something to amputate your feet with."

"Please unlock the cuffs."

"No way. I've brought you some hot tea. Don't try to fight with me when I get near you. I haven't got the keys for the handcuffs on me, so you'd only make your situation worse. No one can help you to get out but me, so be a good girl." He opened the Thermos, filled the plastic cap and handed it to her. He had to hold it to her mouth because her hands were trembling. As on Tuesday morning, he had laced the tea with a sedative and sugared it generously to cover the bitter taste of the drug. He refilled the cup twice and the warmth spreading inside Jessica calmed her. Her eyes, however, looked unnaturally large.

"You've had your revenge. I had the most dreadful of morning crises of my whole life."

Slowly, with set movements, he screwed the rubber stopper on the jug and replaced the cap. "Revenge? You're misjudging my motives. Is there anything else you need at the moment? Apart from tea, I mean."

"I have to . . . go to the bathroom."

"If you must pee, there's a pot under the bed. You can use it when I'm gone."

He saw a flicker of humiliation in her eyes. "What have you done with my tracksuit?"

"Red is such an aggressive color, isn't it? You shouldn't wear red, now that the emphasis of power between us has shifted."

"Why did you exchange my sports shoes for my practice shoes?"

"Isn't it a comfort to share your loneliness with them?"

"Stop being cynical. What day is it? How long will you keep me here? And why?"

"It's Wednesday, the day of the première. You're here for your own good. Things will happen, dark and dire things, my rosebud. I want you safely out of the way. Then there's your correction I have to attend to. You're character is wanting in many respects."

"Things will happen? What kind of things? What are you talking about?"

"You know you deserve to be punished, don't you?"

Tears welled up in her eyes. "You said so before. I remember it now. Believe me, you've punished me already. Free me, please.

Don't let me die here."

"If everything goes according to plan, you'll be free on Friday morning. And then you'll have all the time in the world to try and understand why I had to do this."

"If you free me now, I promise I won't report you to the police."

He got up from the bed, took out the chamber pot, removed the lid and placed the pot at Jessica's side. "I have to leave now." He returned the jug to the bag.

"Don't. Don't go."

At the door, he turned and looked into her large eyes. How lovely she was when she was afraid—like a child scared by imaginary ghosts, creeping under her father's duvet. He loved her more than ever.

"I'll be back tomorrow and then I'll stay longer and we can talk." They would talk about death. Three men were going to die, and Jessica would have to take the responsibility. He was sure she'd get over it, egotistical as she was. That's why he had to do something to her as well. It was her own fault that she cared so little for others and therefore needed a more direct punishment. He closed the door and her muffled pleas and cries followed him as he hurried downstairs.

"Jessica, my love," he whispered to himself, "you will die the longest death conceivable, because you will never be able to dance again."

When surfacing from her sleep—valium-deep and dreamless—Susan had decompression problems like a deep-sea diver. Sleep was the better choice, but it couldn't last forever. She clutched the quilt and pressed her eyelids firmly together. She covered her face with David's pillow. It was the second night he hadn't slept in his bed and his smell was gone. He'd never come back, she knew. With both arms, she pressed the softness of the pillow against her nose and mouth to the point of asphyxiation. She let go and sat up, gasping. The survival instinct—what was it good for when there was nothing left worth living for? What would she do all day? The première would take place without her. And tomorrow? Would she be able to hold her classes? She was fed up with it. Her body was tired of it all. Dancing was not her thing. She had only started dance lessons because she wanted to get close to David. Everything she had ever done had been dictated by his wishes and needs. She would have preferred to stay in New York, close to her friends and family. She hated the terraced house they lived in, hated the whole area here, with its uniform architecture. He had kept promising to find something nicer. Now that he had left her, should she return to New York, back to her roots? In hindsight, she began to comprehend that by shaping her personality perfectly into his she had missed out on the chance to develop a life of her own and thus to play an important, noteworthy part in their relationship. Looking up to David had inevitably led to him looking down on her.

How ungrateful of him to break up with her when she hadn't done anything wrong, when she had always been at his beck and call, failing just once to give him what he wanted—failing so fatally. She should have ended her life after her miscarriage. She should have committed suicide as she had yearned to do. The gynecologist had called her crisis a postnatal depression. Even mothers with healthy babies suffered from them, he had said, making her feel reduced, unworthy of genuine sadness. He had advised her to concentrate on the future, the next pregnancy. When years passed without a new conception, the problem was suspected to derive from infertility on David's side, but he had refused to have his sperm counted.

I didn't want your child and I don't want you. When she had heard Jessica speak these words it had meant the death sentence to all her hopes; David was perfectly able to reproduce, Susan unable to conceive. It was so appalling. Not only had he betrayed her—and how could she have been so blind as to fail to notice?—

he had made Jessica pregnant.

Seeing David flee from the room after Jessica had repudiated him, deadly pale, smarting from her remarks, had made Susan want to smash Jessica's doll-like face and scratch out her innocent blue eyes. How dare she discard what was dearest to Susan!

Later that night, when she had returned from Alan's, David admitted his affair but impeded any discussion of Jessica's pregnancy. Susan couldn't imagine that he would have agreed to an abortion, so what exactly had happened? She would never know because she would end it now. Susan switched on the lamp and opened the drawer of her bedside table to take out the little automatic pistol David had bought for her in New York. It was meant for self-defense. It would now defend her perfectly from having to live her tormented life.

But it wasn't that easy. Susan remained sitting on her bed for a long time, the cold metal turning warm in her palm, her naked toes digging into the carpet. A more rational inner voice warned her not to overreact. Life changes, things get better. She would find another man, adopt a child or two and live on happily forever. There were so many possibilities. What a waste it would be to throw away her life in a moment of despair. She had only to think of Eileen. Her situation had been worse—her boyfriend had left her at the saddest moment of her life. What would Eileen have given to have a perfect body like Susan's? She felt guilty for being so miserable on such trivial grounds. She was too beautiful to dedicate herself entirely to one man.

The question was whether she was strong enough to live without David. The answer wasn't yes, but it wasn't enough of a no for such a final decision. Susan slipped out the magazine of the pistol and removed the bullets one by one, letting them clang into the drawer. There was a sound at the door. She halted. A key turned. Quickly, Susan closed the drawer and clicked the half empty magazine back in place. With her index finger not too close to the trigger, she aimed at her temple. She wanted David to see what he had done to her. Maybe the shock would be healing.

"Sue? Are you still in bed?" The door to the bedroom swung open.

She faked sudden agitation at his appearance. David was with her in two quick steps and snatched the weapon. "Have you gone completely mental?"

It was not the reaction she had hoped for. "Without you, it's all so meaningless."

David fixed the safety catch, then put the automatic in his pocket. "I'm sorry it has to end like this." The way he said it made it sound rehearsed and lifeless. If she had pulled the trigger, she would have died in his arms—which would have been more than what she was getting now. Even a perfunctory kiss would have been a solace to her.

"David, I need you as Jessica never did." It hurt to think that David had preferred Jessica to her. Jessica, who was totally opposite—not only in looks but also in character. Susan was meek and servile, Jessica wayward and recalcitrant.

"Don't lower yourself by clamoring for my love. I can't believe you really wanted to top yourself, at least not in this ugly way."

"I wanted to make you feel guilty."

She expected he would say something along the lines of: "What do you gain from making me feel guilty when you're not around any longer to watch my guilt?" What he said instead sent shivers down her spine that didn't stop for many hours.

"You selfish creature. Can you only think of yourself? Our little boy didn't even have a proper burial. I have to carry his grave in my heart."

Eileen was still standing at the window when Alan joined her a few minutes after Inspector Terry had left. She was brooding. Had she told the inspector too much or too little? Had she painted too negative a picture of Jessica, even discredited her? Should she have had a premonition when Helen told her that Jessica's shoes were missing? Could she have prevented Jessica's disappearance by reacting more quickly?

"How do you feel?" Alan asked.

She looked at the handkerchief the inspector had pressed into her hands. "I'm all jangled nerves and jarred spirits."

"Shall I take you home?"

"I can't leave you alone now. Bad enough that I was away all day yesterday. Are we really having a première today? It's so unreal. Shouldn't you call it off?"

"I'd love to, really, but what about the rest of the troupe? They wouldn't sympathize, not when Jessica might have run away of her own accord. Jessica is the lead of the show, but she's not the show itself. The Caesar is the center of her universe, not the other way round."

"Sure. But running the show seems improper when there is the possibility that she's dead. It's macabre, like dancing on her grave."

"Don't talk about graves. Come here and sit down for a moment. There's something I have to ask you."

She sank into the depths of Alan's settee and he came to sit by her side.

"It's about Jessica," Alan started. The question didn't come easily. "Is it true that she's in love with me?"

Eileen jerked her head at the mention. Was there no secret that was safe any longer? Had Jessica felt that it was high time for her to abscond before her carefully built construction of secrets and lies came tumbling down on her? Or was her disappearance the earthquake that had shaken it all loose?

"Is it true?" Alan insisted.

"Yes, but—"

"I wish I had known it sooner. I could have dispelled Jessica's delusions about me."

How naive he was, always thinking in straight lines. "Jessica doesn't have any illusions whatsoever. She knows that your feelings for her will never be anything but fatherly. That's why she didn't want you to know she loved you. Best you can do is blot it out of your memory." She sounded too stern. "Alan," she went on mildly, "you don't have to think too much about it. Jessica has a different way of loving."

"You don't think she has done something silly because of me—that she was in despair . . . ?"

"After loving you for so many years, why should she suddenly take umbrage at not being loved back?"

"It must have been terrible for her. All those years . . . . How could she stand it?"

Eileen saw that she wouldn't get away with her attempt to oversimplify the matter. "I don't think Jessica wants or expects you to return her feelings. On the contrary. It feels safe for her to love you because she knows you're not seeing the woman in her. She has serious problems with men and her feelings or lack of feelings for them."

"It has to do with her mother, right?"

"Yes, once more." It was a subject Eileen and Alan were tired of discussing. "All of Jessica's problems seem to have their origin in her perverted upbringing. Remember how happy we were when Jessica decided not to move to Auckland with her parents? We thought the trauma would heal. I'm convinced I had a chance of getting through to her. On many a morning when she came round from a blackout in our flat in Islington, she would let me deeper inside her own world. But then . . . . After the fire I had other problems, and when Jessica and I began to socialize again our roles had become inverted, and she started mothering me. I tried to bring the topic of her parents up every now and then but she turned a deaf ear on me."

Alan said, "My theory is that she has managed to suppress the memory completely. That's why I considered it my duty to tell Roger some of it. Just enough so that he would understand that he couldn't expect too much from Jessica because she hasn't learnt to see love as a safe-haven. For her, loving means to be on the open sea with a tornado building up on the horizon."

"Except loving you. It's a feeling she has all for herself, a jewel she is hiding deep in a cave on her emotional treasure island. You were never supposed to know about it. How did you find out?"

Alan stared at her absent-mindedly and gave no answer. "There's always an aspect of longing in love, even when you don't seek sexual satisfaction. What is it Jessica wants? What can I do for her when she returns?"

"If she returns," Eileen murmured sadly. When the inspector had talked about suicide, Eileen had suddenly realized that Jessica, for all her forceful manners, had always seemed insubstantial to her.

"Come on, Eileen, do what you're best at doing—handing out advice. There must be something Jessica is missing or she wouldn't be motivated to feel so much for me."

"She'd love to perform and dance with you," Eileen answered feebly. "This is her idea of sublime happiness." It was futile to discuss this when no one knew where Jessica was and if she was still alive.

"I'm no match for her—and I'm too old for it, too. Then there's my stage fright."

That got Eileen's hackles up. "Go on and find some more lame excuses. The fact remains that you're a far better tap dancer than you pretend to be. You're even better than David, as far as I can judge. I don't know why you're always trying to play your talent down."

Alan rubbed the sides of his nose. "You're looking right through me. Did you know that I can dance all the parts of the choreography for the show, even those of the girls, including Jessica's?" He made an effeminate gesture with his hands.

"You'd make a lovely understudy for her. No, seriously, why did you step down the moment David took over the troupe? You're the boss. You don't have to cringe before him and his smugness."

"I didn't want David to think I was trying to vie with him. You know how he is. I can't risk losing him. He's the best choreographer I could find for Jessica."

"Neat, isn't it? Jessica didn't want to leave you because she loves you. You found David for her because she wouldn't leave The Caesar when she had an offer from a professional troupe, and now you don't want to dance with her because you're afraid to poach in David's preserve, which in turn makes Jessica unhappy because she wants you and not him to perform with her. A perfectly neurotic situation. I'm glad I'm not part of this muddle."

"But you are, darling," Alan said in honeyed tones. "Jessica had an affair with Simon. And who's got him now? You, if I'm not completely mistaken."

Eileen couldn't find it funny. "Alan, for God's sake, Simon is not a prize stallion."

Alan coughed to bring his vocal register down again. "I'm sorry. He likes to refer to himself as a challenge trophy, doesn't he?"

"You know the serious side of him as much as I do."

"Another case of someone-else's-trauma we've adopted and are mothering between us," he acknowledged. "Speaking of Simon, how was the conference?"

Although she knew she was adding more trouble to his difficult situation, she told Alan that she would soon leave London for a long time and jeopardize everything she had gained with his, Jessica's and Simon's help. His reaction was fiercer than she had expected.

"Eileen, how can you be so gullible? Don't you see this renowned doctor is using you to advance his research? He won't be risking anything. He'll always win. If he succeeds, he can brag about his achievements; if he fails, he'll have his mistakes to learn from, and you can't even take legal action because you got it all for free. How you could fall for his propaganda is totally beyond my comprehension—or has Simon talked you into making the arrangement? Is that why he slept with you last night?"

Before Eileen had the time to find out that what she was fighting back weren't tears but the raw impulse to hit Alan, he had already reached out and drawn her close to him. "I'm sorry, God, I'm so sorry. Please forgive me. I can't believe I just said that. The trouble with Jessica must have clouded my senses."

She leaned against his shoulder. This was one of the many ingredients of social grease Jessica had to understand—she had to school herself to ask people to forgive her when she had hurt their feelings. Roger, David and Susan had all been hurt by Jessica. Could it be that one of them had killed Jessica, as the inspector suspected?

"The letter. Well." Roger wrung his hands, warmed them at the fireplace, wrung them again. He had just come in from the cold. Edgar had let Terry in and asked him to wait in the living room for Roger's return.

"It was silly of me not to mention it," Roger said, his back to the room. "Throws a bad light on me, doesn't it?" He turned around and went to the sofa but remained standing. "I didn't think—and still don't—that there's a connection between the letter and Jessica's disappearance. And believe me, I haven't done anything else since yesterday than ponder about possible explanations."

"Can you show me the letter?"

"No. Jessica must have kept it. I've searched for it of course, and asked Edgar and Nurit. You can have the envelope, if you think it helps you, but is it that important? You said you knew who wrote it and I can tell you what was written in it. The words are burnt into my brain. 'Jessica had two lovers. One was David Powell, the other Simon Jenkinson.'"

Alan had cited it likewise. "When you read the letter, what

was your first reaction? Did you believe that this accusation was true even before you asked Jessica?"

Roger paced behind the back of the sofa opposite Terry. His fist rhythmically thudded down on the high back. "Yes . . . no . . . maybe. It was quite a blow for me . . . but in the end, I was ready to forgive her."

"When she came home late on Monday you were certainly no longer in that lenient mood."

"I was seething with anger."

They exchanged a prolonged look.

"The question is, was I furious enough to kill Jessica, isn't it?" Roger spoke it out. "And the answer is no. You can search the house and my car for traces of blood, I have no objections."

"If you strangled her, there wouldn't be any blood."

Roger folded his hands as if in prayer. "Jesus Christ. I make the perfect culprit, don't I? I was the last to see Jessica alive, I was jealous, I had hours to dispose of her corpse and to remove all evidence. Have I forgotten anything?"

"Your irascible, fiery temperament."

Roger laughed hollowly. "Why don't you arrest me straight away?"

"I'm not a man of hasty actions. Telling me the truth will do for a start."

Determinedly, Roger lifted his chin. "I haven't killed my wife."

"I thought so," Terry said sedately. "Have you done anything else to her?"

"Like what? Lock her into the cellar for bad conduct? Or throw her out of the house in the middle of the night with nothing on but her tracksuit?"

"Or like hitting her once more, giving her a reason to leg it." He had no time to pursue the topic because Blockley was shown into the room by the manservant. "Morning, sir. Good morning, Mr. Warner. Something new has turned up. We have a witness who saw Jessica yesterday morning. She was getting into a car just a few houses away at the corner of Chalcot Crescent."

"That exonerates me, doesn't it?" Roger burst out.

"It was dark. How could you discern the color of Jessica's suit when she was about a hundred yards away?"

Aldridge, sitting upright in a club chair, kneaded his bony fingers. "Well, Inspector, it could, of course, have been orange or pink as well as red—but I'm pretty certain it was a shade of red. She passed a street lamp the moment I saw her."

They were in Aldridge's overheated living room in his house at Chalcot Square. Blockley, standing at the window, was taking notes. The dog, Jessica's namesake, lay at Aldridge's feet, her chin resting on slim paws. Terry, who had been bending to fondle the soft fur behind her ears, stood up and looked for a place to sit in the crammed room.

"And you're absolutely certain that it was Jessica Warner and not someone else wearing her suit," he said as he folded himself into a rackety chair.

"I would say ninety percent sure. There was something in the way she walked, almost bouncing on the balls of her feet—but I had only seen her once before, so I could be wrong."

"How much time passed before you finished putting your dog on the leash?"

"Half a minute at the most."

"If Jessica had walked on at a steady pace, where would she have been by then?"

"I'd say at the park entrance. I looked down both sides of the road first, and only then did I see her get into the car."

"Did you have the impression that she got in on her own free will, or that she was forced?"

"Inspector, in the latter case I would have called the police straight away."

"I mean, now that you know she has disappeared and see it

under a different light—"

"I really can't tell."

"Can you describe the car?"

"It was black."

"A taxi maybe?"

"Not a taxi, I'm sure. Just a normal car."

Blockley had brought along the station's book of car makes. "Could you pick one?"

Aldridge scratched his head, pouted his lips and leafed the pages back and forth. Finally, he pointed at a Toyota Corolla. "A bit like this one, I'd say. I really wasn't looking at the car but at the pair of legs that was being pulled inside."

"What made you think they were Jessica's legs?"

"Actually, the door of the car shaded the street lamp, so all I saw were those slim legs and white shoes."

"White sports shoes?"

"Yes."

"How about the driver? Male, female?"

"Could have been a chimpanzee for all I saw. I would have paid greater attention had I known what was at stake."

"It's all right to be vague. Many witnesses invent facts to please us, which doesn't help us a bit. You couldn't know at that time that you were the last person to see Jessica. Were there other people on the street?"

"Not many, and no one I knew."

"Can you think of anything else? A detail that didn't strike you as important at that moment?"

Aldridge scraped the backs of his hands in turn. "The car drove away at a normal speed." With a boyish grin, he added, "Kidnappers in movies always beat it with screeching tires, don't they?"

Despite the prevailing winter grayness, Chalcot Square didn't look all too bleak, thanks to the white, blue, yellow and pink fronts of renovated terraced villas which enclosed a garden square with benches and a small playground. Many houses were swathed in scaffolding—even more were uninhabited and had posts planted in their front gardens with signs offering them for sale or rent. Terry and Blockley walked along Chalcot Crescent toward the place where Aldridge had seen Jessica.

"How did you get on with Susan?" Terry asked.

"I didn't have a chance to see her. It was David who answered my ring."

"David? Isn't he supposed to be staying with a friend?"

"Yes, but there he was, blocking my way and not letting me talk to his wife. He said she was still in bed."

"What time were you there?"

"Five past ten. I tried to ask David a few questions but he only said something strange about sorrows coming not in single spies but in armies."

Terry grinned. "He was misquoting *Hamlet*. It's battalions, not armies. Give me a description of him."

"Blond, ear-ringed, virile," Blockley summed up. "I took an instant dislike to him. I'd say he's emotionally unbalanced."

"Which would be understandable considering the circum-stances—the première, Jessica missing, his marriage trouble."

"It wasn't acute, more a sort of persevering petulance that shimmered through like a basic trait of his character."

"Now there's something you have in common with Eileen," Terry said. "She's also analyzing people all the time."

They arrived at the corner of Chalcot Crescent and Regents Park Road, the place where Jessica had last been seen. To their left stood another empty house, three storeys high, white, shield-ed by a wall. Terry scribbled the house number into his notebook.

"Abandoned," Terry remarked as he looked at the dark win-dows. "No one living there that we could ask about seeing Jessica and the car. We'll ring at the houses next to it—but first, let's test the situation. I'll go to the park entrance to see if I'd recognize you over the distance. When you see me looking at my watch, start walking toward me."

"With a bouncing step, sir?"

Terry rolled his eyes skywards and strode to the park. When he reached his destination he squinted down the road. Blockley, in his brown coat, could have been anyone—his pale face under the mop of brown hair was indistinguishable. Terry inclined his head to look at his watch and waited until the second hand had moved halfway around. When he looked up again Blockley was only a few steps away. In the same lapse of time, Jessica could have walked into Chalcot Crescent, say, and thus have disappeared from the old man's view—if it really were Jessica he had seen. They also knew too little about the car to follow this lead.

"It doesn't take us anywhere," Terry concluded. "Especially since Jessica doesn't have the monopoly of wearing red clothes. I'd say we leave it at that. I've got a court hearing to attend this afternoon. We'll meet at The Caesar tonight."

Blockley's eyes lit up. "That's going to be a real treat."

Terry forced himself to smile, then his face relaxed into an expression of genuine mirth. On closer inspection of his motives, he found to his surprise that what cheered him up was the prospect of meeting Eileen again.

Chapter Eleven

Victor, a lanky young man of Russian ancestry, sat on the massage table and moaned. "It must be the stage fright. It makes my muscles tense and the pain increases."

Simon fixed the bandage he had strapped around Victor's knee. "Once you're on stage, the excitement will make you forget everything around you—and the pain inside you as well. If it gets worse, David can always take over."

"Oh, no. Leave me out," David said and tugged at his earring. "Why don't you give him an injection?"

"Because pain is a warning signal and shouldn't be suppressed," Simon replied.

Alan began to say something to David, but Victor assured him that he would be fine. "I faint at the sight of a syringe, you know." He hopped to his feet and flexed his knees.

"I'll be here all evening. You can always come back for a massage between your numbers."

"Thanks, Simon," Victor said and left.

"I think I'm through. You have a troupe of invalids. I've practically run out of ointment."

Alan grinned. "They all long to be touched by your magic hands. I'll send someone round to the pharmacy." He went away as well, leaving Simon and David alone in the narrow treatment room.

"What does Alan think he's doing?" David spouted venomously. "How can he be so cold-blooded as to run the show without Jessica?"

Simon, ill at ease, concentrated on rolling up a bandage.

"It doesn't seem to concern you at all that she's missing," David went on. "You used her like you use every other woman with your easy-come-easy-go attitude. You never loved her, she was just easy meat. As far as you're concerned, you'd just leave her to heaven, and to those thorns that in her bosom lodge to prick and bruise her."

"Prick and *sting*. And what thorns, for God's sake? That I wasn't in love with her doesn't mean I'm not worried. I'm horror-stricken when I think what might have happened to her."

"Simon, have you ever loved? Have you ever wanted to spend the rest of your days with one special person, to take over responsibility, to have children?"

Simon could have told David that, in fact, he had a child, a sixteen-year-old boy, Peter, mentally retarded due to lack of oxygen during birth, who lived with Simon's elder brother and his family. He could have told him that Peter's mother, Geena, had died perinatally, leaving Simon a young widower in dire straits both financially and emotionally; that these circumstances had forced him to give up studying medicine; that he drove to his family in Sevenoaks every second weekend to see Peter. He could have told him all that, and for a moment was tempted to do so. For while everyone else either worshipped or despised David, Simon had a less drastic attitude toward him. It was often misleading to judge someone by his behavior. In David, he sensed undercurrents of high sensitivity, and he was sure there were traumas in David's past, too. Talking openly to him might be the beginning of a friendship. What stopped him was the stark hatred in David's eyes, not so much directed at Simon but at the distress David was going through at the moment. Acknowledging the situation, Simon said, "I was sorry to learn that you and Susan have broken off."

"Well, you're welcome to console her any time," David said pertly and left Simon open-mouthed. Mentioning Susan had probably been a bit lacking in tact. He was happy when Eileen came in, her strictly upright bearing a distinct signal that she didn't want anyone to see how tired she was.

"What a beehive," she said and closed the door behind her. "There's a Sergeant Blockley who tries to flirt with Claudia and upsets her all the more."

"I met him. Nice chap. He said he's electrified by the atmosphere." Simon helped her to sit on the high massage table. He stood in front of her, his hands on her hips. "How was your day, my love?"

"Laden with work. I had to take a nap in between to get through it."

"And your workout?"

"No mercy, eh?"

He moved his hands up along her sides until his thumbs were on her nipples. They hardened to his touch.

"No, not here, Simon. Someone might come in any moment."

"I don't care." He kissed her thoroughly. A softly stretching feeling extended in his chest. "I wonder why it took me so long . . . five years. Three to discover I loved you, one year to accept that I was possessed by a feeling I had avoided at all costs since Geena's death, and a fifth year to find the courage to seduce you."

"I suppose you had to work down your list of intended conquests first."

He smiled and played with her hair. "How was your encounter with the police?"

"You mean Inspector Terry? He's an amicable man. I hope you don't mind that I told him about you and Jessica."

"It's common knowledge by now. It spread like a—"

"A fire? Hey, since when have you been watching your tongue with me?"

"It's because we're so intimate now. It makes me self-conscious and anxious not to hurt you. It was thoughtless of me to start an affair with Jessica. I'm sure you suffered when she told you all the juicy details."

"Jessica's stories only served to enrich my fantasies about you. I'm not the jealous type."

"As of now, you won't even have a reason to be jealous," he said ceremoniously.

Her eyebrows dipped in disbelief. "You mean you won't sleep around any more? Have you considered that I'll be away in the States for several months?"

"After a month or two, I'll fly over to see if they are treating you according to my standards. When the therapy is finished I'll come again, and we'll have a terrific holiday together. How's that? Why are you looking so sad?"

She leant her forehead against his. "Alan said I was taking too great a risk."

"With your new knee, you'll start an entirely new life. Don't let Alan's pessimism get you down. It's my opinion that counts. I'm older than he is and more experienced."

"Experience sometimes only means that someone is very good at repeating the same mistakes over and over again," Eileen said gravely.

"I love your enigmatic oracles, honey, but what the hell has this got to do with your operation?"

"Nothing, of course. I'm trying to be witty as always." She kissed him tenderly. "I'd love to stay in this romantic little chamber with you, but I promised Laura to watch the show. She says she finds my presence encouraging."

"I'll watch a bit, too, from the wings. Maybe I can get a glimpse into the changing room."

Terry arrived a few minutes before the curtain went up and advanced along the aisle.

"Sir?" Terry turned around and saw Blockley, who said, "I was backstage—I thought you'd come there, too."

"The court hearing wouldn't come to an end." Terry followed Blockley to their seats in the second row and was delighted when he discovered that he was sitting next to Eileen. He leant over. "Hello, Mrs. Lanigan."

"Hello, Inspector." She looked happy to see him. "I've still got your hanky. I cried so much this afternoon that it will take days to dry."

He was so charmed by her he wished he had had the time to drive home in order to shave and change. A minute later he also wished he had brought earplugs. The music roared and thundered. Blockley seemed entranced, Eileen highly concentrated. It was an inspired and eccentric production, but not to Terry's liking. He sat through the first half like the victim of an earthquake. Had the show not been interspersed with a more silent number now and then, he would have felt shell-shocked.

During the interval, while Blockley went to pursue his backstage business, Terry remained seated. Once safely outside, he'd certainly not have returned voluntarily. Eileen told him about the fun they had had choosing the costumes in a fetish fashion shop in Soho.

"The owner kept showing us his selection of whips because he thought we were putting up a special party. He asked if Jessica was our dominatrix. David ordered him to shut up—probably because in a sense it was true and Jessica really dominated him. Simon topped it off by saying that we were staging a hard-core version of *The Taming of the Shrew*." She blushed. "Sorry, I got carried away. I don't know what's happening to me. I'm probably overcompensating for my worries about Jessica."

The second half was more tolerable, yet Terry was relieved when the finale was over. He dutifully joined in the thunderous applause.

"Sir," Blockley breathed into his ear.

"Yes?"

"Alan is here. He says he needs our help."

They followed Alan outside, where he turned to them, his face unnaturally white.

"I think he's dead," he said. "I called 999 and asked for an ambulance immediately after I found him—but it might be too late. I couldn't bring myself to feel his pulse."

"Where?" asked Terry.

He led them quickly down the stairs and then to the last room in the corridor, close to a spiral staircase. "In here."

The inanimate body of a man lay slumped across a massage table. The round handle of what might be a tool stood out grotesquely from his back. Terry felt the pulse at the neck artery and looked at the frothy blood at the corner of the victim's mouth. "He's alive."

"It's Jessica's," Alan intoned in a dead voice. "The red handle . . . . It's her screwdriver. Someone stabbed Simon with Jessica's screwdriver."

"You called the ambulance, you said."

Alan clicked his heels impatiently. "They must be here any minute. I told them to come to the stage door—it's the quickest access—but I didn't ask for the police, because you are the police." He was losing his coherence.

"How long is the tool?"

"About six inches long. And it's cross-headed," he added, his eyes unfocusing at a frightening rate. The sirens of the ambulance were finally heard.

"Make sure no one comes down here," Terry told Blockley. He went to open the stage door at the other end of the corridor. A young doctor carrying a respirator and an oxygen bottle, along with two medical orderlies pushing a stretcher trolley, followed Terry to Simon's room.

"I'm Detective Inspector Terry of Camden CID. I happened to be in the audience. How are his chances?"

The doctor examined the angle of the handle. "Depends on how long the weapon is."

"It's a cross-headed screwdriver, about six inches long."

"That's bad," the doctor said. "Means lungs and heart. It can't have happened longer than a minute or two before he was found or he'd be zipped into a rubber sheet now." He turned to the ambulance men. "His upper body must be kept absolutely motionless." They heaved Simon face-down onto the stretcher. The respirator was fixed and the oxygen bottle opened. Terry let out the breath he had been holding for what seemed a lifetime. He went with them as they raced the stretcher down the corridor. "Where are you taking him?"

"Middlesex Hospital."

"Please try to remove the screwdriver without leaving or destroying any fingerprints."

He watched as they folded down the wheels of the stretcher and pushed it into the ambulance. Terry shut the stage door, closing out the cold and the revolving lights of the ambulance. The sirens started wailing again.

Within twenty minutes, Terry had everything and everybody where he wanted them. The audience had been cleared, with four uniformed policemen taking down the addresses of three hundred people. The cast and crew were now sitting on the upholstered chairs of the auditorium, drinking coffee from Styrofoam cups and complaining that they hadn't been permitted to go to their dressing rooms. He had made a brief statement to the reporters, called on scene by a journalist who had come to review the première. In the basement, the crime-scene crew was dusting every horizontal and vertical surface for fingerprints. Blockley and three constables helped control the situation.

Terry was occupying Eileen's office. On the desk in front of him lay a ground plan of The Caesar, on which he had marked the scene of crime and the three ways of access: through the stage entrance, down the spiral stairs from the stage level or via the lobby down the main stairwell. He had spent the past ten minutes placing calls. When he hadn't been able to trace Mr. Warner, he had sent out a constable from the police station to search for him—at his home address as well as his office.

"Well then, let's get started with the interrogation. Blockley, I'll entrust you with the crew. Every tiny observation might be helpful. Ask if they saw anyone hang around backstage who had no business being there." Terry took a sip of his steaming coffee. This was going to be a long night.

Alan was brought in first. He looked sufficiently recovered to make a useful statement, but Terry knew that a part of him would never get over it. This was what violence did to people, tearing a wound into the matrix of the soul. Every crime was a variation of the rape theme.

"Any news of Simon?" Alan asked.

"They're operating on him now."

"Why you didn't want me to tell the others what happened? Do you think it was one of us?"

"Let's stick to the few facts we have. What exactly happened? Try to remember every detail."

Alan turned his eyes upwards. "The last time I saw Simon was when we were backstage, about quarter of an hour before the end of the show. Victor needed an injection before he had to dance his solo, and they went down together. I remember it vividly because Victor is a chicken when it comes to having a jab. Ten minutes or so later, I went to fetch Simon for the curtain calls, and that's when I found him. You heard what the doctor said—if I had gone down a minute or two earlier I could have prevented it."

"Who else was in the basement?"

"Nobody. They were all on stage for the finale."

"And shortly before?"

"The dancers change in a room behind the stage so they don't have to take the stairs all the time."

"How about the others, the crew?"

"They're all needed backstage."

"Did you see anyone else go down?"

"No, I was watching the show. The stairs are around the corner behind the toilets. I've thought about it very hard but I haven't come up with anything. You don't really see a lot because it's dark behind the stage."

"You went straight into Simon's room, didn't you?"

Alan nodded. "It all happened so quickly. I saw him lying there, ran to the office to call the ambulance and then went to get you."

"And you neither saw nor heard anyone around?"

"No, I didn't. God, just a minute too late." Alan frowned. It finally dawned on him what this implicated. "You mean, the attacker was still somewhere around? Hiding?"

"It's very likely," Terry confirmed.

"And when I was gone he used the chance to flee. Oh, damn it all!" Alan gritted his teeth. "Sorry. But what else could I have done? Gone on a wild-goose hunt in the basement?"

"No, of course not. It could've been dangerous for you. Where is Jessica's screwdriver normally kept?"

"In her dressing room, either on the table or in a drawer. We have lots of screwdrivers around. We need them to secure the plates of the shoes."

Terry uncapped his pen. "Let's have a look at motives. Simon was very popular. Who could be so filled with hatred that he wanted to kill him?"

Alan made a helpless gesture. "Why, Roger of course. He could have used Jessica's key for the stage door. Nobody would have seen him coming."

Terry started scrawling irregular patterns on a sheet of paper. "And he used Jessica's screwdriver to stab her lover."

"How about David? Shouldn't he be warned?"

Terry wrote "David" and encircled the name with tear-drops. "David has a motive, too. He was still in love with Jessica when she had it off with Simon." Terry drew a heart and an arrow right through it. It struck him how aggressive this symbol for love looked.

"If you want to find someone who was jealous, you should have a closer look at Luigi, Laura's friend. He's a very passionate Italian."

Terry frowned. "Wait a minute, you've lost me. Laura is . . .?"

" . . . Jessica's understudy."

"And what's going on between Laura and Simon?"

"I think they had a one-night stand."

"I'll ask Laura about it. That would give Luigi a motive to attack Simon." Terry screwed up the piece of paper and aimed at the wastepaper basket next to the computer desk. It bounced off the edge. "I can't see how he could be connected with Jessica's disappearance."

"With Jessica out of the way, Laura had a chance to dance the lead," Alan suggested, but then changed his mind. "I shouldn't say this. Suspecting anyone of this horrible crime is a crime in itself. It's just that I don't like Luigi. He's a lady-killer."

"As is Simon." A ladies' man Eileen had called him.

"Yeah, but it's not the same. Simon would never ask a woman to marry him because he knows he can't be faithful. Luigi proposed to Laura—and he did it in front of all of us at our Christmas party, the slimy bastard. Laura was so stunned she didn't know what to say. You can't compare Luigi to Simon."

With nothing left to draw, crumple up or aim, Terry leant back and tried to relax. He felt he wasn't on the right track. When had he taken the wrong turn? "How do the others get along with

Luigi?"

"Hard to say. He isn't around that much. The girls either adore or loathe him. David treats him like a fly on the wall. Once, when Luigi criticized David's behavior toward Laura—and he had a point there, you know—David started calling him names and cursing at him in mock Italian. It was in Luigi's restaurant, a posh affair serving excellent pasta. Simon and I often eat there. Actually, Simon is one of the few who knows how to take Luigi. No, it can't have been him. And I can't think of anyone else."

"Thank you. I will talk to Eileen next so that she isn't kept waiting for too long."

Alan covered his face with his hands. "I don't know what it's going to do to her. Let me stay when you talk to her. She'll need someone to hold her when she hears about Simon."

Terry understood this. Her closest friends had both been torn away from her in just two days.

"Eileen, I'm so sorry," Alan began when Eileen joined them, and Terry hurried to interrupt him.

"Please, sit down, Mrs. Lanigan."

"It's Simon, isn't it?" she said. "He's the only one missing. What has happened?"

Terry recited the facts for her. "Since you were sitting next to me all the time you know as little as I do about what happened. All I can ask you is if you know who might have a motive."

"Roger. David. Plus dozens of others," she said with a voice like a robot. "A whole line-up of jilted girls and their betrayed boyfriends and husbands."

"Simon must be a hell of a lover," Terry remarked thoughtlessly. When he saw Eileen's appalled expression, he understood. She had a crush on Simon.

All of a sudden, Eileen began to wheeze asthmatically. Cramps ran through her body.

Terry picked up the phone. "I'll get a doctor."

"That's not necessary." Alan was amazingly calm. "She's having one of her fits. It's like epilepsy. All you can do is wait."

Terry went over to Eileen.

"No. Don't touch her," Alan warned. "It would prolong the convulsions."

Helplessly, Terry waited. "How long will it last?"

"Two to three minutes. I'm not heartless, but I've seen it many times before. If I could have it in her place, I'd gladly—"

At that moment, Eileen sat up again. Her eyelids were pressed down, her mouth was squeezed into a tight line. Her breath whistled through her nostrils.

"I'll take her upstairs with me," Alan said and put an arm around her. "She shouldn't be alone tonight. Please keep me informed about Simon, Inspector."

Terry, who had been kneeling by Eileen's side, got up and nodded. When Eileen opened her eyes, Terry saw the tortured look in them. Suddenly, she took one of her crutches and threw it forcefully at the wall. "Damn," she whimpered. "Damndamndamn!"

David Powell came striding in, reproachfully spreading out his fingers. "Why were our fingerprints taken? What's all this about? Policemen all over the place, not letting us go to our dressing rooms and not even bothering to give an explanation. This is outrageous. You have no right to treat us like criminals."

Terry folded his arms in front of his chest. "Mr. Jenkinson has been stabbed," he said shortly.

David sank into the chair. "Oh. I didn't know that." He combed his blond hair back with an abrupt movement of his right hand.

"When did you last see him?" Terry asked.

"Sometime during the second half." A light shrug, a vague gesture with the hands—David was all body language.

Terry unfolded his arms and, unconsciously, mirrored David's hair smoothing routine. He had a hunch that David was overdoing his part to cover up his discomfiture. "Did you go downstairs during the second half?"

"No, why should I?" Goodness, you're dense, his screwed up face said.

"Did you see anyone else go down?"

"No, I didn't. Look, are you insinuating that you suspect one of us?"

Terry decided to let it pass as rhetorical. "What were you doing during Victor's solo?"

David frowned. "I think I was speaking to Laura and giving her a few instructions."

"And during the finale?"

"I had to go to the toilet. Afterward I met Helen, who was coming out of the changing room."

"Was anyone missing?"

"I don't count my dancers," David said with an inappropriate laugh.

"What a pity," Terry said wryly. "Tell me something about Mr. Jenkinson."

David ran his thumb across his forehead. "Simon was the kind of person you couldn't help liking, although he's said to be a sex maniac. Women found him absolutely irresistible. You can draw your own conclusions." The latter was said in a tone that was only a modicum short of insolence.

"Drawing conclusions is one of the jobs I'm paid for." Terry placed his hands on the desk and studied the structure of their bones. "You're speaking about Mr. Jenkinson as if he were already dead."

"You said he's been stabbed."

"I didn't say he's been stabbed to death, did I?"

"Oh, that was a misunderstanding then." David clearly disliked being on the defensive. He shifted in his chair.

"Does your wife find Mr. Jenkinson charming, too?"

"My good man, you're asking strange questions. Yes, Susan likes Simon. We all do. Susan would never betray me, if that's the innuendo intended."

"Would you?"

"Pardon?"

"Betray her." Terry's reactions came like rapid gunfire now.

"That's none of your business."

"You had an affair with Jessica."

"Who says so?"

"Did you?" Terry persisted.

"What's the connection with the attack on Simon?"

"He also had an affair with Jessica."

"Yes, but that was after—" David blushed with anger. He had stepped right into the trap. "Come on, you're not trying to say that I took advantage of Jessica's absence to assault the lover she had after me."

"Jealousy is a widespread motive for crimes, you know."

"In this case, dozens of jealous men must be queuing to have a go at Simon. Unnatural deeds do breed unnatural crimes."

"Unnatural troubles," Terry corrected automatically. "It's a marvel Simon survived so long."

The sarcasm was lost on David. "You have a distorted view of the world, Mr. Terry. I attribute that to your job. Believe me, you are not surrounded by villains. We are just a hard-working dance company, trying to make the best of our talents to entertain an audience. Simon was . . . is the lubricant in the machinery, and none of us would cut into his own flesh and attack this guileless man. Even you should have sufficient brainpower to . . . . I'm sorry. I've had a long and stressful day." He sounded lachrymose now. "I apologize for being rude. Can't you see how absurd it is to suspect—"

"I got the gist of it, Mr. Powell. I never said I suspected anyone in the troupe. I'm just collecting information."

To this, David said nothing and Terry had time to assess him. He found him handsome with his accurately cut hair, the two golden earrings in one lobe, the sensual mouth. He was good-looking in an intimidating way. It was not so much his arrogance that created this impression but the underlying complacency, this unbecoming I'm-the-center-of-the-universe attitude. He had certainly been his parents' pride and joy. A devoted wife and a meteoric career hadn't helped to put his self-image straight. When Jessica destroyed his illusions, had it unbalanced him enough for him to seek for an act of retaliation?

"Tell me about Sunday night."

"Roger's birthday? A completely normal, boring dinner party."

"With a not so boring episode involving a renewed declaration of love on your part."

David crossed his arms and looked away.

"You had a blazing row. Jessica sent you packing, didn't she? It must have hurt, considering that she had already finished with you last spring."

David's head jerked back. "I suppose Eileen told you about it, and what she said was certainly an exaggeration of what she had been told by Jessica, who was very emotional about the whole business because of the slap Roger gave her—so her story was not exactly objective either."

"You tried to win her back, didn't you?"

"It's not unusual to feel protective about a woman you love."

"You must have been mortified when she told you about her pregnancy."

David's face froze.

"You were so shocked you drove away and left your wife behind."

"I was shocked because of her," David explained. "Susan had overheard Jessica and me. Until then she had had no idea about our affair."

DC Rowlands came in and handed Terry a note. He gave it a quick read. Roger had been located. Terry looked at David. "Sergeant Blockley tried to talk to your wife this morning. Do you know that she wrote Roger a letter?"

"The news has made the round."

"What will she think when she learns about Simon? That Roger tried to kill Simon and that she's responsible? That she has endangered your life, too?"

"I'm not scared of Roger—and he wasn't here tonight, as far as I know."

"No, he was in his office in Bloomsbury, just a short drive away."

"Then you should offer me an escort."

"Where will you be tonight, Mr. Powell?"

"At my friend's house, Norman Patmore. The address is—"

"We've got the address. Were you there on Tuesday morning?"

David put his palms on the desk as if he wanted to get up. "Is this relevant with regard to the crime that took place tonight?"

"It's relevant with regard to Jessica's disappearance."

"I see, you're solving two cases in one go. Brilliant. To save you further questions, I'll give you a complete account of my doings. On Monday evening I saw Jessica for the last time. We had been filming the video. Afterwards I went home instead of going to a pub with the others because Susan was ill and had a temperature. It turned out that she had been in a ferment all day. She attacked me with questions and a quarrel ensued. I decided to move out. Norman, a friend of mine, is staying in Canada at the moment. His flat is not far from our house and I water the plants and collect the post. It's ideal as a temporary accommodation. On Tuesday morning I had to go shopping because the fridge was empty. In the afternoon, I was here for the dress rehearsal. In the evening, I watched TV. This morning I went over to our flat to fetch some more of my things. I found Susan sitting on the bed with the curtains drawn and the bedside lamp on, as if she didn't know how to start the day. That's when your sergeant came. I couldn't let him talk to my wife. She's addicted to sedatives and shouldn't be put under too much strain." His monologue finished, David removed his hands from the desk.

"Do you have a car?" Terry wanted to know.

David's eyelids flickered. "A car? Yes, sure."

"What make and color?"

"A dark blue BMW convertible."

"And your friend, Mr. Patmore?"

"Now, let me think. A silver metallic Ford. Why?"

"Jessica was seen getting into a car on Tuesday morning at the corner of Regents Park Road and Chalcot Crescent." He watched David's reaction. First, the color completely drained from his face, the next second it returned a burning red.

David ran his tongue along his upper lip. "A car, you say? Now that's—em—unexpected. Do you think I drove away with her? In that case, I wouldn't be here, would I?"

"Depends on where you drove with Jessica and what you did to her."

"I drove nowhere with Jessica." He got up brusquely. "And why should I want to do anything to her?"

"She's special for you—was special until she showed you what you must have seen as her true face. Suddenly the rose was all thorns. You called her your red rose, didn't you?"

"So? That which we call a rose, by any other name would smell as sweet. Did I get the quote right this time?" He motioned to the door.

"Dismissed," Terry said to the back of his head. David had cited from *Romeo and Juliet*, which made Terry think of another pair of lovers, Petruchio and Katharina—the parts David and Jessica should have danced tonight. Jessica was a shrew, there could be no doubt. Had David felt the need to tame her? Petruchio takes away Katharina's dress, he deprives her of food, he . . . . Terry shot up from his chair. The jogging suit in the bin, taken from Jessica, mocking the police. David had this mocking streak in everything he said. David also had access to Jessica's practice shoes and the plastic bags. His car was dark blue, a color that could be mistaken for black.

And what had Eileen said? Something about a hardcore version of *The Taming of the Shrew*. That could be exactly what David might be up to—a real-life rendering of the basic plot idea that a woman's duty is to obey and serve a man. If Terry's gut feeling were right, it meant that there was a fair chance Jessica was still alive, held prisoner by David.

"Rowlands," he called into the corridor. "Follow Mr. Powell. I'll organize some backup. I want him under surveillance."

Laura's porcelain paleness was enhanced by the harsh neon light in the office. She tugged at her skimpy dress, sat down and waited, nervously playing with her ginger curls.

"Mrs. McFerrar, I'm sorry I've kept you waiting for so long. I have a few questions."

"What has happened?" she asked shyly.

"Simon Jenkinson has been stabbed."

"God. Simon. Stabbed," she exclaimed. "Oh, no, no! Who—I mean, is he dead?"

"He's alive, but he has been seriously injured. We don't know by whom. When did you last see him?"

Her lips trembled. "During the interval."

"Where were you when Victor was dancing his solo?"

Laura tugged at her hair as if to activate a memory module in her head. "I had gone to the ladies'. When I came out, I ran into David and he began to lecture me on my performance. Why should anyone stab Simon? That's so shocking and unreal. I've always been scared of knives."

"He was stabbed with a screwdriver."

Her eyes widened. "That's perverse, that is. Cripes, only a psychopath would be capable of such a deed."

"You spent a night with Simon, didn't you?"

Taken unawares, she shrank back. "How'd you know? Oh, please, don't tell anyone. Especially not Luigi. He's my fiancé, you know—asked me to marry him and I kind of said yes. He went to Rome for a few days and I thought I had to, well, sort of find out how I felt about it all, and so, when Simon . . . Oh, my God." Laura yanked her curls again. "Promise you're not going to tell Luigi about it."

Terry nodded solemnly. "Can you help us with the investigation? Did Simon mention anything during the time you spent together that could throw a light on this crime?" He hoped this complex question wouldn't result in Laura scalping herself.

Laura blushed. "We weren't talking much, I'm afraid."

At that moment, Luigi came rushing in, flinging his hands through the air as if he wanted to cut it up in slices. "*Dio mio! Che succede?*" he sang rather than spoke in a beautiful tenor voice. "What's all this about? *Cara Laura* is tired, I want to take her home. Why do you keep us waiting?"

Terry grinned. He liked the Mediterranean temperament. It was such a refreshing contrast to the mild-manneredness of his compatriots.

"And wasn't Laura great?" Luigi added with melting eyes. "*Meraviglioso, affascinante!* I am so glad she had a chance to show her true talent."

"Luigi, please." Laura looked at Terry for help.

"You can go to your dressing room, Mrs. McFerrar."

"Can I accompany her?" Luigi asked.

"No, Mr. Manizotti. I'd like to ask you a few questions."

Hesitantly, Laura left.

"There has been an attack on Simon Jenkinson."

"*Madonna! Che sfortuna!* Did you tell Laura? Were you careful not to shock her too much? *La mia bella Laura,* she'll cry her eyes out. She is so fond of him. *Mi dica,* what happened? What bastard did this awful thing to *caro* Simon?"

Luigi spoke English with such fluency that Terry wondered why he had this mannerism of throwing in Italian phrases. Was it just his natural urge to express overflowing emotions in his more passionate vernacular tongue? Or was he showing off, peppering his language with bits of Italian in order to impress or charm his environment? This man was difficult to assess—too much fidgeting and articulating on the surface to know what was going on in the depths of his character. Slimy, Alan had called him.

"He was stabbed in the back," Terry explained.

Luigi was dumbfounded for a change.

"Did you leave the audience during the second half?"

"Me? Leave? *Ispettore*! I wouldn't have wanted to miss a second of Laura's performance. I have come for no other reason, come all the way from *Roma*, you know."

"You live in London?"

"Yes, I do. *Ho un ristorante*." Luigi produced a card and gave it Terry. "I went to Rome on Sunday because *zio Alfredo*, my dear uncle, died after a heart attack and I wanted to attend his funeral. I had planned to stay for a week to console *mia mamma*, but she seemed to cope with her brother's death fairly well, so I spent hours on the phone to catch a flight back to London in time to see Laura dance. Leave the audience, *ridicolo*!"

"I see. So you couldn't make any observations in the lobby or backstage."

"*No, purtroppo*. I'm devastated. Simon and I were soulmates. GMTA. Great Minds Think Alike. Women, you know." Luigi winked. "He's the only British *seduttore* I've ever met."

Terry couldn't ask flat out whether he knew that the *seduttore* had been successful in seducing Laura. "Did Simon tell you about his conquests?" he asked instead.

"*Ma naturalmente no*. Discretion is the most important ingredient in the true art of seduction. Discretion can be a lifesaver—oh, *dio mio, ispettore*, do you think Simon is the victim of a crime of passion?"

"Mr. Manizotti, you and Simon poached on the same hunting ground. Did you not feel tempted to compare your success?"

"*No, no, no, è troppo pericoloso*. It could turn out that we had affairs with the same women. Seduction is not a sport, it's an art form. We're not reducing women to objects of lust. A real seducer cherishes and worships women. Comparing our success! This is not funny. You Brits don't know much about women, do you?"

Terry laughed. "*Grazie*, Mr. Manizotti."

"*Buona notte, ispettore.* And good luck."

Luigi Manizotti was either a brilliant actor and perfect liar, or else he was exactly what he seemed to be: a smarmy but harmless gigolo. Terry looked at the card Luigi had given him. *Il Pipistrello*. Cute name for a restaurant, whatever it was supposed to mean. He turned off the neon lights and enjoyed a few minutes in darkness. A crime of passion or a premeditated attack? Laura had mentioned knives. People normally use knives when they stab someone. If you intend to kill another person, you bring along a weapon. This had not been the case here. Maybe the attacker had only wanted to talk to Simon. Then an argument had developed. The screwdriver had been two rooms away, on Jessica's table or in the drawer—ideal for a crime committed in the heat of the moment; or for someone who had planned the attack and knew the tool would be there. Had it been Jessica herself who was hiding somewhere and had come to attack Simon with her own screwdriver? Or was it another attempt of David to mock them?

Blockley came in. "Bad news. Rowlands watched Mr. Powell's BMW, which is parked in the backyard. When Powell didn't turn up, Rowlands searched the theatre and studios because he thought he was still around—but he wasn't. It looks as if we have lost track of him."

Terry was too tired to swear. He called the station and asked for someone to watch David's house, and that of Norman Patmore. "Let's hope he'll turn up there," he said to Blockley. "Anything else?"

"I've finished with the crew. I drew a blank. Not even Mrs. Blythe-Warren could help. She's everywhere and notices everything, but she was in the wings during the critical time."

"The attacker chose his moment well."

Blockley laid out several small, sealed, plastic bags in front of Terry. "These are the contents of Mr. Jenkinson's coat pockets: a bunch of keys, a handkerchief, a wallet with thirty pounds, his driving license, a credit card and a packet of Durex."

"Thank you, Blockley. Carry on with the male dancers, please. Make them talk about Simon's affairs—and about Jessica and David. I'll deal with the girls."

"If you don't mind, sir, I'd like to do the interview with Claudia Heller."

"Who?"

"The one who danced in the white dress."

"Why have I been brought here without explanation?" Roger accepted the offered chair. "Has Jessica been found?"

"No, I'm afraid not. Something else has happened. An attempted homicide during the performance."

"And again you're suspecting me? Who is the victim then? David or Simon?"

"Simon."

Roger began to sweat. "Well, really? Oh dear. You said 'attempted homicide.' Can't Simon say who attacked him?"

"Not at the moment. Where have you been this evening?"

"In my office. I had to catch up with the workload of the past days. I was in my office tonight from around seven until your men turned up. I thought of course that it was because of Jessica—they wouldn't tell me. I'm in rather a quagmire, right? Circumstances couldn't be more adverse." Ponderously, he got up and paced the room. Terry had never seen him sitting for more than five minutes in a row.

"Is there someone who can corroborate your being in your office?"

"I was alone."

"Did you place any calls?"

"Seven or eight, I'd say. I can write you a list of the people I called."

"Good. Do you have Jessica's keys on you?"

"No, of course not. I see. You think I used them to get in through the stage door. Now that would definitely have been a silly thing to do. Had I come here to have a go at Simon, I would have risked being seen. In addition to that, I wouldn't even have known where to look for him. Maybe somewhere backstage, but there are always lots of people around—it's not the best of places for an attack."

"How about the treatment room?"

"Which room?"

Terry remembered a slight smell of fresh paint that had hung in the air. "It must be new. You don't come here very often, do you?"

"Jessica doesn't want me around. How was Simon attacked?"

"He was stabbed with your wife's screwdriver."

Roger's jaw dropped open. "Do you think there's a connection? That whoever tried to kill Simon is the same person who's responsible for Jessica's disappearance?" He plopped down into the chair. "This means Jessica could have been murdered." Roger kneaded the arms of the chair. "Sometimes people go missing and never turn up again. If that happened, it would drive me mad. It would be better to find Jessica dead than not to find her at all. Isn't it wicked to think along such lines? If this goes on for much longer, I'll lose my mind. I really do hope Simon will soon be able to tell us who stabbed him."

"If he survives."

"That bad? Poor bloke. Poor Eileen, too. First Jessica, now Simon. It's as if someone's trying to deprive her of friends. What about me? Am I under arrest?"

"No, sir. You can go home. We'll keep an eye on you."

Terry watched Roger leave with the heavy steps of a broken

man.

It was the worst picture he had ever painted. From a technical viewpoint it was brilliant, but just looking at it frightened you to death. It showed the perspective of a person falling into an endless tunnel of flames and staring grimaces. Alan put it back into the cupboard where it had been safely out of sight since he had painted it five years ago. He went into the kitchen, took the strainer from the cup and absent-mindedly stirred some sugar into his tea. The Caesar was on fire all over again. Even from an objective and remote perspective the whole matter reeked of sabotage. The lead dancer was missing, the physiotherapist had been stabbed, the secretary was in despair, the choreographer no longer doing his job and someone else—one of the troupe evidently—was dangerously mad. A murderer in their midst, the core of the fire.

Eileen, thank God, was asleep now. Alan went to sit by her side and put the cup on the bedside table. A streak of light fell in from the corridor. She looked poignantly fragile among Cindy's plush animals. To think that she and Simon were lovers . . . . If Simon died, would Eileen get over the loss or would she be falling forever, just as he had painted her?

He heard someone at the front door. "Mr. Widmark?"

Alan beckoned the inspector into the room. He was carrying Eileen's crutches.

"I didn't want to ring or knock for fear of waking Eileen." Terry looked down at her. "She's beautiful, isn't she?"

Like Jessica, Eileen had always been a sexually neutral being for him and Alan was at a loss what to say. He led Terry into the living room. "Any news?"

"Good news. Simon survived the operation. His life functions are stable. There's a fair chance he'll recover fully."

Alan's legs and arms felt disjointed with relief. "Oh, sweet Jesus. Did the interviews bring anything up?"

"Just a vague idea that David might be involved. Do you expect him to come in tomorrow?"

"No. The next performance would have been on Friday. I cancelled it. Why? Is he really a suspect? Well, that's—"

"Call me when you hear from him—and thank you for reacting so quickly and keeping a clear head. It made the investigation easier and it saved Simon's life."

"It's kind of you to say that. Nevertheless, I'll always feel that I was a minute too late. What surprises me is that you aren't suspecting me. The first on scene . . ."

"And you have a motive, too. Someone told me Simon was after your ex-wife." Terry got up and smiled. "But I simply know you wouldn't have done this to Eileen."

Alan saw the inspector to the door. "I wish we had met under different circumstances."

From the way Terry returned his look, Alan knew he had understood.

Chapter Twelve

Eileen switched on the bedside lamp and found herself staring with bleary eyes at a plush elephant. What time was it? There was no clock in Cindy's room. Eileen looked at the shadows on the wall, the silhouettes of toy cars and dolls. There was a numbness inside her, a thick, protective wadding around her psyche which muffled the voice in her head that kept asking: Is Simon still alive? If he were dead . . . . As long as she didn't know, it wouldn't be true, he'd still be alive for her. No, that was wrong, he'd always be alive for her. She would never let go of him.

She was scared now and switched off the light. Maybe she could sink back to sleep if she allowed her mind to wander. She remembered going for a walk with Simon in Sevenoaks—just a short walk of course. It had been such a beautiful autumn night. Looking up into the cloudless sky, she had sensed how her gaze went all the way through the atmosphere into outer space, reaching the milky way and the galaxies beyond. There was life out there somewhere. As a child, she used to imagine what the life forms of other planets might look like and how they experienced their lives. Were emotions universal? Simon put his arm around her and said he wished they were standing on top of Mount

Everest; the stars must seem within easy reach to a probing mind, and you were surrounded by perfect silence. She was tempted to kiss him, but he was having his affair with Jessica at that time. Eileen knew she could have prevented it, simply by telling Jessica that she was in love with Simon. Jessica would not have let him seduce her had she known. On the contrary, being always enthusiastic when seeing a chance to do something for Eileen, she would have taken it as an incentive to play matchmaker, and that was an embarrassment Eileen couldn't face. Love is a luxury. It is for those whose life is built on solid ground, who can risk a humiliation or two without feeling their personality crack.

Looking back, the risk appeared piddling—because if it were Roger who had, in an outburst of jealousy, tried to kill Simon, then Eileen's secrecy about her feelings for Simon got her entangled in the complex structure of cause and effect that had led to last night's catastrophe. Suddenly, she couldn't stand the uncertainty a second longer. She sat up and switched on the bedside lamp once more.

"Alan!" she shouted.

"*Hasta la vista,* baby."

"Not you Ginger," she sighed and called again.

The door opened. On seeing Alan's tired face something inside her broke. "Is he dead? Alan, is he—"

"Simon's all right." He sat down on the bed and pressed her arm. "As far as I know, that is. Before he left, Inspector Terry told me that the operation had gone well."

A warm, mushy gratefulness spread inside her. "I'm sorry I woke you, but—"

"It's okay. I wasn't sleeping very soundly anyway. I had dreadful dreams."

In unison, they tried a reassuring smile. Two myopics squinting at each other's hazy faces. She realized how much she liked him.

"I could take you to the hospital so that we're there when he comes round."

"Who knows how long it will take. To tell the truth, I'd rather you went alone. I'm not up to it, but I'll hold the fort in the meantime. Kiss him for me, will you?"

"With the greatest pleasure." Alan stood up and hesitated. "You know, I'm really sorry about the rude things I said yesterday after you told me about your planned surgery. I didn't mean a word of it. I'm sure you and Simon are going to—"

"Alan, what's eating you? Below the surface, I mean."

He took up the plush elephant and rotated it between his hands. "Someone has to inform Simon's family. I couldn't bring myself to make the call last night. Peter loves his Dad, and its so unjust and all."

"I get the message. I'll call the Jenkinsons later."

"Thank you, Eileen." He kissed her temple and left.

There's nothing like a brisk walk to get the juices flowing and to sweep the cobwebs from the mind. The cold air acupunctured Alan's lungs with countless needles. The streets were deserted and unearthly, just some sandwich bars and newsstands were already open. He ignored the stench of rancid oil and avoided reading the headlines. Leaving Eileen alone hadn't been a good idea. There would be calls from the press and from parents who wanted to take their children out of the classes. Irrational as it was, he could well understand the panicked reaction. The Caesar wasn't a safe place any longer. Every now and then Alan turned around. In his mind's eye, he always saw this picture of Simon with the handle of Jessica's screwdriver grotesquely sticking out of his back. By the time he reached the hospital, his muscles were cramped from the effort of keeping his shoulder blades as closely together as possible.

In the main reception area, a green sign on the wall between the elevators said that the intensive care unit was on the 4th floor.

Alan went up. "Visitors press button and wait for answer," another sign next to the door of the ward told him. Obediently, he pressed the button. A competent looking nurse appeared. When he asked for Simon she frowned, and he feared she would tell him he was dead.

"You can't see Mr. Jenkinson," she said, putting her arms on her broad hips. "Nobody's allowed to see him except his relatives and the police."

"I'm one of his closest friends."

Deep lines appeared on the root of her nose. "I have strict orders not to let anyone in."

"Could you please make an exception in my case? I was the one who found him."

"We don't make exceptions for anyone."

"Good morning," said a loud and friendly bass behind him. Alan turned around and saw a dark blue corduroy coat and, somewhere above, the collar belonging to it. He craned his neck and looked into hairy nostrils and the underside of eyeballs.

"I'm Constable Brick," the giant announced himself in a droning voice. He certainly had the element of surprise on his side. "I've come to ensure the safety of Simon Jenkinson. How is he?"

The nurse kept her head strictly at eye level and addressed the buttons on the constable's coat. "I can't tell you as long as this . . ." she cast a sharp glare in Alan's direction, "individual is around."

The constable looked down at Alan questioningly.

"My name is Alan Widmark. I've also come to see Mr. Jenkinson."

"Mr. Widmark." A hand the size of a frying pan clutched his. "It's a pleasure to meet you. Blockley told me about your gorgeous show."

"He's only a friend of Mr. Jenkinson's," the nurse said derogatively.

The kindly giant smiled, showing huge teeth. He let go of Alan's hand, who clenched it to test if the bones and sinews were still in their proper places. The nurse gave up her rigid posture to show that she was handing over her responsibility to the constable. "You had better talk to Dr. Evans. I'll show you the way."

Alan was about to ask if he could join them when the constable began dragging him along in what he must have intended to be a friendly gesture. Alan was mystified by the constable's physique. He wasn't trying to compensate for height by slouching but held himself upright, carrying his smile like a red flag on a car that announces the transport of oversized goods.

Dr. Evans, mustachioed and bespectacled, sat in his office, drinking coffee and yawning extensively. "Forty-two hours on duty. Or was it fifty? I'm too tired to read my watch and do the math. Simon Jenkinson? We almost lost him during the operation. The screwdriver had gone all the way through the left ventricle. We managed to reanimate him with internal cardiac massage. It's impossible to tell how long he'll remain unconscious."

Alan felt crest-fallen.

"I was told to wait for Mr. Jenkinson to come round so I can ask if he remembers who attacked him. What did you do with the weapon?" Constable Brick inquired.

"We've already sent someone to take it to the police station—in a plastic bag, of course. It's not the first time for us to handle evidence. Ugh, is this supposed to be coffee? Tastes like brewed bone meal." He tried to chuckle but was so tired that his laugh turned into another yawn.

Alan was glad when the constable thanked Dr. Evans and they left his office to take up posts at Simon's side. The surgical overcoats they had to put on were one-size-fits-all. Alan tucked up the sleeves, whereas the Constable looked as if he'd put on an apron. Alan felt frightened and intimidated amidst the beeping apparatus. How much hope could there be when all this effort was required to keep someone alive? He was glad Eileen hadn't come with him. He looked down at Simon's dear face, touched the waxen skin, stroked his cheek and tried to ignore the jagged lines of the electrocardiogram. Simon looked like a cyborg with all the machines and tubes attached to him. "This is from Eileen," Alan said and bent down to kiss Simon's lips.

The Constable brought two chairs. "Here, take a seat, Mr. Widmark."

They began to talk in hushed voices. Were they afraid of waking Simon? Alan forced himself to raise his voice. He was sure that Simon would have liked the way he and the constable were chatting at his bedstead. Maybe the friendly and relaxed atmosphere infiltrated his subconscious.

"You'd make a great tap-dancer. No need to put a microphone near the floor."

Brick laughed, producing a sound reminiscent of distant thunder.

"Are you in the Guinness Book of Records?"

"No, I'm not," he said. "Can you believe this? In England alone, there are two men who are taller than I am. There is one George Par—"

"Constable," the pungent voice of the nurse broke in.

In a reflex, Brick snapped to attention.

"Doctor Evans is on his round. I must ask you to wait outside."

"That's fine with me. I was getting hungry anyway." He smiled broadly at the nurse and they left the ward.

"I'm always hungry," he told Alan. "During meals, my father used to say that I would eat as much as one cared to shovel at me." He delved into the pockets of his jacket. "I've brought something to eat. Help yourself."

After the walk in the cold on an empty stomach, Alan gratefully accepted one of the lavish sandwiches. Brick went to see if he could find a drink dispenser and returned balancing two Styrofoam cups on his palm. They finished their sandwiches and returned to Simon's side. He asked the Constable about Inspector Terry.

"It's said that his parents had an entirely different career in mind for him, as a pianist. He played some pieces on an old untuned piano once when we sat together in a bar to celebrate a solved case. Quicker fingers than Sam the Snatcher. When we asked why he had turned his back on a career, he mumbled something about stage fright." Brick shrugged. The stages of this world were no threat for him. "For some strange reason he took to the Job. He wasn't much of a success as a rookie. The rumor is he drove everybody mad and some of his superiors refused outright to work with him. They said he was insubordinate and unreliable—and his jottings were unreadable, too. He drew stick-figures and the like on them."

"Um, I saw him taking notes last night," Alan fell in with a giggle.

"The problem with him was that, although he never made any real mistakes, he didn't give the impression that he was taking his job seriously. They kept promoting and transferring him to get him out of the way. Actually, he's solved some really bent cases lately. They say it's due to his seri—sependi—blast it, I never get that word right."

"What's it supposed to mean?"

"If only I knew. I wanted to look it up but I keep forgetting the syllables. Seri-something-pity."

Alan made a guess. "Serendipity."

"You're a smart lad. What does it mean?"

"It's the faculty of coming to solutions of problems without trying to solve them, like finding things by deliberately not looking for them."

"That's a terrific description of his style of work. You should see his office. He must spend half his time finding things without looking for them or otherwise he'd never get any of his paperwork done." The Constable frowned. "I think his breathing rhythm has changed."

"What?"

"Mr. Jenkinson took a deeper breath just now."

Alan's pulse went up and he watched Simon closely for a long time. When nothing happened, Brick resumed their talk. "I'm very fond of the inspector. D'you know what he said when we met for the first time?"

"I'd love to hear it."

"Grrnnn." The sound had come from the bed. Seconds ticked by.

"Agggnnn," Simon moaned, the corners of his eyes twitched, then his eyelids began to flutter.

Waking to a memory turned to full volume was a torture. Jessica cringed and flinched inside and tried to withdraw. She didn't want it to be true. She wanted to forget who she was and what was happening to her. She longed for a hot shower, fresh clothes, a sumptuous breakfast, a long dance session and a good talk with Eileen. Most of all, she longed to forget about guilt, self-accusation, fear, and this impotent feeling in her legs, like a Formula One car that got clamped.

It wouldn't take her anywhere to go on rolling in her misery. Practical, Jessica, try to be practical, she commanded herself. That she had awoken without a reality blackout could be taken as a sign that she was gaining strength. As she had so often said to Eileen, when she had motivated her to use her legs despite their muscular atrophy: emotional strength can be trained like a muscle, a crisis is there to be overcome, and so forth. Like an agony aunt. Yet it had helped Eileen, hadn't it? Why shouldn't it help Jessica herself?

Breaking the window hadn't worked. Her shoes stood on the bed, left of the pillow. She touched the smooth leather. Alan's special gift for her eighteenth birthday. Falling in the year of the fire, it had been a sad event, despite everybody's attempts to cheer each other up. Looking at the shoes, she had thought about Eileen lying in a hospital bed, pained and crippled. Eileen, who had been nice and reliable. She missed her—and that was why she decided not to avoid the confrontation any longer, and to go and see Eileen at the hospital the next day, the day that had changed both their lives.

Now, again, she missed Eileen, and Alan and . . . She felt so homesick she wanted to cry like a baby. Home—that was The Caesar, the stage under her feet. It was no use thinking of her feet. She had to find another source of strength now. First of all, she had to do something about him. Would a careful approach to his feelings give her enough leverage to persuade him that he had punished her sufficiently? She wouldn't try to appeal to his love, which seemed to have become distorted and psychopathic. Neither would she, to lull him, pretend feelings she didn't cherish. She would admit her faults and ask him what he expected of her; take a rational approach to this emotional disaster.

In the meantime, she should do something for her body. She could swing and stretch her arms, press her palms together, make some isotonic muscle contractions with her quadriceps. When she sat up and removed the goosedown comforter she found that the room was warm. A gray light filtered through the clouds. Was it dusk and the stove still operating after these few hours, or was it the dawn of the next day—Thursday, right?—and he had been here in the meantime to replace the gas bottle once more? She was so thirsty. Would he bring her tea again? Why had she been asleep all day and probably all night as well? A drug in the tea, of course. She had better not drink too much of the next supply.

The need to pee created a relentless pressure in her bladder. How demeaning it was to have to use the chamber pot. At least it had a lid that closed tightly, or else the room would smell of something worse than mildew now. The discomfort of the procedure made her angry. The chains of the handcuffs were short and didn't give her much room to move. Accompanied by steely clicks, she bent her upper body into an unnatural angle to reach for the pot and lift it up. She sat on the cold porcelain and the gush of urine came so strongly that drops spattered up against her thighs and vagina. What would she have given for toilet tissue. As if anyone cared if she was clean. Well, she herself cared. She didn't like the idea of a stinking body. In her rage, she almost knocked the pot over when she yanked up her underpants. She quickly put the pot back on the floor and began to pummel the comforter to get some of the raging energy out of her system—but anger meant strength, and strength was her only weapon. She would find a way out. She knew she would, because she had to.

She moved closer to the handcuffs so that she could let her knees fall sideways. Remaining constantly in the same position was a torture she hadn't imagined to be so cruel. Jessica scrutinized the handcuffs. Were they solid police things or phony S&M equipment like the ones she had seen in the fetish shop where the troupe had bought the costumes for the production? They looked frighteningly reliable. Fucking reliable and heavy, and much too narrow to allow her feet to slip out. No padding, no escape lever. Her hands were free. Was there anything in her reach she could bend into a shape that would open the lock? She fingered around inside the drawer of the bedside table. It was empty. A spring from the mattress? It was a polyurethane mattress, she remembered. She rattled the top bar of the bedstead, then pulled at the small vertical bars. Not one of them gave way. She then tried to loosen one of the screws on her tap shoes so she could use it as a tool—either to open the handcuffs or to scratch the soldered joint of two bars. No luck. She banged a heel plate against the brass of the bedstead. Neither the brass nor the plate showed any signs of wear.

Ah, the helpless feeling. She so wanted to get out of this bed and away from this place. She'd never sleep in a bed again; in a hammock, or on the naked floor, or dangling by her legs like a bat—but not in a bed, be it her own or the one in the guest room. As she thought of the guest room, Monday night came back to her, too strong a memory to be ignored, even though in her desolate state of captivity it seemed of little significance.

She had come home long after midnight with a guilty conscience. As usual, this sensation soon turned into anger, directed both at herself and Roger. How negligent of her not to have called him when she knew how concerned he would be. How presumptuous of him to think she needed his constant supervision.

He had been waiting for her, of course. When she had unlocked the door she saw him coming out of the living room, still fully dressed, with a small glass of cognac in his right hand. His face carried the familiar expression of righteous irritation. She closed the door with an angry push of her heel and was about to give in to the habitual impulse to sneer at him when she remembered the anonymous letter. They weren't playing the same old game again. Circumstances were entirely different and required a new set of rules. He seemed to sense it too, and was as much at a loss for words as she was. For an eternity, they stood in the hallway and waited for the other one to end the silence and thus to define the situation.

It was as if she were looking at Roger for the first time. He was really there, a genuine person, made of flesh and blood. A shadow of gloom crossed his hard features. No, he mustn't show weakness. She wanted him strong and predictable in his anger. She didn't want to be responsible for this sad look on his face. Without warning, a hot, scary sensation filled her. She longed to be punished, to feel pain.

"Hit me, Roger," she said.

"What?"

"Hit me. I mean it."

"Is this a test of some kind?"

"Just do it." She stepped closer.

Slowly, with dignified concentration Roger lifted his left arm. Jessica clutched her hands together behind her back to keep them from interfering. It felt as if she were gripping someone else's hands. The blow was delivered on her right cheek with the back of his hand. Roger's signet ring scratched her skin fiercely. Strange words came to her mind. *You deserve to be punished, you bitch, for all that you did to him.* It was someone else she was talking to. Just whom it was, she had no idea.

Roger was trembling. "Are you all right, Jessica?"

She brought a hand up to cover her burning cheek. "Thank you, Roger," she said, unable to explain why she felt so pleased and why the odor of blood didn't inundate her with disgust as it had done two nights before. "Thank you."

Then there was a small crushing sound. Roger had clenched his right hand, cognac dripped from his wrist. As he flattened his palm, the stem and the fragments of the balloon glass showered onto the oak parquet. She was relieved to see that there were no cuts in his palm.

"We've been through a bad patch," he said in a mellow voice. "Tomorrow we'll start anew. But tonight . . . it would be better if you slept in the guest room."

Feeling small and vulnerable, she couldn't take her eyes from the fragments on the floor. "Please protect me, Roger."

"Give me one night to get over your unfaithfulness."

She obeyed, convinced that she had regained her grip on their marriage, which had been on the skids for months. But the next morning everything had changed before she had stood a chance to settle down in a new life.

Jessica ran her fingertips along the scab on her right cheek. More light came through the window now, which meant it was morning. She had feared the darkness and now she looked around her prison with doleful relief. Bewildered, she noticed something that hadn't been there before.

A tall vase had been placed on the bedside table, a vase with a single red rose.

"Why are you searching my house, Inspector?" Roger asked,

suppressing his hallmark tone of offense. It was humiliating to watch how they ransacked room after room. That's why he had retreated into the kitchen.

"I have finally managed to get a search warrant," Terry said factually.

"What do you hope to find? I thought you had checked my alibi."

"Of course. Three of the calls you made from your office last night fall into the critical period of time which you would have needed to drive to the theatre, stab Simon and return to your office. The people you called testified it was definitely you they had talked to."

"Then what are you looking for? Jessica's body parts hidden beneath my underwear?"

"The problem is that David also disappeared last night."

"Splendid. What do you expect me to do, burst into tears? And when was I supposed to have done away with David? When you interviewed me? Or when your constable escorted me home? Or sometime during the night when the police were patrolling the pavement?"

"Nobody patrolled in front of your house last night. Consider this a routine search. We're also searching David's flat, that of his friend and the place where Simon lives."

"Leaving no stone unturned, huh? You're thorough."

"And persistent. We were interrupted yesterday as we were talking about Monday evening. Something you said rang a false note. I'm just not sure what it was."

The time for prevarication was over. He might as well tell Inspector Terry the truth. Pour out his heart to him. Why not. It wouldn't help to find Jessica but it would unburden Roger's soul. He realized he was sitting round-shouldered with downcast eyes, and corrected his posture.

"I was lying when I said that Jessica and I had a quarrel when she returned late on Monday night. It was quite the contrary. We never understood each other better."

Terry tilted his head in surprise.

"There were so many words in my head that night, the full set of reproaches and accusations I have ready at hand at these moments—and I knew Jessica's retorts in advance. It was like running in a circle, not getting anywhere. No reason to go through the routine once again. So I looked at her in silence for several minutes. Then she asked me to hit her."

Roger had the inspector's full attention. The chocolate bar he had been dipping into a cup of tea was put aside. "She asked you to hit her? My eye!"

"Take my word for it. I think she was finally facing her childhood trauma, although I'm sure she wasn't aware of it. Denial is her means of self-protection."

"A childhood trauma? Of what nature?"

"Her parents had a violent relationship."

"You mean her father was beating up—"

"No, the other way round. It was her mother who was abusing her father. I can't tell you much about it since I had no opportunity to meet the Greshams. All I know is what Alan told me about them. The Gresham woman must have maltreated her husband regularly. When Mr. Gresham came to fetch his daughter from her dance lessons, he often had a black eye or bruise marks on his arms. Jessica died with shame each time."

"Did Mrs. Gresham beat her daughter as well?"

"No, fortunately not—but what she did to her wasn't much better. She taught the girl that men were born to be slaves and other such brilliant home truths. She hit Jessica's father in front of the girl's eyes."

"A most unhealthy atmosphere for an only child to grow up in."

"Very unsettling. It explains why The Caesar became her home and why she decided to stay in London when her parents moved to Auckland. Alan said he more or less replaced the family for her, together with Eileen."

Terry poked his lips with his forefinger. "So Jessica isn't the spoiled brat she seems to be. She just can't help treating men as her flunkies. All through her formative years she has been indoctrinated. She was forced to witness her parents' altercations and must have felt it was all wrong, even though she emulated her mother's behavior. To escape the dilemma, she fled into tap-dancing so as not to have to deal with her psychological problems."

"I'm sure the source of her blackouts lies there as well," Roger said. "Jessica never talks about her family. She must have buried her memories and closed the lid firmly over them. I think I shook something loose when I slapped Jessica at the party. She treated me with a kind of reverence after that. It was probably what she had always hoped her father would do, to hit her mother back, to defend himself."

"I see. It must be terrible to have a father who is a weakling, whom you can't expect to protect you from all the dangers in the world when he can't even deal with his own wife."

"On Monday night when Jessica said she wanted me to hit her, I knew that, in a way, I had to slip into her father's role and transform Jessica's view of men. I had to force myself to do it. My bad temper is never more than skin-deep. I brought up two daughters without ever raising a hand."

"You don't have to justify yourself."

"Oh, I sure have to, because I hit her harder than I had intended to. My signet ring cut into her skin. Here," he took off the ring and laid it on the kitchen table. "You'll probably find traces of Jessica's blood on it. That's something you overlooked."

Using a plastic bag, Terry picked up the ring. "You could have invented this story to explain the traces of blood."

Roger ignored this. "Your men will find a dark patch on the parquet in the hallway and maybe some microscopic fragments that match those Nurit gave you on Tuesday. They belong to a glass of cognac I had in my hand. I crushed it when . . . ."

"Yes?"

"Jessica . . . . She thanked me for hitting her. It felt as if she were ripping my heart out. Now comes the tricky bit. I can't get it out of my head. Jessica said, 'Roger, protect me.' I thought she was just longing to be hugged and held, but now I wonder if she knew she was in some sort of danger. I can't forgive myself for not asking her. I'm probably a greater weakling than her father ever was."

David's mood was lugubrious when he got up with an aching back. He had spent the night on the hard floor in front of Jessica's room, rolled into his coat on a lumpy mattress—it was the old mattress he and Jessica had removed from the bedstead to replace it by a new one for their lovemaking. Things hadn't worked out the way he had planned them. Simon wasn't dead. It was a toss-up whether he would come round to tell who had attacked him. On learning this, David had known that he couldn't return to Norman's flat or take his car to drive to Primrose Hill. All he could do to prepare the last thirty-six hours of Jessica's captivity was to buy some crackers and two plastic bottles of Evian in Euston Station, from where he took the tube to Chalk Farm, walking the rest of the way.

Bringing Jessica a rose had been a spontaneous idea. He saw it in a flower dispenser at the station and thought it an appropriate allusion to their past. His severed self, the part of him that had been Jessica's lover, had often brought her a rose when they met to make love. The vase he had used was still there, in the kitchen sink, and he filled it with a little water from the Evian bottle. Jessica was deeply asleep when he took the flower to her bed. He stroked her in the darkness. One rendezvous a week, three hours, that was all Jessica had granted him. Now, finally, he had her all to himself for as long as he wanted.

David stretched his tense muscles. His breakfast consisted of a sip of cold water and a dry cracker, then he was ready to face Jessica. It was important that he got everything right, that he made her understand he was not her enemy.

Jessica was sitting at the foot of her bed, massaging her ankles with diligence. At his entry, she didn't look up.

"Morning. How are you?"

"A bit frayed at the edges." She pushed herself back, prodded the pillows into a comfortable shape before she leaned against them, and looked at him through half-closed eyes. She was playing it cool today. She had no idea what was afoot. It would be a walkover for him to get her begging and sobbing.

"Thanks for the rose."

David laughed out loud. "Get real, Jessica. This is not a rendezvous with your bondage-crazy lover or something. You aren't taking me seriously, are you?"

"You always brought me a rose to tell me that you loved me."

"And I do love you, maybe more than you deserve. You're not looking your best at the moment."

"I know. I wish I could wash my hair. My scalp is itching."

"And I'm itching to tell you what happened at the opening night." He handed her the water bottle. "Here's your breakfast."

"No tea today?"

"The service is deteriorating. You should complain to the manager." David sat astride on the chair between the bed and the wall and watched her expression. "It's all Alan's fault, you know."

She put the bottle on the floor and bobbed her head in his direction. "What do you mean?"

"It's a long story. Fortunately, we have all day to talk it through. I have laid out a punishment plan in five stages."

"David, this is entirely out of proportion. I know I was unfair with you. If I could, I would make Sunday night undone." She sounded composed and sincere.

"Why don't you admit that if the truth were known, you'd love to make all of it undone? You regret every second you spent with me. That's what you said on Saturday night."

"I didn't mean it."

"Now, I'll mean everything I'm going to tell you, so you had better listen well. We're talking about the five stages of punishment. Stage one." He tilted the chair forwards and lifted the rose out of the vase. "The rose is taken out of the water. Stage two." He broke the thorns from the stem. "It is robbed of its thorns."

Jessica winced as if the rose were a voodoo doll.

"Stage three. The petals wither." He tore them off one by one. "Stage four. The stem is broken." He bent the stem until it snapped. "Stage five. The bearer of the rose says his final goodbye." He threw away the stem.

Jessica's composure was beginning to show cracks.

"Let's return to stage one. I took you out of your natural habitat. The theatre. You're like a flower without water now. It was no problem to get you inside the house. You were keen to apologize because you were concerned—not about my feelings, to be sure, but about your self-image. You thought you'd always keep the upper hand in our relationship and so you had no suspicions at all when I offered you tea from my Thermos. There was a drug in it. Making you my prisoner was indeed as easy as taking a flower out of the vase." David played with his earrings. "But you still have your thorns. When I have told you about last night, your stem will be smooth. You will feel utterly defenseless."

Her mask of self-control was beginning to slip.

"So, what did I do? At the première, shortly before the finale, I went to the basement and into your dressing room. I took the piece of cloth you use for polishing your shoes and wrapped it around the handle of your screwdriver, which I hid behind my back." He paused for effect. "Thus armed I went into Simon's treatment room."

Jessica breathed a horrified "No."

Pleased that he had put her in a funk, he continued with relish. "He was sitting at his desk and reading one of his medical books. Never misses a chance to catch up on the newest developments, the good man. I said, 'Simon, come quick, Victor has a cramp.' When he passed me on his way to the door—"

"No!" Jessica screamed.

Implacably, David went on, "I stabbed him in the back."

"You beast! You hurt Simon, the dearest—" She began to choke.

"Cheer up, he's alive. That's where Alan comes in. He came downstairs as I left Simon's room. I hid in the next dressing room and waited until he ran past to get help, then I returned the cloth to your shoe-stand and went backstage again. So, Alan saved Simon's life and now I have to hide here with you because the moment Simon wakes up I'm scuppered."

Jessica was no longer listening. She pressed the back of her hand to her mouth and sobbed, her stomach heaving. "How could you!"

"He was the better lover, wasn't he? You had more fun with him. That's what you said. You should have watched your tongue."

"You must be crazy."

"Don't complain. It was you who drove me crazy. However, there's a glimmer of hope for you. I'm sure you told Eileen about our weekly meetings here. She is certainly faltering and unable to think straight, now that Simon's no longer taking care of her fragile frame, but if the inspector tells her that there was an old man who saw you in front of this house on Tuesday morning, it will click, and the police will be here to get you out."

Jessica became very still. "You're not going to hurt Eileen, David, are you?"

"Small fry. I have something bigger in mind. Stage three. Remember?"

"The petals wither," she murmured.

David stood up and took the automatic pistol from his trouser pocket. Jessica shrank back as far as her tethered feet allowed her to. "Now guess, my rosebud, whom I'm planning to kill next."

She was unable to speak.

"Guess. Come on. You won't put ideas into my head, don't worry. My plan is as fixed as the screws on your tap shoes."

"R-Roger?" she quivered.

David had a laughing fit. "Roger? Roger who suffers more from your whims than anyone else? Roger who has put up with your antics like a saint? And now that his obstreperous wife has vanished into limbo, this plush animal of an inspector suspects Roger of having killed you. Strange twist of fate."

"David, this has to end."

"It will, when I say the time has come. Now, have another try. Who could be the next on my list?"

"There's no one."

"No one who means anything to you? Are you sure?"

Wide-eyed, she nodded.

"How about the only man you have ever loved? Your own words."

"I . . . I said that?"

"You did—when you rammed in the message that you didn't want me. But you didn't destroy my love. It is too strong, strong enough to crush you." He hardly managed to keep the triumph out of his voice as he announced, "Tonight I will go and shoot Alan."

Jessica grasped the vase and threw it at him. He ducked and the glass broke against the wall, spattering a gush of water over his trousers. Jessica's practice shoes followed in quick succession. One of them hit his shoulder.

"Now that's enough, you silly girl. I should spank you." He was angry, but only for a moment. "There, there," he said and wrung the next projectile, the water bottle, from her hands. "What do you hope to gain by attacking me? You should pray that nothing happens to me or there'll be no one to free you. The keys to the handcuffs are in the kitchen—far away from your reach. Without me, you'll die."

"I'm going to die anyway," she blurted out. "Stage four, the stem is broken. The rose is dead. Dead."

"You will live, Jessica," he said softly and for a moment the phantom pain in his severed self paused. "Your death is not part of my plan. I'll leave you alone for a while now. Don't worry, I won't be far away. Just in the next room or in the corridor. You can call for me anytime. But don't think you can talk me out of my strategy. The only thing you can do to save Alan is to keep the night from falling."

Chapter Thirteen

Eileen had been working the butterfly, but she stopped when Terry came into the gym. She used the sleeve of her sweater to absorb the perspiration on her forehead.

"Twelve," she said to herself. "I'm not up to it today. Good morning, Inspector. Any news about Simon or Jessica?"

"Simon woke up two hours ago, but his memory hasn't returned yet." He was playing it down. The truth was that Simon was completely disoriented and not even able to speak.

"I had the privilege of living through this experience several times, and I know the state of confusion and . . . . Oh, let's drop it." She tried to smile. "You're accused of making a terrible mess of my office last night."

"Guilty in the first degree." He looked for a place to sit and went to the weightlifting bench. "Have you still long to go?" he asked.

"Theoretically, yes, but I was about to stop. You must think I'm callous to have started at all today, but it's Simon who always insists I don't miss out on my training." She pulled the sweater over her head. Underneath she was wearing a tanktop which left her midriff bare. "Two sets of crunches and that'll have to do for today."

Eileen hoisted herself on her crutches, which had been leaning against the weight casing of the butterfly machine, and went over to a long bench. Fascinated, he watched the contractions of her toned abs as she was doing a set of crunches. He decided to give the butterfly a try. It didn't respond to his first attempt because he had not expected such resistance. He took a deep breath and tried again. After the fifth go his shoulders began to protest. It occurred to him that if Eileen managed twelve she wasn't as brittle as she looked.

"Have you always been a sporty type?"

She sat up and laughed. "No, on the contrary. I've got at least ten times as many muscles now as before the mishap. I should eat a pizza every now and then to get a bit of fat on my bones."

"Talking of pizza, what does *pipistrello* mean?"

"Bat."

"Sorry?"

"The rodent with wings."

"Yes, I know what a bat is, I just thought it's a droll name for a restaurant."

"Luigi was inspired by the wayward names pubs used to have."

"There's one near Kentish Town nick, it's called The Vulture's Perch. You can hardly beat that."

"Nobody Inn."

"Huh?"

"The Nobody Inn is a pub in Doddiscombsleigh. My parents spend their holidays in strange places." She stopped halfway into a smile. "What brought you here, Inspector?"

"I just had some time to kill before going to an inquest and thought I'd pop in and see how you're doing." Terry went to sit beside Eileen on the long bench.

"They do good jobs at the Middlesex, don't they?" she asked

as an afterthought.

"Last year, July it was, a painter had his hand cut off with a Samurai sword in a street attack. The hand was brought to the hospital in an ice-filled plastic bag and was reattached. The next day the victim could wriggle his fingers again. I could tell you more such stories about the first-class surgeons there."

She shuddered. "Talking of fingers, did you find any finger-prints on the handle of the screwdriver?"

"No, just traces of black shoe polish, the same make as they use here, as was to be expected. Let's talk about Simon. You said he was a ladies' man. No commitments. We searched his flat this morning and I was surprised when I found out that he is widowed and has a son."

"Hardly as surprised as I was. About two and a half years ago, Simon said he wanted me to meet his family, father, brother, sis-ter-in-law, nieces and nephews, the lot. That was before I was able to walk. So when we arrived in Sevenoaks, Simon unfolded my wheelchair and steered me along the path to the house. From the front door, a second wheelchair was pushed with a boy in it. We stared at each other. He was a handsome teenager, but he grinned in the way the mentally retarded do. 'Meet my son Peter,' Simon said casually. Now, that's what I call a surprise. The boy is hand-icapped and needs twenty-four hours of nursing a day. Had I not known that Simon is considerate by nature, I might have sus-pected that he had adopted me to compensate for the fact that he couldn't raise his son." Her voice had changed. In the huge mir-ror in front of them Terry saw that Eileen had begun to weep.

"I love him so," she said. "I love him to bits."

When Alan, who joined them a few minutes later, saw Terry hugging the crying Eileen he looked horrified. "Is he dead?" he mouthed. Terry shook his head and Alan breathed a sigh of relief. Eileen wiped away her tears and took the bag Alan gave her.

"I brought you some fresh clothes from your flat," he said. "Inspector, I received a call for you from Sergeant Blockley. He's on the line. You'll find the phone in my bedroom."

Terry replaced the receiver and went over to the living room.

"Have you heard from Susan lately?" he asked Alan, who came in at that moment.

"Don't say she has disappeared as well."

"It seems so. At least she wasn't at home all morning, Blockley said. He was there to supervise the search of the house. He rang all the numbers in Susan's address book but couldn't track her down. She may have some errands to do or have gone shopping, but with regard to her emotional distress I find it unlikely."

Alan let himself fall on his settee. "Oh dear, I'm worried about her. She's got a delicate psyche since her miscarriage three years ago. It happened very late into her pregnancy, sixth or seventh month I think. It was more a premature birth than a miscarriage. Sadly, the child was dead. I think neither David nor Susan have ever recovered entirely from the shock, especially since they couldn't have another child. I wish I had gone to see her today, but there was Simon . . . it's all too much."

Alan would be far more worried if he knew that Jessica, in her attempt to undermine David's persistence, had revealed that she had been pregnant. *I didn't want your child*. She had dealt David a death blow. And Susan had heard these words, taking two blows at a time, and of an even more dire nature.

"If Susan comes to see you, don't let her go away again. And be careful. She might be armed."

"Armed?"

"Blockley found five bullets in the drawer of her bedside table. They belong to a 0.22 caliber automatic handgun with a magazine for eight bullets. The gun is missing."

"I hope she's not about to . . . to commit suicide. She's so fragile. She often comes to cry on my shoulder, as Eileen has just done on yours."

"Eileen has a strange way of crying," Terry remarked. "The tears flow but there's no movement, no sobbing, no heaving of shoulders. Not even a distortion of her face. Like a turned-on tap."

"She had a lot to weep about after the fire. Doing it silently was the only way for her because she had to keep still or it would hurt. Her body was smashed, and the most minute change in position was intolerable. She was in plaster for months and had to restrict her breathing, her speaking and all other actions to the absolute minimum. I suppose crying in this silent way has become a firm neurological pattern."

"God. And all this after a silly accident, a fire that broke out because of a short circuit."

"How come you know?"

"I had a look at the arson file."

Alan stared intently at a fruit bowl on the couch table. Terry saw his ears turn red and knew he had touched on something. Suddenly alert, he pressed on. "I forgot . . . . What exactly caused the short circuit?"

"An old electric heater in one of the studios."

"There's a flaw in the explanation, I think. You told me the building was deserted because of the holiday. Nobody was there to turn on the heater." As he said this, Terry became as hot as if the heater had been turned on inside him. Jessica. She needed to practice daily, even during holidays. She couldn't do without it. So she would come to The Caesar, where the central heating was turned low because no classes were being held, and she had switched on the small electric heater.

"It was Jessica who started the fire, wasn't it?" Terry said. "She forgot to turn off the old thing when she left."

Alan spread his hands in a gesture of defeat. "Jessica came forward with her confession straightaway. She said she'd been in the studio the evening before the fire and that she must have forgotten the heater. The old thing must have overheated, some clothes hanging on a rack nearby had began to smolder, and that was it. Jessica was only seventeen and all on her own. I didn't want her to face a charge of arson by culpable negligence. When the fire investigation unit brought up the theory with the short circuit, I left it at that. The damage was done, anyway. You wouldn't say it was an insurance fraud on my part?"

Terry's thoughts ran wild. Eileen's suffering, her mutilations, her agony, it had all been Jessica's fault. Jessica, who was now her best friend. "Who knows about this?"

"No one except Jessica and me."

"Are you sure Eileen doesn't know?"

"When she and Jessica began to be friends I decided it was best to let sleeping dogs lie."

How long could Jessica live with the guilty conscience? How long had it taken before she considered her relationship with Eileen firm enough to stand the revelation? And if she had decided to tell Eileen, what must it have done to her to learn that Jessica had only helped her in order to make good her disastrous fault? It would have been a complete let-down for Eileen, in every respect. But Eileen was self-controlled, her biggest achievement through her years of suffering. Had she hidden her feelings in a dark chamber of her mind where they had turned into stark hatred? Would the hatred be strong enough to generate the wish that Jessica, too, should suffer? Strong enough to goad her into planning how she could pay Jessica back? And hadn't Eileen just revealed to him that she was in love with Simon? Simon had been Jessica's lover. One more reason for Eileen to feel rancor.

"Hold on," Alan burst into Terry's thoughts, "you can't play with the idea that Eileen has anything to do with Jessica's disappearance?"

Terry, caught in the act of doing exactly this, knew he was jumping to conclusions too quickly. "It's a possibility. Remote, but not to be excluded altogether."

"Oh, come on. She's a cripple."

"Crimes have been committed by cripples before. She would need an accomplice, of course." What was the color of Simon's car? Dark blue, a dark blue Fiat. Was Simon the accomplice? On Tuesday morning, before they drove to Richmond, had they picked up Jessica?

"I refuse to follow this line of talk," Alan warned, "and I forbid you to take this outrageous theory any further. Eileen's as innocent of any crime on God's earth as—"

"Point taken."

"Why aren't you suspecting me for a change? After all, it was my studio that burned down. Jessica caused me a lot of trouble."

Jessica caused everybody trouble, she was trouble on legs. She had that autistic trait, an exclusive devotion to dancing that made her indifferent to other people's interests.

Stunned by David's theatrical exit line, Jessica sat motionless for minutes, not allowing her mind to catch up on this new development. The moment she dropped her guard, her thoughts began to race. She had to stop David before he went to shoot Alan. What could she do? Her eyes searched the room, looking for options. Water stains, fragments of glass, her pair of shoes lying upside down on the dusty plywood floorboards. Petals, thorns, and a broken stem.

How could she stop him?

The flame in the gas stove flickered and went out. In the air, conflicting clouds of dampness and dryness seemed to fluctuate. Five stages of punishment. She wouldn't give up. She would save Alan. How? David had already tried to kill Simon. With her own screwdriver. He was not just mad or furious. He was a lunatic, no longer responsible for his actions—and she had done this to him. She had broken his self-respect. Alan must not suffer as a consequence of her selfishness. Cindy must not lose her father because of Jessica.

Jessica grabbed the water bottle to drink. It slipped from her hands and the water ran over her arms, into her lap. Her vision blurred. She saw the floor in her bathroom in the Villa Cathleen, felt the blood running down her inner thighs and dripping onto the white tiles. She had danced the fetus out of her body. Her intensified training scheme over the past weeks had worked. She was finally bleeding free of the burden. There hadn't been the slightest trace of warm, motherly feeling inside her. The tiny lump of cells in her womb had been but a menace. She was convinced that it was her determination that had caused the spontaneous abortion. The pain was stinging, but she bit her lips so as not to wake Roger with an outcry, sat on the toilet for half an hour and pressed to keep up the bleeding. The red spots of drying blood reminded her of something that was lurking deep in her memory banks. The smell made her sick. She often wondered why no one else noticed that blood smelled of defeat. On the night of her miscarriage, she was afraid of swooning away every second. But then Roger would find her and what would she tell him? She fought the petrifying weakness, repressed her urge to moan so as not to wake Roger, and assured herself over and over again that she had won over her physique. Later, when she cleaned up the mess on the floor she decided that no one would ever master her, neither from without nor from within.

This had happened nine months ago. She could cradle her baby in her arms now had she allowed it to live, had she welcomed it instead of fighting it with all her willpower. Now there was only death. Her child, Simon, Alan—all because of her disregard of David's feelings. It was grotesque, maddening. He was going to kill Alan. Was there nothing she could do about it? Absolutely nothing?

The red petals like tiny pools of blood. The sharp fragments of the vase. Roger crushing the balloon glass, cognac dripping from his wrist. Jessica knew where her thoughts were heading and shrank back, paralyzed with the fear she might really do it, but her decision was already made.

She pushed herself forwards until her knees were bent, then lowered her upper body to the floor. Lying with her back on the floorboards, she reached behind her head. Her fingertips touched a fragment of glass. Not close enough. Her searching fingers felt the smooth leather of the tap shoe she had thrown at David. She hooked a finger under its rim and used it to draw the fragment closer. There it was, she had it. Slowly, she worked her way back on the bed.

The equation was simple. Alan would live when she died. It was him or her. As soon as she was dead, there would be no need for David to act out the last three stages of punishment.

She looked at her right wrist, its white, smooth skin covering muscles, sinews and blood vessels. Her dedication wasn't very strong. Something inside her kept pleading not to do it. So, if she wanted to finish this job properly, she had to act quickly. The first cut had to do the trick, that was all that mattered.

Do it, Jessica. Don't hesitate.

But I love my life. I can't sacrifice myself for Alan.

Stop whimpering, she hushed her ego, and with a quick move slashed open her wrist. She saw the blood ooze from the gash. Had she cut deep enough? The pain was setting in, sharp and burning. Her left hand still clutched the piece of glass, but she couldn't bring herself to cut a second time. Jessica lay back on the pillows. The sickening odor of blood mixed with the mildewy, dry-damp aroma of the sticky air. A metallic ringing was in her ears, she had tunnel vision. At the end of the tunnel, she saw her Dad's bashful smile, just the smile without his face.

"Go away," she wheezed and Dad's smile dissolved obediently. "I have to say my last prayer." It consisted of three words. "I am sorry."

Chapter Fourteen

Eileen had warned Terry. Alan had taken over Susan's afternoon belly-dancing class and the sight, she had said, was a bit odd. Actually, it was hilarious, as Terry discovered when he opened the door to the studio where five young women were rotating their bellies to the wailing of shakuhachi pipes. In their midst, Alan was grinding his hips ferociously, wearing striped jodhpurs and nothing else. With an expert eye, Terry contemplated Alan's muscular upper body, his hairless chest and the thin ring in his pierced belly button.

Alan saw him and broke the circle. "Wanna join us? We could do with a bit of male reinforcement."

Terry lifted one eyebrow. "And I'm wasting away my life as a police officer. It's a shame. Look, Eileen sent me up to inform you that I'm going to take her with me to the hospital. Simon has asked for her."

"You mean he's begun to speak. That's wonderful news! Yes, take Eileen. Tell her she doesn't have to come back in. I tried all day to send her home because everybody kept upsetting her with theories about who did it and how awful it was to be interrogated and all that. I wonder how we all carry on under these circumstances."

Eileen was waiting by the front door. She seemed a different person from the fit woman in the gym this morning. Now that Terry had his doubts about her sincerity, he was uncertain how to behave. Fortunately, she was not in a talkative mood. As they drove, she stared out of the side window, impervious—a total contrast to her openness on previous occasions. Terry didn't know what to make of her, how to read her. Eileen was made up of opposites, frailty and vigor, frankness and impenetrability. Her life since the fire must have been a struggle for balance, for a reconstitution of an inner harmony that had been smashed together with her body.

When Terry had parked the car, Eileen awoke from her lethargy and looked at him. "I've been thinking about Susan. I'm sorry for her. She conserves and cherishes her weakness. She thinks it's what endears her to David. And it may well have been so before Jessica came into his life. David needed a weak wife to make his strength stand out in greater contrast. He can't bear people who display superiority toward him. It must've been an absolute tragedy for him to fall for a woman as self-assured as Jessica."

"And never to win her heart, not even when they were lovers."

Eileen evaluated this. "You suspect him in all seriousness, don't you? That Jessica rejected him so ruthlessly might in itself have been enough to turn his love into hatred. But then to find that Susan had witnessed his humiliation . . . . Well, it would take a stronger character than David's to cope with that." She looked out of the window. "But then again, we often underrate people's power of forgiveness."

It was the ideal opening line for Terry to broach the question of whether Eileen knew that Jessica had caused the fire. "Mrs. Lanigan . . . ." he began, but the right words wouldn't come.

She turned her face toward him. In the fading light of dusk, her eyes looked even darker. "You can call me Eileen."

"Eileen, I've got something to ask you that has to do with forgiveness. The problem is, it's about something you aren't supposed to know."

A smile softened the tense muscles around her mouth. "And when you ask me, you give away the secret. I see. Let's keep it for later. I'm longing to see Simon."

He helped her get out of the car. The sky was pale and unreal, the air laden with the smell of snow like it had been on the evening when Michael died. As soon as they were inside the hospital, Terry was walking backwards in time. The elevator door slid aside and released them into the square waiting space in front of the Intensive Care ward. Under a dusty plastic plant, a wheelchair stood like a bench at the wayside. Nothing had changed in two years. As he waited for the nurse to answer his ring, layer after layer of protective shields was removed. Any second now a doctor would turn the corner and inform him in a low voice that Michael would soon be relieved from his suffering. Blinded by tears, he would shamble into the room where Michael lay dying, where he had to let go of the fatuous hope that this would turn out to be a mere test of his endurance, a practical joke of a whimsical deity.

Deep backlogs cracked open—of sorrow, of words unspoken, and of self-accusations still waiting to be forgiven. Why hadn't he stopped smoking sooner? Why had he allowed his work to keep him away from his lover's death-bed until it was almost too late? He hadn't been prepared for it, although he had seen death come in so many ways, sudden or slow, violent or gentle, tragic or merciful.

Before Terry entered the ward, he took a desperate lungful of the aggressively clean smell of disinfectant and allowed the knife of pain to cut its cold blade all the way into his chest. Automatically, not aware that he was following his routine, he flipped open his warrant card for the nurse. He put on the overcoat and overshoes like a robot following a program.

The time warp was complete when he saw Simon, who was

an altogether different type from Michael, but who now resembled him through his paleness and unfocused gaze. His nostrils and veins were attached to the same set of life support systems and monitoring devices. In this room, Michael's last words still seemed to linger, maimed by gruesome coughing fits. *Hold me. Don't let me die, hold me.*

Terry looked down at Simon's hand, a hand like Michael's—weightless, a bird about to fly away—and he would have been overwhelmed by his memories, had not, at this very moment, Eileen's soft voice parted the curtain of the past.

"He looks so small," she uttered, and with a start Terry found himself back in the here and now. He lowered the rails on one side of the bed and then took two steps back to lean against the wall. Thus retreating into the background, he watched as Eileen began to stroke Simon's hand. In a moment, her face seemed to lose all its edges. With a voice like molten silk, she said, "Simon. I have come. I am here."

Simon turned his head a fraction, their eyes locked. "Eileen, my lovely."

My lovely? Were their feelings mutual?

"What—" Simon's voice broke.

"You want to know what happened? So you don't remember."

"No."

"You had an emergency operation. There was an assault on you in your treatment room during the performance." Eileen spoke slowly to make sure he understood her.

"Wh-who?"

"We don't know. Keep calm, darling. You're going to be all right. You're in intensive care and recovering. Let the memory flow back slowly. Don't force it. What matters is that you get well again. Be patient with yourself."

Simon pressed Eileen's hand.

After a silence, a light frown rippled his forehead. "Jessica," he said.

"She hasn't been found yet."

"Peter. Does he . . . does he know?"

"I called Barbara this morning. She said she'll come soon and bring Peter along."

A young doctor joined them, looked at the displays, adjusted a tube and reprimanded Eileen mildly for sitting on the bed.

"Can I stay overnight?" she begged. "I want to hold his hand."

"No, I'm afraid that's impossible. And it wouldn't do him any good. He has to sleep without disturbance."

Eileen promised that she wouldn't disturb Simon. Now it was Simon who protested.

"You look tired, my love."

"I want to be with you."

"Come back tomorrow." Simon, exhausted by the exchange, closed his eyes. Terry felt like an intruder as he watched Eileen gently stroking Simon's hand and cheek for a long time.

For how long had Eileen and Simon been lovers? Was Eileen so broadminded that she had shared Simon with other women— even with her best friend? Or was she his latest conquest?

"I will, I will come back soon."

"I love you, Eileen." It was but a whisper.

"I love you too, Simon." She bent down, kissed his lips and let go of his hand. She seemed to cope well. It was only when they were back in the car that Terry discovered that she was weeping in that silent way of hers again.

"I'm falling," she said and leant against the side window.

"You shouldn't be alone tonight. Do you want to stay with Alan?"

"Cindy's mattress is a bit too soft for me. I need something firmer to lie on."

"I could take you to your parents."

"I'm used to being alone. I can manage."

"No, you can't manage. You can't even stop crying and I've run out of handkerchiefs. I'll take you home with me."

As if to demonstrate that she could indeed manage, she ended the flow of her tears with the help of a long, deep breath. Then she went on protesting, but meekly.

"I've got a guest room," Terry told her and started the car, "with a reliable mattress."

"I need my medicine."

"We'll pass by your place and I'll get it for you."

She sighed and handed him her keys to underline her surrender. "You're right. I would be a mouse in a trap alone in my narrow room and with no one to talk to. Thank you, Inspector."

"Friends call me Rick."

Eileen wondered if there was a Mrs. Terry who would prepare the guest room for her. Would she be expected to converse with her? Would there be children? A dog leaping up her chest? All those attributes of a cheerful family life? She should have asked him before consenting to his invitation, but she was too tired now to ask, too tired to change her mind, too tired to even tell her thoughts where to go. She let her eyelids close and gave in. She was immediately filled with fear. She was petrified by the possibility of losing Simon and fought hard to push back the picture of Simon lying pale and almost lifeless in the hospital bed.

She replaced it with a different one—from their night in Richmond. She had had no idea a man could be so tender, but she had forgotten the right reactions. So, just as she had done during the first massage he had given her five years ago, she relaxed into his hands and later into his whole body. Eileen felt her heart go wide and warm as the memory flooded her. It was more than love—a deeper emotion, forgiving, lenient and grateful, akin to breathing underwater.

She lost grasp on her thoughts and became aware of the vibrations of the car, the braking and accelerating, the bends, the purring noise of the motor. Something inside her wished that they would never come to a standstill, that they would drive through the night forever, that there were no more decisions to be made, no more obstacles to be overcome, no more pain to be warded off. Her life over the past five years had been a never-ending fight against the odds; she won a battle and then another, but the war she had already lost. And now there would be more fighting in store. Simon and Jessica. Traumas and injuries. It was too much, simply too much. Take the burden off me and let me fall, she prayed to some God of her own invention. It was not death she yearned for, just peace, silence and driving on forever.

"Eileen." Terry's gentle voice woke her. He was leaning over the open door.

"What? Where? Oh!" she exclaimed when she recognized him.

"We are here. I'll carry you up."

"I can walk," she said lamely.

"I live on the first floor. I've already taken up your crutches."

He bent down to lift her carefully out of the seat. "Is it okay? I'm not hurting you, am I?"

"No, not at all." It wasn't true. Her left shoulder was aching and her back felt crooked. But it couldn't be helped, her muscles were too flabby at that moment to support her efficiently. She put her hands around his neck, leaned her head against his chest and closed her eyes again. She heard him close the passenger door with a push of his foot. He walked up the steps to the front door. "I hope I'm not too heavy," she said, her voice muffled against the rough wool of his coat.

"You're a lightweight."

She was a boat lost in the vast ocean.

"Here we are. I'll put you down on the sofa."

She untangled her arms and they fell to her sides. The lighting was subdued, coming from a table lamp and a rectangle of light through the open door. She was far from home, suffering from hunger, thirst and fatigue, not to speak of the pain that had her in its firm grip now. One thing at a time, she commanded herself. But it was too late. The fit came quickly and developed its full intensity within a heartbeat. The nerves of her left leg were on fire, the left side of her body felt as if it were being folded backwards. She tried to breathe, but all she managed were throaty sobs. Desperately, she tried to do what Simon had taught her . . . to visualize waves running gently along a shoreline, back and forth, licking her feet that were rooted firmly in warm, soft sand. It didn't help this time. The gentle waves turned into fierce, froth-peaked breakers, the sand around her feet was swirled loose, her body was lifted and then smashed against the cutting sharpness of weather-beaten rocks. With an appalling mixture of horror and gratitude, she felt herself sinking into nothingness, the rushing and gushing of the waters around her getting louder and more distant at the same time. Her lungs burst with the saltiness of ocean water, giving no room for air, stifling her, gagging her even as she tried to cry for help.

Then she was on her back and someone was above her, breathing for her, breathing into her mouth until her breath was flowing on its own again. With a gurgle, the water receded, the rocks retreated into the depth of the sea and her body was washed ashore.

Eileen gasped and coughed, which caused new stings of pain. The cramp dissipated, leaving her sore and temporarily paralyzed. Terry was stroking back her fringe that was wet with sweat. She turned her head sideways and saw him kneeling on the carpet by the sofa.

"That was the worst fit I ever had," she whooped. "I think you saved my life."

"I want to get you some water and your tablets. Can I leave you alone for a moment?"

"Sure."

When he returned, he helped her to sit up. She swallowed the tablets, emptied the tumbler and leant against his shoulder. "What I need now is Simon's special variant of a Shiatsu massage. It would make me feel like a human being again."

"I'm afraid the only substitute on offer here is a bath. It's a Jacuzzi, very relaxing."

Floating in water, not drowning this time. "Sounds good." A small peristaltic wave, an after-effect of the fit, rippled down her left side.

"I'll go and run it for you."

"Wait. There's a problem. I can't get in and out alone."

"Then I'll help you. I suppose that dozens of doctors have seen you naked." More understandingly, he added. "I know how important it is for you to preserve a bit of decorum, but it can't be helped." Terry got up. "I'll come back to fetch you in a minute."

She took off her coat and shoes and looked around the room. It was large and sumptuous, with a cream-and-blue color scheme, multiple layers of carpets, comfortably upholstered sofas and chairs, floor-to-ceiling bookshelves, and a grand piano. Terry's living room was twice as big as her bedsit. It held the most impressive library Eileen had ever seen. There was a profusion of paraphernalia and souvenirs, the flotsam and jetsam of an interesting life. The books covered all horizontal surfaces, interspersed with journals and catalogues. Earmarked books were arranged in untidy piles. The coziness was brought to perfection by a large grandfather clock, swinging its pendulum with slow dignity, and the warm glow of dancing flames from the fireplace. Eileen felt much better just from taking in the atmosphere of the room. Terry had leaned her crutches against the couch. The effect of her medicine was setting in and she found the energy to stand up and walk over to the piano. The wood was black, as polished and shiny as Jessica's tap shoes. She touched it reverently, lifted the lid and tried to play the tune of *Oh Come, All Ye Faithful* with one finger. On the mantelpiece, she saw a photo in a gilded frame. With a slight sense of trespassing, she went to have a closer look at it. Terry, some ten years younger, was with a man apparently a few years older than he, fair and handsome. They were leaning, side by side, against the same grand piano she had just desecrated and were smiling into the camera. The older man's arm was round Terry's shoulder.

"His name was Michael," Terry, who had come back, said in a strangely solemn voice. "Your bath is ready."

The bathroom was all veined marble and golden fittings. Terry had laid out a fluffy white towel and a pair of blue flannel pajamas for her. I must be dreaming, she decided.

"Here, sit down on that stool," he instructed her. "Which fragrance would you prefer, lavender or cedar?"

"Lavender, please." She watched Terry pour the scented oil with graceful movements. His hands were that of a younger man, fineboned and smooth.

"I'll leave you alone now. Call when you need me."

She undressed, neatly folded her clothes, had a pee and considered climbing into the tub alone. No, it was too dangerous. With her back to the door, she called for him. He remained practical, asked her how to help her best and a moment later she was in the water. "Is the temperature right?"

"It's perfect." Velvety warmth enveloped her.

He explained to her how to adjust the Jacuzzi and left her alone. She experimented with the three settings of the jet streams and found the medium intensity perfect. She had never been in a whirlpool before. The massage stimulated and relaxed her at the same time. The tub was large enough for two persons and perfectly molded to receive the form of her body. She spread her arms and legs and bent them again. It was easy to move in the warm, gurgling water. The sinking feeling was anodyne to her senses.

Terry returned a few minutes later with a cup. "I want to make sure that you don't fall asleep in the water. Do you like it?"

"I love it."

"I've brought you some tea."

If this Jacuzzi was heaven, then he was an angel. "Thank you." She took the cup and emptied it. "I could cry with relief. You've saved my life a second time."

He smiled down at her. "Fine. I hope you like ham and cheese sandwiches. I've also got chicken salad."

"Sounds splendid."

"I'll have a shower now."

Eileen looked at the shower cabin in a corner of the room. "Here?"

"No, in the other bathroom," he laughed.

Two bathrooms. She shook her head. What luxury. It was probably a housemaid who had lit the fire in the library for his return—and he was just a DI. Most peculiar. It was good, though, to busy the mind with trivia. She counted the tiles, listened to the bubbling of the Jacuzzi and found life agreeable for a change. Although her thoughts were still running around Jessica and Simon, she managed to put the troubled part of her mind at rest and enjoyed the delicacy of the bubbling water that felt like a twenty-handed Simon. When Terry returned he was dressed in pajamas and a gown, both of burgundy silk.

"Time for dinner," he announced, switched off the jet and helped Eileen up. He wrapped a towel around her and made her sit down once more on the stool. Then he crouched in front of her and gently began to rub her shins.

"I don't need your help with the towel, Terry—em, Rick," she said, both embarrassed and amused.

"Of course. I was just . . . em . . . You'll find me in the living room."

The air of confusion became him. What a remarkable man—caring, soft-spoken and reliable. It was good to be with him. Eileen dried herself slowly and put on the pajamas. She had to turn up the sleeves and trouser legs twice. It was the third night in a row she would spend in a bed not her own, dressed in a man's pajamas—first Simon's, then Alan's and now Terry's. She was really getting around these days.

Terry had started to play on the grand piano. Eileen listened with delight as she went to join him. She sat on a chair which allowed her to see his profile. His parted lips moved in a silent recital with the flow of the Chopin nocturne. The repetitive tune of the left hand carried the melody to a superb musical climax.

"Beautiful," she said warmly when the last note had died away.

They sat down side by side on the sofa where he had laid a low table. At the first bite into a sandwich, Eileen realized that she was even hungrier than she had thought and for a while all she could do was eat. He looked pleased about her appetite and asked her if she'd like a glass of wine.

Time had gained new qualities. It seemed dense like a viscous liquid, opaque like frosted glass. It was no longer measurable in minutes or hours. For a stretch of time he couldn't name, David had been sitting by Jessica's side, holding her cold fingers, looking at her closed eyelids until dusk and beyond. The colors had taken on shades of gray, the red petals on the floor had turned black when the night fell. Without shadows moving, the darkness crept in like air getting thicker with smoke, as if all the undisturbed dust of the last year had been sent flying.

Guarding Jessica was like watching a snowflake fall to earth all the way down from the sky in endlessly slow motion. Yet, time was moving—the snowflake would touch the ground, Jessica would wake up. She would.

She was such an important part of his life. She was connected with the most recent watersheds. It was not a coincidence he had chosen five stages of punishment for her. His life could also be broken down into five stages. There was the time until Dominic's birth and death. Before that David had felt secure, sure that everything would always work out for him the way he expected it to. His career, his love life, his marriage, his family. Susan's miscarriage had been a crack in a perfect picture. The second stage had been the year when he hadn't known where to turn, what to make of it all. It was the first crisis in his life. Running away was the only option, away from friends who kept asking when he and Sue would have another child, away from dancers who complained he no longer had the authority to lead a troupe. The move to London had been lifesaving.

And there he had met Jessica and entered stage three. His authority returned, his ability to love, his hope to have a boy. The day she called him into her dressing room, quietly telling him that she was no longer going to meet him once weekly, David had felt the shift from stage three to four, like a train being set on different rails, rails that lead nowhere. A dull throbbing had engulfed him, suffocated him.

Insofar, stage five was a relief. The first shock over on Saturday night after the party, he had somewhere to go. The burning of his phantom pain fired an engine that drove him on. He wouldn't leave the tracks now. The course was set.

At intervals, David felt Jessica's pulse, massaged her body to stimulate blood circulation, moistened her mouth with water and said her name. With the fading of daylight, his voice had turned lower, his thoughts milder. It touched him that Susan and Jessica, who were so different, had both wished to kill themselves for him. Only Jessica, as always, had been the valiant one. She had made the step over the threshold. Fortunately, her dedication hadn't been strong enough to take her all the way. When he had found her, the cut on her wrist had almost stopped bleeding.

It was so important that she lived, that she understood he was doing all this for her; not for himself, not for as foolish a concept as revenge. By trying to kill herself for him, she had shown that she had already learned the cardinal lesson. Submission. So he could abandon stages three to five of his plan, couldn't he? It had worked. This time it had worked. The last time he had failed fatally. His first plan had turned into a terrible defeat. The layout had been simple. He wanted to make Jessica pregnant, thus forcing her to put her cards on the table, to stand by him and quit Roger.

Jessica wasn't on the pill because Roger had been sterilized. David used condoms. Each time before they met he would pierce holes in them, right through the plastic wrapping. He knew from his and Susan's visits to countless gynecologists that making a woman pregnant wasn't that easy. The quantity of semen that went inside the uterus had to be sufficient. He wasn't discouraged when nothing happened during the first months. He cut larger holes into the condoms. If Jessica noticed he could always blame the rubber. He waited and hoped in vain. At least, that was how the situation had looked by the time Jessica broke off the relationship.

Since Saturday night he knew that, in truth, he had been close to success. Jessica had been pregnant, she had carried his child, his boy. Dominic had had a second chance and David hadn't known about it. Jessica had killed the boy without even bothering to tell him. He was fairer than she had been, wasn't he? He had given Jessica time to plead for Alan's life, while he had stood no chance to save his boy's life. But instead of fighting, Jessica had yielded to despair. Seen like this, her attempted suicide no longer seemed heroic to him but cowardly. Did she deserve a chance at all when it was so obvious that she wasn't able to love?

Jessica moaned, and her body stirred slightly. David touched her cheek. "Jessica. Wake up. Come on, say something." He felt her lips move and began to feed her crumbs of crackers and drops of water. She needed salt and carbohydrates to compensate for the loss of blood. Finally, her eyes opened. He couldn't see it in the darkness, but her lashes brushed against his fingertips.

"Jessica, can you hear me?"

She didn't answer. Maybe she was having one of her blackouts. He told her who she was and where she was. She remained still. He explained the situation to her.

"You remember? I told you I was going to kill Alan." No reaction. He had to get harsher. "I will have to leave you soon. I must walk all the way to the theatre. When I've completed my task, I'll take the car. It's still there. I'll be back before sunrise. And then I'll tell you Alan's last words." Even this provoked no reaction. "The rest will be over quickly. I'll untie your feet, put on your shoes and then you will dance for me. Gather your strength, my rosebud. It will be your last dance. Remember? Stage four, the stem will be broken. I intend to shoot you in the knee."

Was there a response? A pained murmur?

"Stage five is my final gift of love to you. I will kill myself. I am the third man who will die for you, my beautiful rose. After that you must somehow make your way downstairs and out of the house to call for help. You'll be in a state of shock. That will help you to deal with the pain. I'm sure you'll make it."

His hand turned wet with her tears. So she had understood him. Would she beg him not to do it? He was prepared to let her off the last stages of her punishment. If only she said the right thing.

"Stop crying, Jessica. I have used my clean handkerchief to bandage your wrist."

He got up. Would she ask him to stay?

"Please," she whispered.

He turned around expectantly, feeling his engine slow down and the pulse of his throbbing grow softer. Then she made a mistake, such a silly little mistake.

"Protect me," she whimpered, "please, Roger, protect me."

Terry was once more amazed how quickly Eileen could change. He had never seen her so relaxed. "Are you warm enough?" he asked, for her feet were bare.

"Sure. I'm warm, well-fed and a mite tipsy." The soft glow of her cheeks underlined her words.

Terry began to unwind. He found her company restful. An hour or two ago, when he had dreaded that she could die, when her agony had pervaded his body as well, he had been thoroughly shaken and momentarily on the edge of panic—but his job had taught him to remain self-controlled against all odds. Later, in the bath, there had been emotions of a different kind that he preferred to dissemble. The sight of her body had touched him deeply—to think that she was actually living inside it. Everything was askew, lop-sided, her hip bones jutting and displaced, her skin criss-crossed with scars from many operations. She was so emaciated he could see the outline of muscles under her transparent skin. She looked like an athlete in danger of starvation. He hadn't felt repulsion but deep affection, a tenderness of an unexpected sort, different from the sexual desire a man's body could arouse in him. The disturbing sensation had been intensified by the memory of something he had seen in her flat when he had searched for her medicine: a blown-up photograph on her bookshelf that showed a comely young woman in a swim-suit standing on a beach. She was about twenty-five, tanned, well-proportioned. Long brown hair fell over her shoulders. She shaded her eyes against the sun and smiled. It was the smile that had made him recognize that this was a younger Eileen, unharmed and optimistic. The contrast to her present condition was painful, even for him, but what would it be like for her? And why had she framed and displayed the photograph that could only serve to remind her of what she had lost?

She had finished her meal. Terry put an arm around her shoulder and drew her toward him. He had become more confident in handling her and no longer felt the need to screen his feelings. Her head against his heart she asked where they were.

St. John's Wood, he told her and began to stroke her sunken cheek. His fingers softly traced the groove of scar tissue. His other hand raked through her hair upwards from her neck. She pushed a hand against his chest and withdrew.

"I'm sorry," he said, "but there's no need to worry. Nothing will happen. It's impossible, you know."

She looked at him with puckered brows. "You don't have to tell me."

"Oh, no, you're misunderstanding. It's not because of what you are, but because of what I am."

She tilted her head. "Impotent?"

"No, gay."

She giggled. "What am I supposed to say now? That I'm shocked, or that I've always dreamed of seducing a homosexual man? Sorry, I'm afraid I drank too much wine." She nestled up to him again. "Who pays for your luxurious lifestyle?"

"I inherited this house from Michael, the man I lived with for ten years. You saw him on the photo. He was an interior decorator. He died of lung cancer two years ago. He led such a healthy life, and I used to chain-smoke. I'm not sure if I'll ever forgive myself."

"He might have contracted cancer anyway. I don't believe in the value of statistics for individual cases. That's why I don't care that my chances to benefit from an artificial knee aren't all too great."

An artificial knee? Terry remembered reading something about it only recently. Where had it been? In Simon's flat, on some notes he had taken down in Richmond. "Are you going to be operated on by this Professor Johnson?"

"Yes, though I'm no longer sure if I can carry it out now that Simon is so badly off." She watched as he poured her another glass of wine. "What was it that you wanted to ask me about forgiveness?"

The question caught Terry unawares. "Uhm, that was when I was on duty and my world was divided into categories of crime and punishment. That I've brought you here doesn't mean I took work home with me."

"I'd really like to know what it was."

"Please forget it."

"Shall I have to wait until tomorrow when you're on duty again?"

"Okay, but I know I'll regret it." How could he ask her without giving away too much? "What was the hardest time you had forgiving someone?" he worded carefully.

She put her right foot gingerly on the sofa and hugged her knee. "I can't tell you, it's too personal."

"It has to do with the fire, hasn't it?"

She showed him her profile and nodded. "To know that it needn't have happened. That I could still be . . . ." She said no more.

"So you knew that it was Jessica—"

"Jessica?" Her head swung in his direction. "What has the fire got to do with Jessica?"

"Well, I thought she told you."

"Told me what?"

"That she was responsible for the outbreak of the fire."

Eileen shook her head. "I don't see how she could have been. What are you talking about?"

"I shouldn't have mentioned it. Honestly, I'm sorry."

"Too late for a retreat. My fantasies might be worse than your truth."

"Alan told me that on the day before the fire Jessica forgot to switch off the electric heater and that this caused—"

"What?" she cut in. "I can't believe it! Oh, Jesus Christ and all the Saints in Heaven. This is . . . it's so absolutely dreadful."

Her face had turned all red and glowing. What had he done? She let go of her knee and covered her mouth with her shaking hands. "Poor Jessica. Poor, dear Jessica. Why didn't they ask me? Why does Alan always think he must protect others? God, in all those years Jessica thought that she was responsible for the fire. I wish she were here now and I could take the burden from her." She was biting her fingertips now. What she said didn't make sense to Terry.

"What do you mean?"

"I told you that Jessica and I were flatmates at that time, didn't I? I had soon found out how scatterbrained she was. She forgot to shut the fridge, to lock the door, to switch off the lights when she left, and even to flush the toilet. She was hopeless. And I knew of course that she went to the studio every day, also during holidays. On that morning when I was at the theatre all alone, the first thing I did was to check if Jessica had left open a window or the lights on when she had practiced the day before. Sure enough, I found the heater turned on and switched it off. I bloody well switched it off!" Eileen kneaded her calves with trembling fingers.

So Jessica had taken the blame for nothing. What a terrible misunderstanding.

Eileen turned to him. "Can you see why I'm so agitated? I never thought of telling anyone about the heater. It was a minor detail, a matter of routine. How could I have known that it was of significance? They told me the fire was caused by a short-circuit, and that's probably exactly how it happened. Maybe the center of the fire was indeed in the studio where Jessica had danced. The heater might have had a short-circuit because it was so bloody old. It makes me mad with anger."

"I'm sorry." Terry took her hand but she withdrew it immediately.

"No, don't say that. I'm glad you told me. Now I can rectify things." She let out her breath between half-closed lips. "I have to put things right. Where is Jessica? I must tell her it wasn't her fault."

"Doesn't it hurt you to think that Jessica only helped you because she wanted to make good what she had done to you?"

Eileen grew calmer. "No, not much. It makes a bit of a difference, but it's the outcome that counts, not the motive—and our friendship stands on firm ground now. I told you a lot of unpleasant things about her because they are true. I love her with all her shortcomings and faults. None of us is perfect, not even Alan who always sees himself as the heart and soul of his troupe. He tends to forget that people have a will of their own." She immediately wiped her words away with a quick movement of her right hand.

"I shouldn't say that about him. He's like a mother to Jessica."

"Mothers can be bothersome." Terry stood up, gathered the empty plates on the tray and carried it into the kitchen. When he returned he saw a new storm gathering on Eileen's face. She looked up at him with a sternness that would have done the Spanish Inquisition proud.

"I've got you sussed. You suspected me, didn't you? You assumed I hated Jessica for what you thought she had done to me."

"I did, but not for long."

"Did you take me home with you to keep me under surveillance?"

He sat down again by her side and put a hand on her shoulder. "No. I did it because I wanted to make sure you're not alone tonight."

She let out a long sigh. "Of course. And I'm glad I'm here with you. I overreacted."

Terry felt relieved that the question was cleared. Jessica hadn't caused the fire, and Eileen hadn't got a motive any longer. But if it wasn't Jessica whom she had to forgive, who was it then? He asked her, but all at once he knew the answer before her reply.

"Myself. I had to forgive myself for my misplaced panic. I should have waited for the fire brigade. It took me years to accept that I wasn't acting rationally at that moment."

"I see," he said. "I saw the photograph on your bookshelf. Doesn't it hurt you to look at it?"

"It helps me to keep the young and healthy Eileen alive within me. To a certain degree, that is." She leant against him once more, and as her pain had transferred into him earlier this evening, so did her weariness now.

"I think I should take you to bed," he said and hooked his arms under her back and knees. He had become very fond of carrying her. When he had laid her down and covered her with the sheets, he went for her crutches and propped them against the bedside table.

"Is the bed comfortable?"

"It is. But I don't think I'll be able to sleep. There's too much on my mind."

"Then I'll sing you a lullaby."

Eileen pressed his hand. "You're starting to mother me, too."

Go to sleep my little one, he sang for her. At first, Eileen giggled and wriggled a bit, then she responded to the soporific tune, her breathing becoming slow and her hands falling open. Terry was touched by the very intimacy of witnessing this beautiful surrender.

Chapter Fifteen

Restlessly, Roger ambled through the house, upstairs and downstairs, from room to room, opening and closing doors, cupboards, drawers. The police had searched his house. There was nothing left for him to find, no clue as to what might have happened to Jessica. He had lost his trust in the efficiency of the police. He knew he shouldn't complain. Inspector Terry took the case seriously enough, but he concentrated too much on the psychological aspects, as if to satisfy his own curiosity.

It was late. He should go to sleep. He looked at his bed and found it impossible even to fold back the duvet. In the bathroom, he stared at his mirror reflection. Bloodshot eyes, slack cheeks, unkempt hair; the cliché of a desperate man. Why had he sent Jessica to sleep in the guest room on that critical night when she had asked for his protection? He touched the few items on the board that belonged to her. Toothbrush, lipstick, cream pots. There was so little in this house that she owned. She had never made herself really at home here. A guest in his house. A guest in his life.

With a shudder, he passed the guest room and went downstairs. There, in the entry hall, was her rucksack, made of garish red leather. Maybe there was too little brightness in this house. All was cream-colored, or blue, or mahogany. If she felt at home in the kaleidoscopic interior of The Caesar, she couldn't possibly warm to these distinguished surroundings and their muted colors. He should have encouraged Jessica to contribute to the decoration.

Roger fumbled inside the rucksack and took out Jessica's bunch of keys. The fob was a miniature tap shoe, a wedding present from Eileen. Inspector Terry had given the keys a lot of attention. He had wanted to know if there was a key missing. They had sifted through the keys together. Roger had recognized those for the front door of their house, the garage, the red Renault and the white Mercedes. The remaining three keys, he guessed, were for The Caesar. Front door, stage door and probably another door inside, the electrician's room, say.

"How about a key for your office in Bloomsbury?" Terry had asked.

"She doesn't have one." He could have added that Jessica didn't even know exactly where his office was, for she had never been there. She had the phone number, that was all. A loving wife, indeed. And yet, he missed her so. He had seen her potential to change.

Roger took the keys into the living room and spread them out on the couch table. What about the three keys for The Caesar? Two of them, made of steel and looking new, were keys for safety cylinder locks, so they certainly belonged to the front and stage door. The third was a brass Yale-type key and had a square head. It was old, stained and greasy, the web rounded by use. He saw keys like this one very often when he showed clients around old houses. Well, The Caesar was an old house, but it had been rebuilt and renovated only five years ago. All locks, he was sure, had been replaced. So if the key didn't belong to the theatre, where did it belong? He could call Alan and ask. Roger glanced at his watch and saw that it was past midnight. Alan's phone didn't ring at night. He could drive there and have a look himself, taking the opportunity to look for clues in Jessica's dressing room. No, the police had done that after Simon had been stabbed. The violence of this crime cast a dark shadow on his faint hope to find Jessica alive.

He wished the night wouldn't last so long. The day had already seemed endless. After the house search, he had walked all the way around Primrose Hill again, hoping for a miracle to happen, for Jessica to come to meet him, apologizing for being late. He had stood in front of the house where this old man had seen Jessica. It had the number 102 in golden lettering on a green door. One of the many empty houses in the vicinity. Had she really been persuaded to get into a car? Whose car? Why?

Back home, he had a most awkward phone conversation with Jessica's father. Having never met his in-laws, he had no idea how to socialize with them at such a difficult time. He tried not to upset them further, tried to play it down. He didn't mention the car, and with it the possibility of a kidnapping, because Mr. Gresham clung to the theory that Jessica had done a bunk.

Roger considered getting drunk, substituting sleep with a delirium of sorts. Without sleep, how would he get through the next day? He had an appointment with Inspector Terry early the next morning and . . . Oh, no. He had forgotten to take home Jessica's file from his office this evening. He was beginning to be as absent-minded as Jessica. Well, was this silly folder so important?

"We couldn't find your wife's documents," Terry had said. "Birth certificate, employment contract and so on."

"I have them all in a file in my office," Roger had told him reluctantly. "I hope you're not going to search the office as well."

"All I want is to have a look at the folder."

"Then send round a constable to fetch it this afternoon."

"That is not the proper procedure. You must be present when I go through the papers."

And so they had agreed on meeting at the police station on

Friday morning.

Roger decided that, since he wasn't able to sleep anyway, he might as well drive to Bloomsbury and get the folder. On his way back, he could pass The Caesar and test into which of the locks the keys fitted.

Images of rape and violation in gruesome variations were on Susan's mind all the time as she walked her erratic course through the streets of London. She had spent the day at the Barbican Center in commemoration of the penultimate happy day of her life, two years ago, when she and David had enjoyed a wonderful time there, looking at the Foyer Exhibition, strolling through the Art Gallery, watching a film at the cinema, taking afternoon tea at the Cappuccino Bar, holding hands and kissing furtively during a Shakespeare play at the Barbican Theatre. It had been a new beginning after the crisis they had been through in New York.

The following day David had received the invitation to an interview at The Caesar, and the day after that he had met Jessica. Subconsciously, Susan had been aware from then on that something had changed, but she had flinched from analyzing what it was that estranged David from her. In her obsequious way, she had accepted his retreat.

Her mind was weary. This morning she had found herself unable to face another day alone at home. She had decided that she would inundate her bereaved little soul with nostalgia. She would suffer once and then move on to a future yet unknown. In this grimly optimistic mood, she had started her excursion. Soon a sense of defeat undermined her resolve and she was forced to admit that what had really taken her to the Barbican was the hope of finding David wandering the same paths of memory.

She lost her way more than once in the vast complex, and found that losing her way was so symptomatic and symbolic for her current state of mind that it felt like coming home, like being herself in a basic sense.

She bought a ticket for a comedy at The Pit. As if to spite her, the play on show was *Three Hours After Marriage*. There was adultery in it, bigamy and a kidnapping. Susan left after the first half.

Walking alone through the nighttime streets, she remembered how afraid she had always been in New York when she had had to walk home at night, her hand tightly wrapped around the butt of the pistol in her coat pocket. Now, although David had the pistol, Susan felt better protected than ever. With a fierceness new to her, she thought how splendid it would be if someone tried to rape her now. She was in the perfect mood to hit the assassin back with all force, to pour all her hatred out at an unknown aggressor. That grubby young man who was shambling toward her, for instance. Come on, rape me. Try me. Let's see who is stronger. She would kick him in the privates. Boom—slash—wang. She would give the bastard what he deserved. Anger was the coarse side of despair. Or was this how you felt when you stopped taking antidepressants and began sliding back into your own personality?

She didn't know for sure in which direction she was walking and why she didn't hail a taxi when it started to snow. To her surprise, she saw Brunswick Shopping Center in front of her as she turned the next corner. She wasn't far from The Caesar. Simon lived just a few houses away. Simon, who was in hospital now. The police had called late last night to ask if David was with her. David was suspected of having attacked Simon. If David had also killed Jessica, it would be a perfect tragedy, wouldn't it? The adulterer killing his girlfriend, when she, the wife, was the one who should kill for jealousy.

She was losing her mind. She was thinking about rape and murder as if those were natural human interactions. The only person who could save her was Alan, of course. Tonight she would accept his invitation and sleep in Cindy's bed, and next week she

would start working for him again. It hadn't been fair of her to let
him down. She had missed two belly-dancing classes today and
hoped that Alan had been able to find a substitute for her.

David passed Roger's house, turned into Albert Terrace and
began to run, the heavy coat flapping around his knees, the pistol
in its inner pocket knocking against his hips.

Protect me, Roger.

He ran faster. What made him feel like hunted game? Guilt?
Urgency to bring his mission to an end? It was stupid. He was
going to attract someone's attention. He slowed down, but the
impulse to run took over again. There were steps, not behind him,
but inside him. Quick, heavy steps. Whoom, whoom, like a double
of Jessica stomping a tribal dance. When he had to stop at the
traffic lights, he realized what it was. His severed self, throbbing
louder than ever, driving him on mercilessly. There was no way to
outrun it. If he walked all the way to The Caesar, the throbbing
would soon drive him crazy. He decided to better take a small risk,
flagged down a passing taxi and said, "Euston Station, please."

Protect me, Roger.

Why did women, even such self-confident creatures like
Jessica, appeal to a man's protective instinct? And why did men
slip into their roles so naturally? David had always protected
Susan. Two years ago, when they had been at the Barbican Center,
an oil painting had hung in the exhibition showing a woman with
a sleeping baby in her arms. The pale child's limp body had looked
like a corpse. Instinctively, David had taken Susan by the elbow
and shoved her away from the painting before she could see it.

Susan had never spoken those words, *David protect me*, but
her passive manner had perfectly communicated her need to be
held, shielded and spared the truths of life. Did she also feel phantom pain now, the burning of a severed self, the part of her that
still loved David? What would she do until she found another

man? Or rather, until another man found her, since she was such a passive individual. She wouldn't kill herself, he was sure. Her act with the pistol had been a showpiece, the classical tableau of a broken heart.

David paid the driver and got out. For a second, he was without orientation. What was he doing here? Alan was just a nice, harmless, slightly perverse artist. He hadn't stolen Jessica's love from David. Alan was completely unaware of Jessica's devotion, like a rich man ignorant of other people's poverty. David didn't hate Alan. Now that he came to think of it, he felt certain that he had never hated anyone. He was a saint, not a killer.

An onrush of snowflakes, driven by a cold wind, made him shiver. The cold permeated his motionless body and, as if in self-defense, the burning inside him set in, sending waves of heat through his veins. David could feel his severed self take over. The phantom pain grew so strong that it blocked out all other notions. The engine was back on track. Stage three waited to be carried out and The Caesar was just around the corner.

You must never tell anyone, not even if your or my life depended on it.

Eileen woke up with this sentence in her mind like a loudspeaker announcement. Jessica had said this to her when she had disclosed her biggest secret, that she was in love with Alan.

Why was she thinking of it now? Was it a message from her subconscious? What, Eileen's slowly oncoming rationale pondered, what if someone else's life depended on it? Alan's life. Suddenly she understood. She called Terry's name, but the door panel and the goblins on the walls seemed to swallow every sound. Automatically, she had already started her usual process of flexing and stretching her muscles to prepare her body for getting up. Her heart was thumping when she finally sat with her legs dangling over the edge of the high bed. Eileen ignored the needles of pain in her left leg. She found a lamp on the bedside table, switched it on and reached for her crutches.

"Rick," she shouted once more when she was in the corridor. Seconds later, a door opened.

"Eileen?" He looked at her with concern. "What's the matter?"

"We must warn Alan. I think he's in danger."

"Come in." He motioned her inside his bedroom and he held up the sheets for her. Gratefully she crept into the pocket of warmth.

"Why do you think Alan is in danger?"

"Because Jessica is in love with Alan. And if David knows . . . she might have told him. It's all a bit vague, I know." Her shoulders sagged. She felt foolish all of a sudden. She wasn't even convinced that it was David who had attacked Simon. "It was just an idea."

"Jessica is in love with Alan? Tell me about it," he encouraged her.

"She doesn't really fancy him. It's different, difficult to explain—and nobody is supposed to know. That's why I haven't told you before."

"So, if no one knows, where's the problem?"

"On Wednesday after you had interviewed me, Alan asked me if it was true that Jessica was in love with him. So he knew. Jessica must have mentioned it when she chased David away on Saturday night. She had completely lost control over what she said."

He snapped his fingers. "Jessica told David, Susan heard it and she's the one who told Alan." He picked up the phone.

"It's no use calling Alan. His extension doesn't ring at night. Unless he's awake and sees the little light blinking, he won't notice."

He tried nevertheless, but there was no answer. "I'll send someone round to the theatre to warn Alan and to give him my home number so he can call back."

It was a futile thing to do, but Roger couldn't help it. Steering his car, he kept looking at the pavement, scanning everybody he saw for a resemblance to Jessica. Luckily, there was hardly anyone around at this hour. Driving by day with all the masses of pedestrians had turned into an ordeal.

In his office, he went straight for the file and was about to leave when it struck him that he should have a look at its contents to make sure there was nothing in it that threw a bad light on him. He was, after all, a suspect in the case.

He switched on the halogen spot on his desk and opened the folder. The documents were filed in reverse order, on top the newest, Jessica's life insurance. Roger rubbed the root of his nose. Life insurance is always a delicate matter. He had taken out the insurance policy shortly after their marriage, together with a health and liability insurance for Jessica, who had never wasted a thought on these practical matters. With a sigh, he turned the pages and skimmed through their marriage certificate, Jessica's rental agreement for Eileen's flat, her contracts with The Caesar as a dancer and before that as a dance teacher, her O-levels, her registration as a pupil at several dance classes and her birth certificate. Roger leaned back and rested his chin on his fingertips. Something had registered in his mind, a minor detail. He shook his head. His tired, tortured brain was unable to concentrate. Slowly, he shifted the papers back over the metal ring and closed the lid. His fingers nervously tapped the desk. To be sure nothing had escaped his attention, he opened the folder again and scrutinized the documents once more.

He let out a cry of bafflement when he found it. Was it possible? Had he found a trace? *Jessica Gresham, 102 Regents Park Road*. That was the address given in her registration as a pupil at The Caesar in 1982. It was the address of the empty house at the corner of Chalcot Crescent, the very house in front of which Jessica had last been seen on Tuesday morning. That was too significant to be dismissed as a coincidence. There had to be a connection.

Roger reached for his phone, then had second thoughts. At the police station, the night shift was on duty. They wouldn't understand the importance of what he had unearthed. All they would do would be to send round a constable to knock at the door. Thinking of doors immediately shifted his attention to Jessica's bunch of keys. The old, greasy key. It might belong to the empty house. Why had she never told him about it?

He broke into a sweat. Although he had no fixed idea what his findings indicated and was too excited to figure it out, he knew beyond doubt that he had found the clue that would enable him to do what Jessica had asked him for. He hadn't protected her in time, but maybe it wasn't too late to rescue her.

Alan was awakened by two things at the same time. The light on his phone was blinking and Ginger and Fred had started to croak. He yawned. When he fumbled with the receiver the blinking had already stopped. Alan sat up and switched on the light. There were steps in the corridor. "Susan?"

The bedroom door swung open and someone came in. Alan squinted. He was too short-sighted to recognize at once who it was. "Susan?" he asked again.

"I'm sorry I have to disappoint you. Is she a regular nightly guest in your bed?"

The familiar snooty voice. "Oh, it's you David. The police are looking for Susan. That's why I thought it might be her."

"They are looking for Susan?" He sounded edgy. "They are searching for me as well, aren't they?"

Alan didn't know what to say. He couldn't read David's expression. Alan smiled to pacify David and got up to step closer.

"Stay where you are," David said sharply.

Alan shrank back when he saw what David held in his right hand. Not Susan but David had the handgun Terry had mentioned.

Scared, but trying not to show it, Alan offered, "You can hide here, if you want to."

"Hide?" David laughed. "You're always so considerate, aren't you? Must be the reason why Jessica is smitten with you."

"Jessica? Do you know where she is?" Alan asked.

"She's at the place where we used to meet to make love, waiting for my return." He moved from the door to a place opposite the bed. "Waiting to hear your famous last words—because I have come to shoot you."

Alan began to tremble. Nothing made sense. "You mean, Jessica sent you to kill me?"

"You don't understand anything at all but it doesn't matter what you think. The important thing is that Jessica understands that I am doing this for her, to teach her the meaning of love and submission. Sit down on your bed."

Slowly, Alan followed the order. "And after you've shot me? What will you do?" Alan asked to gain time, feeling as unreal as a cartoon. "Will you flee with Jessica?"

"She won't be able to go anywhere because the next bullet is for her knee."

With a voice that sounded to him as if it were a recording played back to his moving lips, Alan asked, "David, you didn't stab Simon, did you? You wouldn't hurt someone who's your friend."

"Are you trying to talk me into a guilty conscience? Friends, God, as if I've ever had any in this city." David took a few steps back until he was against the wall, as if thinking of Simon had unsettled him and made him feel vulnerable without rear cover. "Actually, I did it," he said in a taut voice.

"David, what is all this about?" He had to be insane. What could stop him from pulling the trigger now, when he had had no scruples about forcing Jessica's screwdriver into Simon's back?

"It's about Dominic, my boy. He was so tiny, but so perfect already. There was nothing wrong with him. No one had an explanation why he died."

What was the connection between Susan's miscarriage and Jessica? "Let's be reasonable, David. Put down that thing in your hand. We can talk about—"

"He had a second chance. He was even tinier when he died this time. She killed him. She stopped his heartbeat once more. She doesn't deserve my love." For a moment, David lowered the pistol. "If only I could hate Jessica for this, then I wouldn't have to kill you."

Blockley had just arrived for the second night shift at the police station when he got Terry's call. He had thought it better not to send a constable who didn't know his way around in the building but to drive to The Caesar himself. He parked his car on the other side of the street. He saw a light in one of the dormer windows on the second floor. So Alan was still awake. Looking down again, he saw someone unlock the front door. It was Susan. Quickly, Blockley got out, followed her and reached the door before it swung shut. Susan was going up in the elevator. Blockley took the stairs. When he rounded the stairs at the first landing, the elevator came to a halt on the second floor. Blockley felt a sudden sense of urgency and began to take two steps at a time. He was at the door of Alan's flat when he heard a scream and simultaneously a shot. In the dead silence that followed, Blockley cursed that he hadn't brought a second man with him and stepped inside. The next moment, David was coming toward him. When he saw Blockley, he hesitated for a second, then aimed a pistol at him. "Get out of my way," he hissed.

Blockley lifted his hands and let David pass, then he went to the room that was lit. Susan's golden hair was streaked with red. She lay halfway across the bed, her head and upper body diagonally over Alan's chest. Alan lifted his hands and stared at them. "It's blood. Oh, my God. Susan? Susan!"

Blockley put his fingertips on Susan's artery. "She's dead," he stated and shifted the body to free Alan and check if he was injured. Then he was on the phone to arrange for the pursuit of David.

"But . . . he wanted to kill me. Not her, me," Alan jabbered and began to weep, muttering incoherently about a drowning mermaid.

Chapter Sixteen

It's your fault. Don't forget this for a second. It is entirely your fault that Alan has to die.

With these words, David had left Jessica. The echo of his voice was in her head, which was aching as if it had been screwed into a vice. She tried to recall the things he had said before, about killing himself. She wasn't sure. The pain in her head had been like a noise, blocking out most of his words. Jessica stirred to change her position. There was a sharp stinging at her right wrist.

It's your fault that Alan has to die.

The mist in her head cleared slowly. David was on his way to The Caesar. He had said that he would shoot Alan, return in his car and then . . . Something with her knees. Jessica moaned. Better to leave the memory hazy. Better not to think about it, to withdraw to somewhere far away from reality, inside herself where she'd be safe.

It's your fault. Your fault.

It was no longer David's voice. It was her Mum's. Mum coming back from the hairdresser's, her smooth black hair permed to a frizzle. Jessica cried out in shock. "Mum, what have they done to your hair?" Dad, sitting on the sofa, went all pale. "It looks nice.

Takes a little getting used to, but . . ." He couldn't finish his sentence because Mum was hitting him with her handbag. "It's your fault. You said you wanted me to change my looks and now see what they've done."

That wasn't true. Jessica knew it wasn't. Her Dad had told Mum to be careful with experiments, hadn't he? What was happening? Why was she hitting him again? Why was she always hitting him when something went wrong?

Dad lifted his hands over his face. "Send Jess upstairs," he said, but Mum wouldn't listen. She never listened to Dad. Jessica disappeared into the far corner of the living room. She covered her ears, pressed her eyelids together, but she knew without looking or listening what would happen. Mum would use her fists while her Dad would shrink, make himself smaller, shield himself with his trembling hands. Then she would kick his shins until her temper had subsided.

It was always the same procedure. Whenever something didn't go exactly according to Mum's wishes, Dad had to take the blame. Afterward, Jessica would help him to cool his bruises. He'd just sit there, on the stool in the bathroom, smiling sheepishly and apologizing. "I'm sorry you had to see this Jessica. Your mother's got a wild temperament, you know."

Sometimes it was so bad that there was blood dripping from Dad's lips, red stains on his shirtfront and on the bathroom floor, smelling of defeat, of weakness, and of guilt. She had never found the courage to defend Dad. She often felt like hitting him, too, in order to wipe that stupid smile from his face. There were moments when Jessica wanted to be like her mother, with strong kicking legs and an air of invincibility. But most of the time Jessica was sorry for her Dad and wished he would hit back. Maybe he was afraid of Mum's cold-bloodedness, for there was nothing uncontrolled in her demeanor, no perfervid anger. Did she feel anything at all when she was beating up Dad?

Then, amazingly, the painful scenes stopped when Jessica was about twelve. She soon discovered that this was because her Mum was having an affair. Mothers are not supposed to do this, and Jessica was ashamed for her. She wondered if Mum was now beating up her lover instead of Dad. A most bizarre situation, which must have helped Dad to make up his mind when he had been offered a job move to New Zealand. Since then, her contact with her family had consisted of letters from Mum and phone calls from Dad. Somehow all the kicks and hits and reproaches had vanished from her memory until David's words had brought them back.

It's your fault.

Jessica was crying as the pictures from the past flickered in front of her mind's eye. It had happened in this house, over and over again, and not once had Dad tried to fight back. She had admired her mother for her strength and had hated her for her brutality; she had pitied her father for his sufferings and had loathed him for his weakness. He loved his wife, adored her, accepted his miserable role in this unbalanced marriage. That was the lesson Jessica had learned: to love means either to suffer or to make the other one suffer.

Jessica wiped away her tears with the handkerchief David had fixed around her wrist. No more tears, no more regrets and accusations. Nothing was anybody's fault. Jessica understood that the key to redemption was forgiveness.

"Mum," she said in a hoarse voice, "I forgive you. And you as well, Dad."

It was like a vow. She repeated it to make sure she meant it. Her headache was gone. If she was able to forgive her parents, why not do the same with herself?

"I herewith forgive myself every mistake," she said solemnly, "and every nasty thing I've ever thought, said or done. I forgive myself for the things I failed to do, like protecting Dad or switching off the heater which caused the fire."

Could she forgive herself for being responsible for Alan's death? She was responsible because she had told David about her feelings for Alan. But more than anyone else, David needed to be forgiven. He was about to commit murder. New tears welled up as she said, "David, I forgive you." She did not quite feel it. It was more natural to hate him, and yet she knew she had found fortitude and the only way to get along with her life no matter what was going to happen.

The other thing she needed was physical strength. She tried to sit up, but with the rise in blood pressure the splitting headache returned. Take it easy, she encouraged herself. Then she began to work her muscles—legs, bottom, back, shoulders. She had to be prepared for David's return. What had he said about her knees? She couldn't remember.

It had begun to snow. As she stared at the dancing flakes that froze against the window, David's words came back to her.

The stem will be broken. It will be your last dance.

Had he really meant it? Could this be true? No, no and no and no. He hadn't attacked Simon and he wasn't going to shoot Alan. He was just mocking her. Psychological torture, that was what it amounted to. She had been so confused by her blackouts that she hadn't questioned his freakish threats, had even felt desperate enough to attempt to kill herself.

Sounds interrupted her inner monologue. Steps stomped upstairs, the door was whooshed open. In the darkness, all she could make out was a quickly moving figure. What she heard were short-winded gasps. A hand fell on her shoulder.

"She's dead. You killed her." David began to grope around on the floor among the fragments of the vase. "I told Alan where you are," he panted. "We'll have to end it now, quickly." He had found what he was searching for. "Here are your shoes." He banged them on the bed. "Put them on."

Jessica did as he had told her. "Who is dead?" she asked with as much composure as she could muster. A few seconds before, she had been convinced that David was playing a cruel game. Now she was sure that he was absolutely serious—and that meant that he was beyond reasoning. Her only chance was to stay calm and hope for an opportunity to escape.

"Susan. You killed Susan. The moment I pulled the trigger she was there, out of nowhere. Her blood was all over Alan. He wasn't prepared to die for you, the squeamish bastard. Have you laced your shoes?"

Alan was alive. He was alive. She was glad David couldn't see her face now. "Yes," she replied quickly, trying not to think of Susan.

A short metallic sound, then a dull thud. David had thrown something onto the bed. "Take the key and open the cuffs. No sudden moves now. I've got a gun."

She was amazed at how steady her hands were. Feeling for the lock, she concentrated on what she was doing and tried hard to ignore the fact that David was aiming a pistol at her. Was all this real? Or was she in the grip of a blackout that had not only wiped out reality but shifted her into another one? She turned the round-barreled key once, twice—and her feet were free.

"Okay," she said, rubbing her ankles to get the blood flowing. This was real enough. "I've done it."

"Now get up, quick."

She put her feet, still numb from constriction, on the floor and pushed, but her head was reeling. She had to play for time. She wasn't sure if the darkness was a drawback or an advantage. She would have to keep on talking, to make sure he knew where she was and what she was doing, so that he wouldn't harm her out of panic or uncertainty. The problem was that she couldn't see him either and couldn't read his reactions.

"I will dance for you, David," she said. "As you wanted me to."

Just how could she maneuver into a standing position? She remembered what Dr. Shelley had said when he had seen Eileen walk. *It must be sheer willpower that keeps her upright.* If it worked with Eileen, it would work with her. "I'm getting up now, David. My legs aren't in good working order, I'm afraid." They felt boneless, indeed. Straining her eyes and ears, she took a hesitant step away from the bed into the darkness that seemed filled with invisible tripwires.

"I can hear where you are. Don't try any tricks. I want you in front of the window."

On tottery legs, Jessica walked over. The dull clicks of her tap shoes on the dusty floorboards gave her a far better power charge than her mental replay of the wisdom she had poured out on Eileen over the years.

"And now dance," he ordered. "Dance your last dance. Dance until I tell you to stop. Until I make you stop."

"What will you do?"

"Take my aim at your knees. I'll empty the magazine on you to make sure I don't miss. Don't you ever listen to what I tell you?"

"I do want to listen to you. I want to know why you are doing all this."

He didn't answer immediately, and for a fearful moment she thought he was already aiming at her. What would come first? The deafening report of the gun? Or the pain, the impact of the bullet, the cracking of her kneecaps, her precious legs giving way under her? Terror gripped Jessica, but she had to keep her head.

When he finally spoke, his voice was infirm, as if a part of him that still held on to reality was trying to put a silencer on the voice of madness that must—she was sure—have been pounding away in his head since the party, steering his actions like a puppet-master.

"You killed my boy, Jessica."

"What?" Wrong reaction. She had better try to get through to the real David.

"You said you didn't want my child. You had an abortion."

"You got it wrong, David, it was a miscarriage. I didn't do any harm to . . . ."

David seemed to falter but then he went on with renewed malevolence. "Did you do anything to keep him?"

"There isn't much you can do to keep a child. I woke up one night and—"

"Did you stop dancing when you found out you were pregnant? You killed Dominic. You're responsible for all of this, for Susan's death most of all. Now dance before I change my mind and shoot you right away."

This was not a moment for pleas. Jessica understood that she had to be strong, not just for herself but for him, too, in the same way as she had been strong for Eileen. Maybe David wasn't lost entirely yet.

"I will dance now," she announced, feeling ridiculously like a show host. *And here is our surprise guest, the fringe show shooting star, the untamed Jessica Warner.*

She began to dance cautiously. For the first time during her detention, she felt alive and real. Her feet switched to the good old auto-pilot as if they had already forgotten three days of immobility. Wasn't it paradoxical that it had been David—who was about to destroy her legs—who had brought out her full talent, who had taught her all the frantic jumps with clicking heels? Jumps! That could be the way to stop him. Would she be able to do it? A purely academic question. Of course she would, because it constituted her only chance. You don't discard the chance to fight for your life—and her legs were her life—just because you're so vertiginous you'd see the world swaying around you were it not for the darkness.

David sensed her determination. He backed away as she moved closer. When his back was against the wall, he shouted, "Stop." Just then, all the bridled energy in Jessica's legs was set lose like water from a high-pressure hose. Going for the small metallic reflection which had to be the pistol in David's hand, her left leg came up, the tip of her plated shoe crashed into his wrist, sending the pistol flying. He cried out in agony. Jessica heard the pistol land on the floor close to the bed and went down quickly to grab it.

And so they stood, motionless all of a sudden, David somewhere at the wall, holding his fractured wrist, Jessica in front of the dark sky framed by the window, clutching the pistol. Time had been suspended.

"Why is it taking Alan so long to return the call?" Eileen asked. "Are you sure Sergeant Blockley sent someone to The Caesar right away?"

The minutes ticked by. Eileen stared in turns at the phone and the digits on Terry's alarm clock. "The waiting drives me mad. It could already be too late."

He covered her restless hands with his. "We're acting on half-baked suppositions, so cool down. It's a remote possibility we're pursuing. The fact that we've just thought of it doesn't make it more likely to happen."

"It must be a psychological trapdoor, just like I never feared I could be HIV positive until I had my blood taken for a test. All of a sudden I could think of nothing else. It had become a real threat."

"Why did you have an AIDS test at all?" asked Terry, happy about the diversion.

"Simon wanted me to, because of all the transfusions I've had over the years. The test was negative, thank God. I've got enough trouble with my life the way it is."

When the phone finally rang, Terry leant over and took the receiver. Eileen pushed the button of the loudspeaker.

"It's Blockley, sir. Sorry, I'm calling back so late. I had to bring in a scene-of-crime team and the police surgeon."

Eileen gripped Terry's wrist so hard that the receiver almost dropped off his hand. "What happened?" he asked.

"David killed his wife with a shot to the head. I'll explain it all later. We have to find David before he has a chance to destroy Jessica's legs."

Eileen's grip loosened. Terry was acutely aware that her hand had started to tremble.

"It wasn't easy to get the information from Alan because he is suffering from a severe shock," Blockley went on. "It seems that David is holding Jessica prisoner at the place where they used to have their rendezvous. His car is gone. I've already given out the license number to all patrol cars."

"Hold the line."

Eileen's breath was getting more and more restrained. Her face was livid.

"Eileen," Terry said firmly. "Do you know where David and Jessica used to meet when they had their affair?"

She couldn't hear him, her eyes were empty. "He killed Susan, his own wife. What will he do to Jessica?"

"Nothing if we get there in time. Listen to me. Answer my question. Eileen, for God's sake, come round."

"What will he do to Jessica?" Her voice had taken on an alarming shrillness, the tremor of her hands had spread all over her body. She was getting on of her fits.

He tried once more to soothe her. "Eileen," he said, looking straight into her widely staring, unseeing eyes, steadying her with his hands on her shoulders, "Eileen, please, it's me, Terry. Talk to me. You can save Jessica. You can save her. Can you hear me?"

It was obvious that she couldn't. Her teeth were chattering, her breathing was flat and quick. He decided to try shock treatment, grabbed her crutches and slammed them against the wall, in imitation of Eileen's reaction the night before. The sudden clatter brought her round.

"Terry, what the hell are you doing?"

"You must tell me where David and Jessica met to make love."

"The old house," she said. "Her parent's house, I mean. But what for—"

"Give me the address."

"102 Regent's Park Road," she answered mechanically.

"Blockley?" Terry said into the phone. "Send as many cars as you can get to the empty house at the corner of Chalcot Crescent where Aldridge saw Jessica. She's inside."

"Sir? You mean it was right in front of us all the time?"

Jessica's heart pulsed heavily. She had saved her legs, but her reserves were exhausted. Would David feel threatened by a pistol aiming at him in the dark, would he give in? "Let me go," she said. Her fingers held the weapon so firmly they were beginning to cramp.

"You bitch. You broke my wrist."

"I can do more damage now. I have the pistol."

David laughed with derision. "Thanks for the warning. I've already said my farewell to the world. Do it. Come on, shoot me, Jessica, so I can die at your feet, your almighty feet, and through your hands. It's so perfect it's Shakespearean."

"I don't want to kill you. I am sorry for you, David, sorry for what I did to you."

The spasms expanded into her shoulders. Jessica felt tempted to lower the pistol, to go over and comfort David. He had killed Susan. Somewhere deep inside he had to know that he had killed the woman who had loved him to the point of forgiving his betrayal, and that he couldn't put the blame for it on anybody else.

"Shoot me, Jessica. Finish what you've started. Loving you has been a death sentence right from the start."

Jessica knew she couldn't keep the situation at bay much longer. In a bout of light-headedness, she felt like returning to the bed, just to sit down for a moment and reconsider the situation—but she had to get the hell out of here before the tables were turned once more. She aimed at the wall to her right and pulled the trigger. A deafening explosion filled the room, followed by the stench of smoke and the drizzling sound of powdered roughcast.

"Bad aim. Try again. Show your mettle."

He was coming closer. Desperately, Jessica shot once more, a bit to the right from where she could make out the white of his shirt, and then, before the echo of the explosion had faded and before David had a chance to recover from the shock, she ran past him through the open door and along the corridor to the stairs. She heard his steps behind her, hardly audible against the clanging of her shoes. They were wonderful shoes for dancing, but running in them was difficult, outrunning David impossible. He caught her as she reached the landing. He grabbed her and turned her around. In the light of the street lamp that was coming through the high window, she could see that her second shot hadn't missed, his left arm was bleeding, the blood looking black on his white shirt.

"Let me go!" she screamed.

"No way. First you have to kill me."

His left arm and right wrist were injured, but he was desperate enough to motion the pistol against his heart. He got hold of her wrist and wriggled his thumb around her index finger. She couldn't stop him as he pressed the trigger. A hollow click. The magazine was empty. David cursed. His right hand shot up to cover the wound on his upper arm. Although Jessica was free to move now, she was afraid to turn around and try to escape down the stairs as long as he was so close to her. Could she use the pistol to knock him down? In the distance, she heard a police siren, then another. They were coming. Thank God, they were coming.

The next second David's blood-smeared hand was on her face.

"Taste my blood, Jessica," he said and pushed.

The pistol clanged down the stairs as Jessica's hand reached out for the banisters. With her left hand, she tried to hold on to David. He pushed harder, crying out in pain as his broken wrist folded back at an unnatural angle against his arm. Jessica stumbled backwards and began to fall. The overpowering odor of blood was everywhere now.

Suddenly, unexpectedly, before she hit the ground, there were

hoped he would come to meet her.

Terry frowned. "Did she say anything else?"

"No, she just gave me this message."

"Hm, that's strange. Well, thanks."

Terry had only met Barbara Jenkinson, Simon's sister-in-law, once at the Middlesex Hospital when she had come with Simon's son Peter. He vividly remembered the motherly middle-aged woman pushing a wheelchair with the kindly youth who suffered from cerebral palsy. Why could she want to see him? The only reason he decided to go was that it would make a perfect escape from tidying up his office.

Whistling the melody of Peer Gynt, he drove out to Golder's Green, turned left at the station and soon reached the gates of the cemetery. With some difficulty, he found a place to park his car down Fortune Green Road and walked back to the gate. The broad main drive before him looked as inviting as the entrance to a cemetery possibly can. The chirping of birds in the mature trees filled him with a sense of peace. He was ten minutes early and began to stroll, subconsciously looking for Susan's grave, which also held David's urn.

"The Powells are buried farther north," said a female voice as if in answer to his thoughts. "I knew you'd look for their grave."

The voice was familiar, although he couldn't place it immediately. He turned, expecting to see Barbara Jenkinson, but the woman who had walked up behind him was younger. The sun reflected in her brown hair, a soft wind played with her white skirt. A short-sleeved blouse spanned over her firm, juvenile breasts. For a few seconds all he saw was a pretty woman with an easy smile and striking eyes; then, with a sweet shock, he recognized her.

"Good God. Eileen."

Her hair had grown to shoulder-length, her face was tanned and fuller. She stepped closer, her arms outstretched for a hug.

"Eileen." He kissed the side of her mouth. "When did you

return?"

"Yesterday. I'm still jet-lagged, but I had to see you as soon as possible. I missed you so, Rick."

"You look gorgeous. What did they do with your face?" Where her scar had been, there was a narrow line of rosy skin now.

"The latest in laser surgery. Professor Johnson said that once I was anaesthetized he might as well bring in a plastic surgeon. He's a perfectionist."

Terry kept stroking her cheek. "And where are your glasses?"

"I thought I could round things off a bit by wearing contact lenses. I'm made up of spare parts when you come to think of it."

He wanted to drown in the warmth of her smile and the glow of her eyes. "You look like a new person. You don't even need a cane now."

"Only for longer walks."

He couldn't take his eyes off her. She was like a restored painting, all brilliance of colors and shapes. They hugged and kissed once more.

"Are you as fine inside as you look from the outside?" he asked.

"Even finer. Some of my letters must have sounded pretty gloomy. You see, I was thrown back to where I had been after the mishap—well, I shouldn't call it a mishap. It's a silly euphemism Alan brought up to cover his dismay. It was a catastrophe, nothing less. Anyway, after my surgery in the States I went through a fast-forward replay of the past five years. Immobility in plaster cast, traction, hydrotherapy, the wheelchair, physiotherapy, a walking frame, and then, at the end of May . . . ." She glanced down at her legs as if to make sure they still stood there. Terry saw her eyes turn liquid for a moment.

"It's so good to be back," she went on. "I feel as if I've returned from a hiatus between two lives. I had massages, too, but they were rude compared to Simon's."

Suddenly he knew it. Eileen was the Mrs. Jenkinson who had

called. "You married him. I can't believe it. You married Simon!"

Eileen flushed. "In Las Vegas last week. Simon said we were made for each other because I have artificial joints and he's got a pierced heart."

Terry was so happy he couldn't stop smiling and shaking his head. "My congratulations."

She giggled like a young girl as he picked her up. "What are you doing?"

"I'm kissing the bride," he said and pressed his mouth on her lips. "I want you to know that, even as a married woman, you'll always be welcome in my Jacuzzi."

She laughed and he put her back on her feet.

"Have you and Simon already found a place to live in?"

"Well, that was a special treat Simon, Jessica and Roger prepared for me. They had the old house renovated and redecorated, with an elevator built in, in case my surgery wasn't successful."

"The old house? You mean the one where Jessica—? But . . . doesn't it hold too many painful memories?"

"Not for me. I'd never even been in the house before. And as for Jessica—"

"She's very good at putting memories aside, isn't she?"

Eileen shook her head and in the light breeze, her soft brown hair swung around her chin. "She has found a better way to cope. I'll show you."

Her arm on his, skin touching skin, they strolled along the gravel path. She walked with the faintest hint of a limp.

"Here," she pointed when they came to Susan's and David's grave. A smooth, unpretentious stone headed the rectangle covered with heather. In front of it, in a tall, slim vase, a single rose stood, the calyx full, the dark red petals flawless.

Eileen's hand tightened around his fingers. "Jessica brings a fresh one every week."

When Terry looked at her he saw that one thing hadn't changed. She still wept in her quiet way.

Dead Wrong

by Robert L. Iles

Sheriff Walker Whitlow must solve the murder of a beautiful young girl as he struggles to keep his job, his family, and his belief in himself.

ISBN 1-929613-15-6 $5.50 US/$7.50 Can

The Rhythm of Revenge

by Christine Spindler

D.I. Rick Terry sifts through a storm of suspicion when tap star Jessica Warner disappears. Devious secrets are revealed as Terry delves into the intimate lives of the dance troupe.

ISBN 1-929613-18-0 $5.99 US/$7.99 Can

Song of Innocence

by Margery Harkness Casares

From the moment she first sees Charles, Mignon San Marco knows he is her true love. Through the perils of the Napoleonic War, treachery, and other intrigues, they struggle to find their way together.

ISBN 1-929613-02-4 $6.50 US/$8.50 Can

Ask for these books at your local bookstore, or order them below

---

Mail to Avid Press, LLC 5470 Red Fox Drive Brighton MI 48114-9079, or fax to (503)210-6765

Please send me the books I have checked above.

☐ My check or money order (no CODs please) for $_____ is enclosed (please add $1.50 per order for postage and handling--Canadian residents add 7% GST). Make checks payable to Avid Press, LLC.

☐ Charge my VISA/MC

Acct#_____ExpDate_____.(please add postage and handling of $1.50 per order; Canadian residents add 7% GST).

For faster service visit our website at
http://www.avidpress.com

Name:_____ Telephone:_____

Address:_____

City, State, Zip_____ Email:_____